"Jonah showed up today at the shelter with his nanny. And he presented me with flowers. He said they were from his dad because his dad wanted to say he was sorry."

"Well, now that's what I call a true gentleman," Mavis Anne said. "That was a very kind gesture."

"It was," Iris agreed.

"What's this dad look like? I wonder how long his wife has been gone," Yarrow asked, making me laugh.

I shrugged and realized I had given barely any thought to the father. It was the boy who had stirred emotion in me. However, when I recalled the father I had to admit he was rather sexy in that nerdy sort of way.

"The dad is good looking," I told her. "But I have no idea how long his wife has been gone."

"Hmm," Mavis Anne said. "Well, you never know what can develop."

"Yeah, right," I retorted. "The father thinks I'm a busybody. Not much chance of a romantic involvement there. Besides which, I'm definitely not looking for a relationship."

Iris laughed. "Famous last words."

# Unraveling the Pieces

## Terri DuLong

LYRICAL SHINE
Kensington Publishing Corp.
www.kensingtonbooks.com

LYRICAL SHINE BOOKS are published by

Kensington Publishing Corp.
119 West 40th Street
New York, NY 10018

All Kensington titles, imprints, and distributed lines are available at special quantity discounts for bulk purchases for sales promotion, premiums, fund-raising, educational, or institutional use.

Special book excerpts or customized printings can also be created to fit specific needs. For details, write or phone the office of the Kensington Sales Manager: Kensington Publishing Corp., 119 West 40th Street, New York, NY 10018. Attn. Sales Department. Phone: 1-800-221-2647.

Lyrical Shine and Lyrical Shine logo Reg. U.S. Pat. & TM Off.

First Electronic Edition: November 2016
eISBN-13: 978-1-60183-555-0
eISBN-10: 1-60183-555-8

First Print Edition: November 2016
ISBN-13: 978-1-60183-556-7
ISBN-10: 1-60183-556-6

Printed in the United States of America

*For Rose White. Thank you for many years of friendship and for your support*

# ACKNOWLEDGMENTS

Readers ask me where I get my inspiration and ideas for characters and plots. The answer is: everywhere. So I want to give a big thanks to my high school classmate, Cheryl Crotty. We lost touch after school and like so many others we reconnected on Facebook a few years ago. Cheryl frequently posts photos of her handsome grandsons Liam and Jaxson. I was captivated with the younger one, Jaxson. His photos melted my heart and over time, the character of Jonah emerged in my imagination. Although Jonah is about seven years older, Jaxson's photos were my inspiration. So thank you to both of you.

Another huge thank you to my BFF, Alice Jordan, for your help coming up with the title for this story. I'm looking forward to celebrating both the book release and our seventieth birthdays in Florence, Italy in the spring!

I'm very fortunate to have such an extraordinary editor. A multitude of thanks goes to Alicia Condon—for all of your assistance, suggestions, and most of all, for always making my story better.

As always—thank you to my loyal readers for your support and especially to all of my Facebook followers. You're the best!

# Chapter 1

M y mother had been a firm believer that the past should remain in the past. Maybe she was right. Maybe not. But Rhonda Garfield kept the identity of my father a secret that she took to her grave three years ago.

I glanced at the black-and-white photo in my hand—my mother holding a baby in her arms, sitting beside a good-looking fellow on a beach, and the name Peter Maxwell written on the back—and I let out a sigh because I was no further ahead in figuring out whether perhaps this man was my father.

The name Peter Maxwell had never come up when I was a child. Whenever I questioned who and where my father was, the only answer my mother would give me was that he had died and that was the end of the conversation. After a while I simply stopped asking.

"Yoo hoo, Petra," I heard Mavis Anne call from downstairs. "Are you busy?"

I smiled as I stood up and replaced the photo in the box I had found after my mother passed away.

"No. I'll be right down," I said, heading to the staircase.

I had arrived at Koi House for an extended stay the day before. This gorgeous Victorian structure had been the childhood home of Mavis Anne Overby and her siblings, David and Emmalyn. Mavis Anne now resided next door with her brother and his partner, Clive. Emmalyn had passed away years ago in a tragic car accident at age twenty-eight, leaving behind a daughter, Yarrow.

The house had then stood empty until Chloe Radcliffe Wagner discovered it when she relocated from Cedar Key to Ormond Beach. When my best friend, Isabelle, was going through difficult times, Chloe was in the process of marrying Henry Wagner. She invited

Isabelle and her daughter, Haley, to relocate from Atlanta and stay at the house while Isabelle attempted to start over. Call it fate, but my best friend ended up meeting the love of her life last year and was now married to Chadwick Price. So Koi House had once again become empty. I wasn't going through a crisis, nor did I need a place to stay. I owned my house in Jacksonville, had a well-paying job I could do from home, and although my social life was lacking, I could have stayed put. But I was lonely. I loved visiting Isabelle in Ormond Beach. During the past year I'd gotten to know Mavis Anne, Yarrow, and the women at the yarn shop. And when Mavis Anne and Isabelle suggested I stay at Koi House for an extended visit, I decided to accept the offer.

"Hey," I said, walking into the kitchen to find Mavis Anne removing dead leaves from the begonia plant on the table.

"How are you, sweetie?" she asked, and I found myself enveloped in a bear hug. "Did you sleep well your first night at Koi House?"

I smiled. "I did. Very well. I was just going through some of the boxes that I brought with me and getting settled in."

"Oh, good. Well, the reason I came by is because we're having leftover turkey this evening for dinner. David and Clive insist that you join us, especially since you missed Thanksgiving this year. Yarrow will be with us and Isabelle, Chadwick, and Haley are coming too."

I had been busy packing and getting things ready at my house in Jacksonville so I could leave my home in the capable hands of a property manager; having a turkey dinner two days before hadn't been important.

"That sounds great," I said. "And I'll enjoy that turkey so much more sharing it with all of you. So yes, I'll be there. What time?"

"Come over around five-thirty. Cocktails on the patio first, of course."

Lotte must have realized we had company and came running into the kitchen.

Mavis Anne smiled as she bent down to scoop my Yorkie into her arms and place a kiss on the dog's forehead.

"And of course Lotte is invited," she said. "She's such a sweet, well-mannered girl."

I laughed. "Thanks. Lotte accepts your invitation. We'll be there."

"Okay." She placed Lotte on the floor. "I have to get going. Louise is picking me up shortly. She has to drop off towels at the animal shelter and then we're going out for lunch. Oh, would you like to join us?"

"Thanks, but no. I have some more chores to finish around here, but why is Louise dropping off towels at a shelter?"

Mavis Anne waved a hand in the air. "Oh, you know Louise. Always getting involved in something. About a month ago she began volunteering at the local shelter. They can always use towels for the animals, so she cleaned out her closet to donate her older towels."

"What a nice thing to do," I said.

Mavis Anne nodded. "Okay. I'll see you later today."

I was heading back upstairs when my phone rang. I answered to hear Isabelle's voice.

"Hey, my BFF, all settled in?" she said.

"Not quite, but I'm getting there. I didn't bring that much with me, so I'm mostly sorting clothes in the closet and bureau. What's up?"

"I just wanted to be sure that Mavis Anne contacted you about dinner this evening."

"She just left and I accepted. I'm looking forward to seeing the three of you."

"Same here. Great. Then I'll see you at Mavis Anne's later. Love you."

"Love you too," I said before hanging up.

I walked into my bedroom and smiled. I had a lovely home in Jacksonville, but Koi House was special. Picturesque and filled with vintage charm. My room here had a turret that jutted out to overlook the front driveway and French doors that led outside to a small balcony. According to both Chloe and Isabelle, who had also stayed in this bedroom, the spirit of Emmalyn Overby still lingered in this room. I had to admit that the temperature was always a few degrees cooler than the rest of the house, but I had no belief in ghosts. Even though Mavis Anne insisted that Koi House had a soul and was at its happiest when inhabited by people.

I shook my head and smiled before I resumed getting my room in order.

Carrying Lotte across the lawn to the gate that separated the two houses, I could hear voices coming from the back patio of David and Clive's home.

"Hey," Isabelle said, jumping up to hug me. "You're here. Oh, Petra, I'm so happy you're going to be living close by."

I laughed and returned her hug. "For a while anyway."

"For a very long while," I heard Mavis Anne say as Chadwick and Haley came to embrace me.

"Right," Haley said, as she took Lotte from my arms. "You can't leave us, Petra. Ginger would miss Lotte."

I laughed as I watched Lotte reacquaint herself with Haley's small dog.

"See," Haley said. "They're BFFs."

I marveled at how fast my best friend's daughter was growing up. Having recently turned fifteen, she'd had a couple of difficult years with the death of her grandfather, the divorce of her parents, and bullying at her school in Atlanta. But Haley had managed to come through all of it more self-assured and even more mature than before. She was a daughter to be proud of.

"Here we go," I heard Clive say and looked up to see him walk onto the patio carrying a tray of champagne glasses. "We need to toast Petra and welcome her to Ormond Beach."

When everybody had a flute, David raised his and said, "Here's to Petra. May you be so happy here that you'll never want to leave."

All of us laughed, and I felt moisture sting my eyes. Growing up an only child with a single parent had been lonely. Isabelle always said that I was her rock, when in truth she had been mine. Always there for me since we first met in kindergarten, through high school and then college. And because of her, I had acquired this group of people who made me feel welcome.

"Thanks," I said, swallowing the lump in my throat. I took a sip of champagne and looked around. "Where's Chloe and Henry?"

"Oh, they took the dogs and rented a place in North Carolina for Thanksgiving. They'll be back tomorrow," Isabelle said.

"Yeah, isn't that romantic?" Haley nudged my arm. "They retreated to the mountains."

I laughed. "It is," I agreed.

We sat around the table and conversation flowed. Isabelle and Mavis Anne caught me up on the news at the yarn shop.

Just then Yarrow came through the house onto the patio. She was out of breath and her cheeks were red.

"I'm so sorry I'm late. The traffic coming over the bridge was horrible," she explained.

She bent to kiss Mavis Anne and accepted the glass of champagne that Clive extended in her direction.

"Thanks. Cheers," she said, lifting the flute. "What have I missed?"

We laughed as Mavis Anne said, "We were just welcoming Petra to Koi House."

Yarrow shot me a smile and nodded. "It's so nice that you decided to come here. Let me know if I can do anything to help you settle in."

"Have you heard from your mother?" Yarrow asked Isabelle.

"That's right," I said. "Wasn't she going to Key West for a few days?"

Isabelle nodded. "Yes. She's with her friend, Charlotte, and two other women. They rented a condo there over Thanksgiving weekend. They'll be back on Monday. I spoke with her yesterday and it sounds like she's having a great time."

I smiled. Iris Brunell was another problem my best friend had had to sort out the previous year. Iris had left home when Isabelle was fifteen, and after a thirty-year separation, they had been able to reconcile after Isabelle moved to Ormond Beach. They now shared a close mother-daughter relationship.

Following dinner, we sat around the dining room table, enjoying coffee and pumpkin pie.

Coming to Ormond Beach had been the right decision for Chloe and Isabelle. Each of them had found her direction and in the process had even met a man she planned to spend the rest of her life with. Not that I was looking for a special relationship, but staying at Koi House made me feel that I was in my element.

*Yes, Petra Garfield,* I thought. *You are precisely where you're supposed to be.*

# Rhonda Garfield
## January 1969

The bus made its way along I-95, heading south. With each mile we left behind us, I felt the coal dust from my small western Pennsylvania home town drifting away. I glanced beside me and smiled as Cynthia quietly snored, preferring sleep rather than looking out the window to watch the landscape flash by.

If not for my best friend, Cynthia, I wouldn't be on this bus heading to Amelia Island in Florida, where a new job and a new life await me.

It was Cynthia who had seen the ad in the classified section of the Pittsburgh newspaper. We were finishing up our waitress shift at the only eating establishment in town that served more than hot dogs or burgers. It also offered better tips.

"Look," she had said, pointing to a square at the top of the page. "This swanky hotel in Florida is looking for winter help."

I leaned over her shoulder and saw the name, Broadglen's. The Broadglen family was well known in the Pittsburgh area. Originally their wealth came from the coal mining industry but over the years family members had branched out to own various enterprises. Charles Broadglen was the owner of the hotel catering to winter residents from the north and prestigious Amelia Island families.

"What's that have to do with us?" I asked.

"We could apply for a position. We could be spending the winter in Florida making money. Away from this godforsaken town. Mr. Broadglen is known for hiring staff from this area. He likes to give people a chance. Why shouldn't it be you and me?"

At the time I had doubted Cynthia's optimism. We were nineteen, out of high school one year. Leaving western Pennsylvania wasn't something I thought we would ever do. But we had.

We had mailed the applications along with two letters of recommendation; three months ago we had been notified that we were scheduled for an interview in Pittsburgh. Within a week following the interview, we each received a large packet in the mail, informing us we had been hired. If we agreed to the employee regulations included in the envelope, we were to get a doctor's letter stating we were in good health and had no physical limitations.

I smiled as I recalled Cynthia's excitement. She had flown into my house waving the envelope in the air, jumping up and down.

She pulled me into a bear hug before grabbing both my hands to include me in her jumping. "This is *it*," she had said. "We are finally going to get out of this town and *do* something with our lives."

My mother had walked into the living room and joined our excitement. I knew she would miss me, but she encouraged me to leave because she didn't want to see her daughter stuck in a small town the way she was. With only a high school diploma and no money, a good position wasn't easy to find.

My plan was to work at Broadglen's until I had saved enough money to attend a secretarial college, which would, I hoped, secure me a decent job with a good company.

I felt Cynthia stir beside me. She sat up in her seat, rubbing her eyes, and yawned.

"Are we there yet?" she asked.

I laughed. "Not yet. But we just came over the Georgia border."

She yawned again. "A few more hours and we'll be in the Sunshine State."

I looked down at our winter attire. We had left Pittsburgh at seven the previous morning and it had been thirty-eight degrees. Each of us wore a turtleneck sweater with slacks, a winter coat, knitted hat and mittens when we arrived at the bus terminal. I was looking forward to shedding our clothes for the warmth of Florida temperatures.

Cynthia shifted in her seat to look toward the back of the bus.

"Sally and Carol are still sleeping," she said.

We had met the two sisters at the bus terminal and discovered they had also been hired to work at Broadglen's. Like Cynthia and me, they would be sharing a cabin provided by the hotel.

"They seemed nice," I said, and smiled as I recalled how excited Sally had been about our new jobs. She marveled that the hotel had provided our bus tickets and would pick us up in Jacksonville in a van to take us to Amelia Island. Her sister, Carol, had been quieter, and I wondered if perhaps she had been coerced into accompanying Sally.

"They did seem nice," Cynthia agreed. "Maybe we can hang out with them when we're not working."

She removed a compact from her handbag. Flipping it open, she assessed her face in the mirror. "Look at me," she wailed. "I look like a ghost. I plan to soak up every bit of that sun on the beach and get a nice tan."

Looks had always been important to Cynthia. I laughed. "Right. You better work fast. We're going to be working six days a week."

Cynthia groaned. "I know. That's really going to cut into my fun time. With my luck, it'll probably rain every day we have off."

I shook my head and smiled as I leaned my head back on the seat. Cynthia pulled out from her tote bag the Danielle Steel novel that she had begun reading hours before.

The movement of the bus along the highway made me drowsy, and I must have dozed off. I awoke to Cynthia nudging my arm.

"Look, look," she said, pointing out the window. "We just passed into Florida!"

I glanced out the window to see the bare trees of the north replaced by palm trees. Sunshine streamed through the window, and I smiled. Within a short time we would be arriving at the Jacksonville bus station—where my new life would begin.

# Chapter 2

I had made plans to have lunch with Isabelle on Monday but decided to call her in the morning just to double-check on the time. Since her marriage to Chadwick, she had left her coffee and muffin delivery job with Yarrow to work in Chadwick's real estate office.

"Hey," Isabelle said when she answered. "What's up?"

"I'm just calling to confirm lunch at twelve. We're meeting at Frappes?"

There was a pause on the line and then Isabelle moaned. "Oh, no. Was that today?"

"Yeah, it was. Why? What's going on?"

"Oh, gee . . . well . . . I forgot and told Chadwick I'd have lunch with him. He booked a table for us at Café Margot in Cocoa Beach."

I felt disappointed but managed to say, "Well, that's okay. Isn't the office open today? You're driving down to Cocoa Beach?"

"Things are slow around the holidays. We're here at the office now but leaving shortly to take the rest of the day off."

"Okay. Well . . . enjoy your lunch and your time together. Give me a call when you get a chance."

"Will do," was all she said, and the line disconnected.

I sat at my kitchen counter sipping the rest of my cold coffee. That was odd. Not even *I'm sorry* from her. I understood that she was newly married, but it was the first time I could recall Isabelle canceling a lunch date with me.

I heard Lotte whining at my feet and smiled. "Have to go out, girl?" I asked her and opened the French doors to let her outside. I stood watching her sniff the shrubbery before she squatted to pee and ran back into the kitchen.

"So," I said, rinsing out my coffee mug and looking down at Lotte, "it's just the two of us. What would you like to do today?"

I had my work with the software company caught up. The last part of the year was a slow time for me, and when I lived in Jacksonville this was normally the time I took for extra projects around the house, reading books I'd put aside, and finishing off knitting projects. But I was now living at Koi House and there were no projects that required my attention. My to-be-read pile lacked any books that interested me, and I wasn't in the mood to work on my socks.

I could spend some time on the computer doing research in an attempt to locate my father, but the idea that had excited me a few months ago had begun to lack appeal. Did I really want to find him? What if I didn't like what I found? What if my mother had been right about the past staying in the past?

"Come on, Lotte," I said, heading to get her leash. "We're going for a walk on the beach."

I had made myself a promise that when I stayed at Koi House I'd make an effort to enjoy the ocean more than I did when living in Jacksonville. It was just a short drive over the bridge and onto A1A and there she was: the mighty Atlantic.

I drove a short distance to Andy Romano Park, where I left the car.

I carried Lotte to the edge of the sand and put her down as I wrapped her leash around my hand. "Let's walk," I told her as I breathed in the fresh, salty air.

It was a gorgeous November morning with the sun shining, no humidity, and the temperature hovering around seventy. We had gone quite a distance, and I realized we'd been walking for more than an hour. As we got closer to the park I saw a figure farther down the beach waving at me and realized it was Louise, Mavis Anne's friend.

"Hey, Petra," she called as I got closer. "I thought that was you."

"How are you, Louise? And Ramona, how're you doing?" I bent down to pat her small dog as Lotte excitedly greeted her.

"I'm great," she said and smiled. "I think our girls like each other."

I nodded. "So are you off for a walk?"

"Yes, and then I was planning to get some lunch before going to the yarn shop. Can you join me, or do you have plans?"

I felt my earlier disappointment lighten, and I smiled. "No, actually I have no plans at all."

"Great. Well, how about if we meet at twelve for lunch. Is Peach Valley okay, just up there on Granada?"

She pointed toward the west, and I nodded again. "Sure. That sounds good."

"Wonderful. I'll see you there. and then we'll head over to Dreamweaver to do some knitting."

Louise was already at the restaurant when I walked in. She was waving to me from a table in the back.

"Hi," she said. "I'm so glad you could join me."

"Me too," I told her as I sat down. I had liked Louise Blackstone when I met her on my previous visits to Ormond Beach and I was looking forward to getting to know her better. She was in her early seventies and had been a good friend of Mavis Anne's for many years.

"Are you settling in at Koi House?" she asked.

"Yes. It's very comfortable and such a beautiful home."

"It certainly is and the apple of Mavis Anne's eye. She's so happy you're staying there." She picked up her menu. "They have some nice sandwiches here."

I glanced at the options and settled on a chicken salad sandwich with ice water.

After the waitress took our order, Louise said, "Mavis Anne mentioned you have no family."

I nodded and realized how pathetic that sounded. "My mother passed away a few years ago and I never knew my father. He died when I was a baby and there was no other family left."

Louise took a sip of her iced tea. "My husband passed away years ago and we had no children. I do have a wonderful nephew and his family. They live in New Smyrna Beach and we try to see each other often. But he still works and doesn't have a lot of free time."

"It's nice that you have him nearby."

"It is," she said. "But I've always maintained that we really end up forming our own families over the years, and they don't have to be blood. Look at Mavis Anne. She's become my family and so have Yarrow, David, and Clive. I think family can be more than just genes. I think it's two or more like-minded people who love each other."

I smiled and saw that Louise Blackstone was a very wise woman.

"Yes, that's true. I've always considered Isabelle and Haley my family, and Isabelle's mother, Iris, was like a second mom to me while I was growing up."

She nodded. "That's exactly what I mean. And of course, my Ramona is family. She just happens to have a furry coat."

I laughed as the waitress placed our lunch in front of us. "Yes, I can relate to that. Lotte is my best companion. Dogs and cats are such a comfort, aren't they?"

"They certainly are, and it's easy to see that you love them as much as I do."

She took a bite of her sandwich and seemed to be thinking.

"I was wondering," she said. "Do you think you'd be interested in volunteering at the animal shelter? We could certainly use help. Especially this time of year."

"Mavis Anne mentioned that you dropped towels off there the other day. Do you also volunteer at the facility? What exactly would I be doing there?"

"I go a few times a week and walk the dogs for their potty breaks. The hardest part is when I have to put them back into their cages. They all want a forever home. Well, we do need somebody right now to manage the front desk. Answering the phone and assisting the people who have come to pick up their adopted pet."

"Really? Now that sounds uplifting. I know my limitations, and I don't think I could handle dealing with the dogs that have to stay there. I'm afraid I'd find it too heartbreaking and would end up taking them all home."

Louise laughed. "Yes, I can understand that. But it's a no-kill shelter and I just know that eventually every single one will find their forever home. But listen," she said, reaching into her handbag and passing me a business card, "this is the name of our director. Suzanne is a wonderful person and I know she'd love to have you join us. Give her a call and see what you can work out."

"Thanks, Louise. I think I will. My work schedule allows me to be flexible, so I can certainly volunteer a few hours a week."

"That would be wonderful. I don't think you'll be sorry, and who knows where it will lead. A new adventure always opens new doors for us."

*Right,* I thought, *as long as I don't end up with a house overflowing with dogs and cats.*

\* \* \*

I walked toward Dreamweaver and smiled. It was the perfect venue for a yarn shop. Located behind Koi House, the structure reminded me of an English cottage with the oval dark wood door, brick chimney, and window boxes filled with seasonal flowers. I inhaled the scent of wood smoke as I stepped inside and saw that the center fireplace at the back of the room was glowing. The flickering fire added coziness even if all the windows were open to let in some cooler air. Mavis Anne had a thing about lighting the fire if the temperature dropped below seventy-four degrees outside.

Chloe came running over to give me a hug. "Welcome, Petra. We were hoping you'd stop by. With Henry and me away for the weekend and the shop being closed for Thanksgiving, I haven't had the chance to see you since you arrived on Friday. How are you?" She hugged me again and I smiled as I recalled what Louise had said about family.

"I'm great, and you look terrific. Married life must agree with you."

She laughed and nodded. "Oh, it certainly does. And Henry said to be sure to say hello if I saw you. He also wanted me to extend a dinner invitation to you. Some evening this week if you're free."

"That would be great, so yes."

Mavis Anne looked up from the lace shawl she was working on. "Come join us, honey. Brought your knitting, didn't you? And where's my sweet buddy Lotte?"

I laughed and held up my knitting bag. "Yes, I brought my socks to work on. Lotte is taking a nap in the house. We had a long walk on the beach this morning. Actually, I bumped into Louise and she invited me to have lunch with her. She's on her way. Just had to stop off at her house to let Ramona out first."

"Oh, good," Mavis Anne said. "Well, you remember the others, don't you? Fay and Maddie, and Paige called to say she's on her way."

We exchanged greetings and I glanced around to see what the others were working on.

"Oh, Maddie. That's a gorgeous sweater. For your granddaughter?"

She held up the beautiful piece with lace edging around the cuffs of the sleeves and neck. She was knitting it in a shade of pale lavender.

"Yes. I think Tori will like this. I'm hoping to have it finished for Christmas."

The afternoon flew by with knitting and conversation. The women brought me up to date on the news in the community. With Christmas approaching it appeared there would be a lot of various events to attend and fun things to do.

Just as I was getting ready to leave, Chloe said, "Weren't you supposed to have lunch with Isabelle today? I thought maybe she'd stop by here."

"Yeah. We did have a lunch date," I said and realized that although Isabelle had forgotten, Chloe had not. I had mentioned it when she'd called me the day before. "But . . . well, I guess she forgot and made plans with Chadwick for the day."

"Oh. That's too bad," was all Chloe said, but I couldn't help but feel the expression on her face said more than her words.

# Chapter 3

On Wednesday morning I decided to contact Suzanne Palmer at the rescue shelter.

"Oh, yes," she said when I told her who I was. "Louise Blackstone mentioned your name and said you might call me. That's great because we can always use the help here."

"Louise told me you needed some help with the front desk and the phone?"

"Yes, we do. About how many hours a week do you think you could volunteer?"

"Well, I work from home and my job is pretty slow this time of year, so I could be available about six hours a week if that would help."

"It certainly would. In addition to handling the phone, we need somebody to drive around the area to pick up donations for our thrift shop. Would you be able to do that too? Maybe one morning a week for a couple of hours? It doesn't involve any heavy lifting or anything. Mostly knickknacks, clothes, books, that sort of thing."

"Sure. I'm fairly new to the area, but if I had directions, that wouldn't be a problem."

"Wonderful! Also, we're having an adoption day this Saturday at Petco on Granada Boulevard. Is there any chance you could volunteer a couple of hours to assist with that?"

My calendar was pretty empty at the moment. "I'd love to. That wouldn't be a problem, and I'd enjoy seeing a few dogs get a good home."

"Louise told me you have a Yorkie who is a rescue dog?"

I smiled. "Yes, my Lotte."

"Please feel free to bring her with you on Saturday. Sometimes it helps when people see that other dogs have been rescued and now have a loving home."

"That would be great. I'll definitely have her with me."

"Okay. Is there any chance you could stop by here in the next couple of days? I'll get your information and explain the phone system to you."

"Sure. I can come later this afternoon."

"That would be great. I'll see you then."

I hung up the phone and looked at Lotte, who was curled up beside me on the sofa.

I hated to think what might have happened to my precious dog if I hadn't rescued her three years before. She wasn't quite a year old when she was found abandoned and filthy along the highway, and some kind person had brought her to the shelter where I was able to adopt her. Every single dog deserved another chance for a good life, and I wanted to give back and help make that happen.

I planned to go over to the yarn shop before lunch but decided to give Isabelle a call first. I hadn't heard from her since she'd had to cancel our lunch on Monday. I didn't want to bother her on the business phone at the office, so I called her cell but it went to voice mail.

"Hey, it's me. I haven't heard from you. I know you're busy working, but give me a call. Maybe we can reschedule our lunch date."

I had hoped to chat with Isabelle for a little while, so I was disappointed that she didn't answer my call.

I let out a deep sigh. "Well, Lotte, why don't we pay a visit to the yarn shop before lunch?"

She barked and danced in circles before following me along the walkway to Dreamweaver's.

I walked in to find Iris and Chloe sitting at the table knitting.

"Petra," Iris exclaimed, jumping up to embrace me. "I knew you were busy getting settled in and I didn't want to bother you, but it's so nice to see you."

I smiled and returned her hug. I had always liked my best friend's mother. My own mother had been withdrawn and seldom displayed affection. She was the opposite of Iris Brunell, who always welcomed the company of Isabelle and me during our growing-up years.

"It's great to see you too, Iris."

"Did you bring your knitting?" Chloe asked. "Come and join us."

I glanced to the back of the shop and saw that Yarrow was busy waiting on customers.

"Thanks," I said, as I sat down and removed my socks from the tote bag.

I noticed that Chloe was working on a cabled hat with a cream-colored Aran yarn.

"How was your trip to the mountains?" I asked. "Is that what the hat is for?"

She laughed. "We had a wonderful time. And yes, we enjoyed it so much that Henry has booked us to return in February for a week. So I thought I'd knit up some hats and mittens for us. How are you settling into Koi House?"

"Very well. Lotte and I feel right at home."

Chloe smiled. "Yes, Koi House has a way of enveloping a person with love. You're still coming for dinner this evening, right?"

"Definitely. Oh, and I called Suzanne Palmer at the rescue shelter. I'm meeting with her this afternoon and I'm going to be volunteering there a few days a week."

"That's wonderful," Iris said. "I'm also volunteering there now. Will you be at the adoption event at Petco on Saturday?"

I nodded. "Yes, and Suzanne said to bring Lotte. It's good advertising."

"Right. I'll have Fred there with me too."

I recalled how Iris had adopted Fred a few months before and had also gotten Ginger for her granddaughter, Haley. I also recalled that Isabelle hadn't been happy about that at first, but had come to love the little dog.

"Have you heard from Isabelle lately?" I asked.

Iris shook her head. "No. Not much. I get most of the news from Haley. It seems between working at the office and being a new wife, Isabelle is being kept busy. How was your lunch with her on Monday?"

"Oh, well, it didn't happen. She forgot. So it got canceled."

I looked up to see Iris staring at me.

"Really?" she said. "Hmm. She seldom comes to the yarn shop anymore either. I hate to say it, but that can be typical Isabelle. Caught up in her world to the exclusion of others."

"Well, I'm sure it's an adjustment for her—being married again and working at the office." I had to admit it sounded as if I was making excuses for her.

"Could be," was all Iris said as Yarrow joined us.

"How're you doing?" she asked me.

"Great. How's it working out with your deliveries?"

"I really got lucky," she said. "I have Kim and Stacy. They're both college students and share the hours. They're very reliable and it's working out well. Actually, I'm looking to hire one more person. Not interested in delivering coffee and muffins, are you?"

I laughed. "Sorry. My plate is filling up. I'm going to be volunteering at the shelter and my work will pick up again after the first of the year."

"Yeah, I know. I was only kidding you."

"Oh, I wanted to ask you guys who I should use as a vet. Lotte is due for her annual checkup."

"Dr. Wellington," all three said at the same time, causing me to laugh.

"I take it he's good?" I said.

"Oh, he is," Chloe said. "We take Delilah and Basil to him. They adore him."

"Yup." Yarrow nodded. "I've been taking Merino to him since I found my cat."

"Absolutely, Dr. Wellington," Iris agreed. "I take Fred to him. He's very compassionate and excellent with the animals."

"Not to mention, easy on the eyes," Chloe said, and we all laughed.

"Okay, then Dr. Wellington it is. I'll call his office later and set up an appointment." I saw that it was almost twelve. "I need to get going. Time for lunch and then I'm going to the shelter to meet Suzanne. Five-thirty for dinner?"

Chloe nodded. "Yes. And be sure to bring Lotte. Delilah and Basil will want to visit with her."

I smiled. "Okay. See you then."

I parked in the underground garage of Chloe and Henry's building and took the elevator up to their condo. I had Lotte's leash in one hand and a bottle of wine in the other.

Chloe opened the door followed by the two dogs. Delilah had been Henry's dog before they had married. She was a well-behaved and beautiful golden retriever. Basil was an adorable terrier who had belonged to Gabe, Isabelle's father and Chloe's significant other, before he passed away a few years before.

Lotte strained at the leash to greet her two buddies. They had met during our visits to Ormond Beach, and it appeared they hadn't forgotten each other.

I unclipped her leash and laughed. "I think they're excited to see each other again."

"I think you're right. Come on in."

Henry came from the kitchen area wearing an apron with *Kiss the Cook* in red lettering across the front. He pulled me into a hug. "We're so happy you could join us, Petra."

"Thank you for inviting me," I said, passing him the bottle of wine.

"Let's have a glass of wine before dinner. You and Chloe can sit on the balcony and I'll bring it out to you."

I followed Chloe outside and inhaled the salty air from the Atlantic beyond the beach area below.

"You have such a lovely location here," I said, taking in the view to the north and south.

She nodded. "I know. That's why we can't decide if we want to sell the condo or stay put. Right now I think we're going to stay here."

"I can't blame you at all. The condo is ideal for two people, and you're centrally located, not to mention this fantastic view."

I recalled how Chloe had first met Henry. She had rented his condo for a month while she attempted to put her life back together after the loss of Gabe. Henry had been on a work assignment doing photography for *National Geographic* out of state, and when they finally met in person, it was love at first sight.

"Here we go, girls," Henry said, joining us on the balcony.

He placed a tray holding three wineglasses on the table and then passed one to me and one to Chloe.

Lifting his own glass, he said, "Welcome to Ormond Beach, Petra. We hope you'll be happy here."

"Thank you," I said before taking a sip.

"What are your plans for Christmas?" Henry asked.

With my recent move and settling in, I found it difficult to believe that Christmas was less than a month away.

"Oh, I really don't have any specific plans. Mavis Anne mentioned we should have a Christmas party at Koi House for friends and women from the yarn shop."

Chloe nodded. "Yes, she was talking about that the other day. I think it's a great idea. There would be a lot more room there rather than at Dreamweaver's, but of course, that's your home now."

I waved a hand in the air. "Oh, no, that would be fine with me. I can just picture a huge Christmas tree in the family room in front of those gorgeous windows. And the seating area would be perfect. I'll talk to Mavis Anne about it tomorrow and see if we can get a date confirmed."

"Right. Tomorrow is December first, so we don't have a lot of time. Of course I'll help you decorate. We could hire Marta to make pastries and have the party in the afternoon as a Christmas tea. Have you seen Marta since you arrived?"

I shook my head. "No, she'll be over tomorrow to clean."

Marta was a Polish immigrant whom Mavis Anne adored. She had been hired years before, when Mavis Anne still resided at Koi House, to clean and cook and had continued on in this capacity for both Chloe and Isabelle. Although the cleaning duties were twice weekly, the cooking had become less. She was now only hired for special events—mainly for her expertise with pastries.

"You might give her a heads-up," Chloe said. "Let her know we'll be needing some of her wonderful goodies."

We finished our wine and then I was treated to a delicious pasta dinner prepared by Henry.

By the time Lotte and I returned home, I was filled with good food, good conversation, and the knowledge that I was fortunate to have Chloe and Henry Wagner as friends.

I recalled what my mother had shared with me when I was growing up. The sense of family she felt when she had gone to work in Amelia Island, Florida, with her best friend, Cynthia. The friendships she made had ended by that time, but it seemed they had been very important and helped to make her feel welcome in a new area. Which was exactly how my Ormond Beach friends made me feel.

# Rhonda
## January 1969

I looked around the cabin and smiled. No, it wasn't elegant. Not by a long stretch. Two twin beds with blue chenille spreads, separated by a small maple table holding a lamp. One maple bureau containing three drawers on each side and one brown Naugahyde chair that would prove to be even less comfortable than it looked. But it was ours. Our own place. Temporarily, anyway. A small bathroom with sink, toilet, and minuscule shower completed the cabin.

"Oh, God! No tub?" I heard Cynthia wailing.

I turned from unpacking my suitcase to see her facing the bathroom door, hands on hips, and suppressed a smile.

"I think our employers feel we're here to work, not to soak in tubs," I told her.

She let out a groan and shook her head. "Well, yes, I'm here to work. But I think I'd work a bit better if I had the luxury of soaking in a tub *after* I work."

I continued sorting my clothes. "I'll take the three drawers on this side of the bureau, if that's okay."

She waved a hand in the air. "Sure, fine."

It was then that she realized we didn't have a proper closet, something I had already noticed.

She spun around in a circle and let out another groan.

"What? No closet? Where are we supposed to hang our clothes?"

I pointed to the metal rod that had been braced in a small cut-out in the wall. A few hangers hung empty. "Right there."

She threw her arms up into the air. "I need a cigarette," she said, reaching for her pack and the matches in her handbag and proceeding to light one.

I ran over to grab it from her hand. "You can't smoke in here. You read the rules."

I steered her outside. "You're lucky we have this porch."

Granted, it was a small area with only two plastic chairs, but it did have a roof and was screened.

She lit up the cigarette, lifted her head to blow the smoke up, and let out a sigh. "Sorry," she said, after a few moments. "I guess I just thought it might be a bit more upscale."

I looked at the grounds that surrounded us with the hotel in the distance and beyond that, the beautiful blue ocean. "But look how pretty it is, and we're only going to be sleeping here."

Cynthia nodded. "It *is* pretty." She continued puffing on her cigarette as her glance took in the area.

The brick walkways, palm trees, and large flowering bushes looked exactly like what we had seen in the brochure.

"And isn't this weather to die for?" she said.

It was sunny and it felt like the temperature was in the seventies. "It's certainly a far cry from Pennsylvania in January. I'm going to finish unpacking and then change my clothes. We have to be at the hotel for lunch at twelve and then we have the orientation."

"Go ahead," she said. "I'll be right in to unpack."

Following a delicious lunch of crab salad, warm crusty bread, and something called sweet tea, which I'd never tasted, six of us were assembled in a room with a long table where we would begin our orientation.

A tall, slim woman who appeared to be in her early thirties walked in. She wore a brightly colored cotton skirt and a white sleeveless blouse. Her dark ponytail was caught back with a red scarf.

"Hello," she said and smiled. "I'm Joyce and I'll be your supervisor while you're employed here. If you have any questions, any problems, I'm the person you need to find and speak to. I'm in charge of the dining room and kitchen, and this is the area the six of you have been assigned to. Any questions yet?"

All of us shook our heads.

"Okay, then. Let's begin with you introducing yourself to me and the others. Tell us your name and where you're from." She pointed to the girl at the end of the table.

"I'm Barbara, and I'm from North Carolina." She paused for a second before adding, "And I'm so happy and excited to be here," which caused Joyce to smile.

"And I'm Susie." The girl reached back to pull her ponytail tighter in the elastic. "Oh, and I'm from Louisiana."

This was followed by Sally, Carol, Cynthia, and I giving our names and where we were from.

"Okay," Joyce said. "Four of you from Pennsylvania. Did you girls know each other before coming here?"

"We're sisters," Sally said. "But we didn't know those two."

"And we're best friends," Cynthia explained.

"Well, I'm sure within a few weeks all of you will know each other well. When you're off duty you'll probably socialize together. There isn't much to do in Amelia Island, but there is a bus that will take you to Jacksonville. There's a movie theater there, bowling, restaurants, and various things to do. But right now we need to focus on your job."

She reached into a box she had on the table and walked around the room, placing rectangular plastic name tags in front of us. I glanced down at mine, saw *Rhonda* written in large block letters, *Dining Staff* below my name and a small palm tree etched beside it.

Joyce returned to her seat at the head of the table. "You are to wear these name tags at all times when you're on duty." She pointed to an eight-by-ten sheet of paper that had been taped to the wall beside the door. "That's your schedule for the week. Be sure to check it at least once a day because sometimes there might be a change due to somebody being sick or unable to work their hours. You will rotate between the breakfast, lunch, and dinner shifts. When your duties in the dining room have been completed, which means when the final guest has left and you have finished removing the plates, you will return to the kitchen for various tasks. This is when salt and pepper shakers are refilled, linen napkins folded, and you'll be instructed by the kitchen staff what needs to be done. Any questions?"

"Yes," Sally said. "Are the guests only from the hotel?"

"No, they're not. For breakfast they are mostly guests staying here at the hotel. But during lunch and especially dinner we have a fair number of local residents or tourists who book a reservation. For lunch and dinner on the weekends, which is Friday, Saturday, and Sunday, we operate a little differently. Many of the guests booking during that time are local residents and they prefer to not only have the same table but the same server. I won't lie, these are prominent people in the community and they're used to being catered to. We will help you get to know them, but they like to be greeted by name and some of the men tip very well if they know their server has checked the reservation book ahead of time and has made note of their preferred cocktail, so it's waiting for them when they're seated."

Cynthia nudged me, and I knew she was thinking the same thing I was. We would be organized, we'd get a notebook to jot down the names and preferences until we knew them all by heart—and we would make extra money with our tips.

I saw Carol raise her hand, and Joyce nodded toward her.

"We do have Mondays off, don't we?" she asked in soft voice.

"Yes," Joyce said. "The restaurant is closed on Mondays. Guests staying at the hotel can go to the reception area for coffee and various pastries for breakfast, but no formal meals are served in the dining room. Any other questions?" When the room remained silent, she said, "I'm going to go get Earle. He's our head waiter and I want to introduce you to him."

All of us sat there quietly thinking about everything we'd just learned.

"Sounds pretty good to me," Cynthia whispered, and I nodded.

A few moments later Joyce returned, followed by a tall, good looking fellow. His blond hair contrasted with his deep tan, giving him movie star appeal. He wore his hair longer on top, which reminded me a bit of Fabian, the singer who appeared on *American Bandstand*. He wore a crisp white shirt and black slacks and stood at attention beside Joyce.

"This is Earle. He's our head waiter and has been with us for three years. Earle will be circulating the dining room while you're working. He's there to help you with any problems you can't handle."

Cynthia leaned over and whispered, "He can help with my problems any time."

"For instance, if a guest complains about how something is cooked or the wrong side dish was put on the plate or the wrong dessert. Apologize to the guest, find Earle, and he will take care of it. He interacts with the kitchen staff. Also, if you have a large party and your trays are exceptionally full, get Earle and he will help you carry them into the dining room. Any questions?"

Cynthia leaned toward my ear again. "Yeah, is he single?"

"No? Okay, then Earle would like to say a few words."

The moment he began to speak I swear all six of us swooned. He had a voice that was very different from what we were used to in Pennsylvania. It reminded me of slowly melting butter oozing out of his mouth in the form of words.

He stood with his arms clasped behind his back and had a friendly air of assurance. A smile lit up his face. "Welcome to Broadglen's. I hope you'll be happy working here. As Joyce said, if you have any problems in the dining room, I'm there to help you, so don't be shy. I'll see all of you over the next few days as you begin your shifts. Any questions?"

"Yes," I heard Cynthia say. "Where is that accent from?"

He threw his head back, laughing. "That would be Alabama, miss. Birmingham, Alabama."

It didn't escape me that even before he had asked if we had questions, his eyes had been riveted on Cynthia's face.

# Chapter 4

By the time Marta arrived at eight the following morning, I had had breakfast, showered, gotten dressed, and was ready for my walk on the beach with Lotte.

I was finishing up my coffee when she came in the back door. She pulled me into a hug and said, "I'm very happy you'll be staying here, Petra. Mavis Anne would be sad if the house stayed empty after Isabelle moved out. If there's anything I can do for you, just let me know."

I thanked her and began to clip Lotte's leash to her collar.

"Oh, Marta, I wanted to ask you something. Mavis Anne is planning to have a Christmas party here at Koi House. Would it be possible to hire you to make the pastries? We don't have a date or time yet, but it will probably be a tea in the afternoon."

"Of course." She smiled before adding, "Just let me know when you have the details, but I'd be more than happy to do that."

After walking the beach with Lotte, I stopped at the farmer's market downtown to purchase some fresh produce.

When I arrived home I saw that Marta had finished cleaning, so I decided to have lunch and then spend the afternoon at the yarn shop.

I walked in to find the table filled with our regular knitters and everybody talking at the same time. Mavis Anne sat at the head of the table, her head bent over a notebook. She looked up from writing and pointed to the last empty chair.

"Oh, Petra, good. I'm glad you're here. We're discussing our upcoming Christmas party at Koi House."

"Yeah," Maddie said with a smile on her face. "Nothing like whisking your house out from right under you."

I sat down and shook my head. "I don't mind. Really. Actually, I think it'll be a lot of fun. So what have I missed?"

Mavis Anne tapped the calendar in front of her. "Well, today is December first already. I suppose we should have begun planning this sooner, but not to worry. How does Sunday, December eighteenth, sound? That's one week before Christmas. Will that work for you, Petra?"

"Yes, fine. And I spoke to Marta this morning. She'd be more than happy to make the pastries. I told her it would probably be an afternoon tea."

Mavis Anne nodded. "Yes, wonderful idea. In my day teas were quite common. Why don't we say three o'clock? How does that sound to everyone?"

I looked around the table and saw nods of assent.

"I'd like this to be a thank you to our loyal customers, so maybe we could post an invitation announcement here in the shop to let people know."

"I can do that on the computer," Yarrow said. "And we'll put it on the door so knitters will see it right away."

Mavis Anne nodded. "Good idea. Okay, but I'd also like to give each customer who attends a little knitted item and something from the shop. Nothing big. Just a little gesture of appreciation for their patronage."

"I agree," Chloe said. "I have some lovely spa cloths I knitted and put away for future gifts. We can buy some of that nice Mistral soap online and include a bar with each facecloth. And maybe put together little pouches with point protectors, markers, scissors, things like that which always come in handy for knitters."

"I also have spa cloths that I've knitted and put away," Iris said. "So we'll get together and see about how many we might need."

"Right," Fay said. "We need to have a sign-up sheet. So we'll know how many women are planning to attend."

Yarrow nodded. "Good idea. I'll do that on the computer also and print it out."

"What can I do?" Louise piped up. "I don't have a task."

"You can help Chloe and Iris put the gift bags together once we have all the items. And we can't leave all the decorating of Koi House to Petra, so why don't we gather on Sunday to do that? As much as I love real trees, I have a huge lovely artificial one we can put up. The tree and decorations are in the upstairs closet, so we will need help getting everything down to the family room. Can everyone come on Sunday afternoon?"

All of us nodded and I said, "Oh, I bet Haley would love to help and be part of the decorating. Why don't you call her, Iris?"

"I'll do that," she said. I noticed that she neglected to mention Isabelle's joining us.

After cleaning up the kitchen following supper, I settled outside on the patio with my knitting. Lotte was curled up in the chair across from me. I recalled Iris's offer to call Haley with no mention of her daughter. This made me realize I still had not heard from Isabelle since she had cancelled our lunch date. And that was three days ago. What the hell was up with her?

I reached for my cell and dialed her number.

"Petra, hi. How are you?"

"I was wondering the same thing," I said. "I haven't heard from you and wanted to be sure everything is okay."

"Oh, yes, fine. Great, actually. I've just been so busy working and then after work, well . . . I am still a new bride, you know." Her laughter came across the line.

I guess she was right. Isabelle and Chadwick would be married three months on Christmas Eve. "Well, listen, I wanted to touch base with you about the Christmas tea we're having here at Koi House on the eighteenth. Mavis Anne wants to do this as a thank you to her customers. So I hope you and Haley will come. Your mother is supposed to call you with details. But we're having a gathering here on Sunday to get the tree decorated. Do you think you could come? I'd love to see you."

There was a pause before she said, "Oh, gosh, Pet. I'd love to. Really I would. But Chadwick and I are leaving tomorrow. We closed the office for the day. We're flying to New York City to do some Christmas shopping and taking a long weekend."

Oh. This was the first I'd heard about this.

"Well, that sounds like fun. Is Haley going too?"

"No. She's flying up to Atlanta to spend the weekend with her dad and Gordon."

"Well, that's great. Okay. You have a nice time and say hello to

Chadwick for me. Maybe we could get together next week after you come back."

"Sounds great. Yes, absolutely. I'll call you."

I disconnected the call and sat staring at my phone. Silly, I know, but I was feeling rejected by my best friend. Of course, I understood that she was newly married and wanted to spend time with her husband. But I'd never thought that getting married meant you had to relinquish your female friends. Especially a female friend who was more like a sister to you than just a friend.

Then it hit me that perhaps this was just Isabelle being Isabelle. I had to admit that she'd always been a little self-centered. But it was part of who she was and something I had always accepted. I knew I was feeling left out, and maybe it wasn't intentional on her part, but that didn't make it hurt any less.

I picked up the sock I had almost finished and continued knitting. *Maybe you really need to get your own life*, I thought. I had never considered this a problem before. I had my job, my house. and a fair number of failed relationships that had never been too serious from the start. So when they ended, I was ready to move on. And through all of it, I always had Isabelle in my corner. To share my ups and downs. But all of a sudden, she was caught up in her new life and very absent from mine.

Were we drifting apart? I wasn't sure. All I knew for certain was that for the first time since we became friends in kindergarten, thinking about our friendship made me feel sad. Sad and alone.

# Chapter 5

I was getting Lotte and myself ready on Saturday morning to go to Petco for the adoptions when Louise called, sounding terrible.

"I've been up all night coughing," she said. "My throat is scratchy and I'm not going to be able to make it this morning."

"Oh, I'm sorry," I told her. "You take care of yourself and I'll call you later to check on how you're doing."

"Thank you, Petra. I've called Suzanne to explain and I'm going back to bed."

I had met Suzanne a few days before and liked her immediately. I've always felt that most people who love animals are good people, friendly and compassionate and a pleasure to be around. Suzanne was no exception.

I walked into Petco with Lotte on her leash to find a large crowd of people milling about. I made my way to the back of the store and found Suzanne talking with another shelter volunteer. She spotted me, waved, and held a finger in the air indicating she'd be right with me.

"Oh, I'm so glad you're here," she said when she walked over. "Louise called to say she's sick and I have another volunteer out sick, so we're really grateful you could help us today."

"Not a problem," I said. "I'm looking forward to it. You said I'll be outside?"

She nodded. "Yes. Come on, I'll get you set up." She leaned over to let Lotte sniff her hand. "And you must be Lotte. You are one pretty girl and so chic all dressed up in your pretty outfit," she said, laughing.

I had chosen a pink-and-white-striped knitted sweater for Lotte to wear along with a tiny matching beret on her head. "I brought her doggie stroller, if that's okay. I thought she could stay in that next to me and be safe."

"Very good idea," Suzanne said as I followed her out of the store.

"Okay." She pointed to a large crate containing two medium-size dogs that appeared to be part wheaten terrier. She reached into a packet of papers she was carrying and passed me a few. "This will tell you about the dogs. Their ages, possible breed, and other info. If somebody shows an interest, send them inside to find one of us and we'll take it from there. Any questions?"

I shook my head as I went to the crate and allowed both dogs to sniff my fingers. "No, I don't think so. They sure are beautiful. I hope we're able to find them a home today."

"Oh, I almost forgot. Here's your name tag. If you send anybody inside about an adoption, be sure they know you're Petra and you have the dog they want."

I pinned the name tag to my sweater and nodded. "Okay, will do," I said as I set up the stroller, lifted Lotte and placed her inside.

"Great. If you need anything, just come and find me."

"Thanks, Suzanne," I said as she headed back inside.

"Hi there," I heard the man next to me say. "I'm Bob."

I looked and saw he was standing beside a crate of beagle puppies.

"Nice to meet you. I'm Petra."

"Have you volunteered before?" he asked.

I shook my head. "No. First time. How about you?"

He laughed. "Oh, I've been doing this for many years. Ever since I retired. My wife used to join me, but she passed away a few years ago. I feel it's a good thing to do, so here I am."

"Same here. I wanted to help find homes for these lovely dogs."

"Your dog there." He pointed to Lotte. "Is she a rescue?"

"Yes. I don't know what I'd do without her."

He laughed again. "They sure do have a way of working their way into our hearts, don't they? I have three at home. Two Chihuahuas and a bulldog mix."

We chatted a bit more and then I sat on the folding chair to scan the information on the two dogs in my charge. Both were wheaten terriers and they were purebred. I kept reading and discovered they were sisters, one year old, and their owner had recently passed away.

*God, how sad*, I thought, glancing into the crate to find them snuggled up beside each other, both of them looking up at me with soulful eyes. I took a deep breath. I wanted nothing more than to scoop them both up and take them home with Lotte and me. But I knew I couldn't.

More people were now beginning to arrive, and I crossed my fingers that these two beauties would go to a forever home before the day was out.

A couple in their thirties approached my crate, and I smiled at them. "Hi," I said. "Looking to take a dog or two home with you today?" My information didn't say both dogs had to be placed together, but the thought of separating the siblings broke my heart.

"Aw, look," the woman said, bending down to put her fingers into the crate. "They're so cute. Are they related?"

"Yes. Sisters and a year old. Very nice dogs and they really need a good home."

Her husband or boyfriend made no attempt to pat the dogs and took a step back.

"What do you think, sweetie?" she asked. "Can we get them?"

He shook his head. "I told you not to even stop. No dogs. Come on. We have to get food for my ferret."

She stood up, looked at me, and shrugged her shoulders before following him inside.

I won't lie. I was thankful they'd passed on taking Lucy and Ethel. I smiled again at the previous owner's choice of names.

A middle-aged couple walked toward my crate. I was beginning to feel like a social worker at an orphanage, trying to do a quick assessment of whether people might be the right fit for my two charges. They were holding hands and seemed happy. Both good signs. Nicely dressed. Also good, because having pets could be expensive.

"Hello," I said, giving them my biggest smile. "Meet Lucy and Ethel. They're sisters and looking for a new home."

Both the man and the woman reached into the crate to pat the dogs. It was obvious they were dog lovers. Maybe this was it. Maybe Lucy and Ethel would find a new home with this couple. But then the man shook his head and laughed. "I'm afraid it can't be us. We're at our limit. We've rescued four dogs over the past year."

"Really?" I said, disappointed but impressed.

The wife nodded. "Yes, really. As much as we'd love to take another one or two, we have to be practical."

I agreed. "I wish you could take them too, but yes, I agree. I'd say your family is complete."

They each gave a final pat before stepping back. "Well, we wish you luck," the man said. "I sure hope they find a good home. They're beautiful dogs."

"Thanks," I said as they walked inside the store.

I heard a commotion going on farther down the line and looked to see a little girl of about five or six jumping up and down with excitement.

I saw Bob smiling and said, "What's going on?"

His smile broadened. "The parents of that little girl just told her she can have the little shih tzu she fell in love with. Looks like that one found a home."

The volunteer reached into the crate, removed the dog, and put it into the little girl's arms. She cuddled it and kissed the top of the dog's head. The look on the little girl's face was pure bliss, and I could feel moisture stinging my eyes.

"That is *so* sweet," I said, wiping at my eyes. "I'm thrilled for both of them."

Bob nodded. "I know. It always warms my heart to see a dog get a new home."

Over the next few hours, I was able to witness a few more adoptions, and each one was special. But it was looking bleak for Lucy and Ethel. I hated the thought of them returning to the shelter rather than a forever home.

I had just given Lotte some water in a bowl and was placing her back into her stroller when I heard a young voice say, "Why is that dog in a baby carriage?"

I turned around and I felt my heart flip over. Not the romantic kind of flip-flop. It was different. More like how my heart feels when I see a dog or cat. That feeling that grips your heart and doesn't want to let go.

Standing in front of me was a young boy who appeared to be around seven or eight. He was scrawny, wearing nice jeans and a designer pullover jersey. His medium brown hair fell across his forehead, making him look vulnerable; black-framed eyeglasses surrounded the dark eyes that were staring at me.

I swallowed and smiled at him. "Oh . . . well . . . this is Lotte and she's my dog. She's helping me with the adoptions today and I want to keep her safe, so she has a doggie stroller."

He nodded matter-of-factly and then pointed at the crate before going down on both knees and looking up at me. "Can they be adopted?"

"Yes, they can. Do you have any dogs?"

He shook his head as he pushed his glasses up the bridge of his nose but didn't take his eyes off Lucy and Ethel. "No. Are they related?"

"They are. They're sisters. How old are you?"

Still not taking his eyes from the dogs and slowly putting a finger inside the crate, he said, "I'm ten."

Ten? He was small for his age. I noticed that both dogs were licking the boy's hand as their tails wagged.

"Do you think you might want to take a dog home today? Are your parents here?" I now realized the boy was alone.

"My dad's inside. Buying food for our bird. Yeah, I keep telling him I want a dog, but he doesn't listen."

There was something about this little boy that was tugging at my heartstrings. Just then I saw a frazzled looking man exit the store, look around, spot the boy at my crate and come over.

"Jonah! How many times do I have to tell you not to wander off. Come on, we have to go."

"But, Dad, look." The boy stood up but his hand remained inside the crate caressing the dogs. "They're sisters and they really, *really* need a home. Can't we take them?"

Dad ran a hand through his curly dark hair, shook his head and let out an exasperated sigh. He was tall and good looking in a nerdy sort of way. I noticed that he wore the same type of black-framed eyeglasses as his son. "No, Jonah, we cannot. We've discussed this before. It's not a good time to get a dog."

I could tell the boy was reluctant to leave.

"But when *is* a good time?" he questioned.

Thinking this was my cue to jump in and help the boy out a bit, I said, "Sometimes we just think it's not a good time." I flashed the father one of my warmest smiles and continued. "Usually our dogs choose us, and it's clear that these two adore your son." Really pushing the envelope, I bent down to the boy's level and said, "I bet if you asked your mother, maybe she'd agree. Sometimes it takes a mom to convince the dad. Is she here? Still in the store?"

Neither one replied. Trying for a playful attitude, I cocked my head to the side and said, "Where's your mom? Maybe you could ask her."

"His mother is *dead*," the father retorted with ice dripping off his words. He leaned forward, adjusted his glasses, and read my name tag. "And I'll thank you very much, *Miss Petra*, to mind your own business."

With that, he took the boy's arm and steered him toward the parking lot, but not before the boy looked back at me with eyes just as sad as Lucy and Ethel's.

*Well, I clearly screwed that up*, I thought. I could feel the tears forming in my eyes at my own stupidity. I obviously had absolutely no experience with children and I had just proved it. Who did I think I was interfering like that? But there was something about that little boy—Jonah—that compelled me to reach out to him. That was when I realized that he was just as lonely and alone as I was.

# Chapter 6

The incident from the day before bothered me a lot; I was having a hard time getting Jonah out of my mind. This was the sort of thing I'd normally discuss with Isabelle—but she wasn't around.

So I was glad to have Mavis Anne, Iris, and Yarrow at the house to help decorate the tree. David and Clive had come over earlier to bring it down from the upstairs closet and set it up in the family room.

"You're quiet today," Iris said as we placed brightly colored ornaments on the tree branches. "Everything okay?"

I let out a deep sigh and shook my head. "Not really. Something happened yesterday at Petco that is really bothering me."

I proceeded to explain the whole encounter to them. "So I feel like a total shit," I said when I finished.

"Oh, my," Mavis Anne said as she straightened a shiny silver ball. "That sounds like a sticky situation. I never had children myself, but I do know parents get funny about people interfering."

"Right," I agreed. "And making it worse, I'm a complete stranger."

Yarrow gave me a pat on the back. "Yeah, but gee, you didn't mean any harm. You were only trying to help the little boy who wanted the dog."

Iris nodded. "Yarrow's right. It was innocent on your part. But it's true that getting between a parent and child can be tricky."

"I just feel terrible," I said. "Bad enough the poor boy lost his mother, but I made it worse by suggesting that if she was there, maybe he would have the dog. And there was just something about him that tugged at me. He looked sad and lost. I think I felt that a dog might help."

"No doubt it would," Mavis Anne said. "But it seems the father doesn't agree."

"Which just goes to show you why I have no children." I stepped back to assess our work on the tree. "I know nothing about them and end up saying the wrong thing."

"I don't think that's true," Iris said. "You're a great mom to Lotte."

I smiled but couldn't help thinking that being a mom to Lotte and being a mom to a boy like Jonah were miles apart.

"The tree looks gorgeous," I said, wanting to change the subject. "I think we're ready for the garland and bows."

When we completed the entire tree, the four of us stood back and agreed we had done an outstanding job.

"Now we're ready to switch the lights on," I said, reaching to plug the strands in.

*Ooh*s and *aah*s filled the room. The white fairy lights were the finishing touch and added exactly the festive atmosphere we had hoped for.

"Okay," I said. "We earned ourselves a glass of wine, and I made a pot of coffee." I headed to the kitchen and returned with wineglasses and mugs on a tray.

"Is Louise feeling any better?" I asked.

"I spoke to her this morning," Mavis Anne said. "No. Not really. She's going to see the doctor tomorrow."

"And now Chloe is sick too?"

"Yes, Henry called earlier to say she couldn't join us today. She woke up coughing this morning. It seems to be going around. If she can't make it into the shop tomorrow, do you think you could help me out, Iris?"

She took a sip of coffee and nodded. "Of course I can. Just give me a call. I'd be happy to spend the day at the yarn shop."

We all laughed because we knew that for any knitter this was never an imposition.

"Have you heard from Isabelle in New York?" I asked Iris.

"Yes, she called yesterday and said they were having a great time shopping. They'll be back tomorrow."

"Ever since that girl got married, we barely see her at the yarn shop," Mavis Anne said, and I sensed a trace of annoyance in her tone. "Did she stop knitting just because she got married?"

Iris shrugged. "I can't begin to figure Isabelle out. I seldom hear from her and when I do it's a rushed, brief conversation. How about you, Petra? Have you seen much of her since you got here?"

I shook my head. "No. Only last weekend when she came to dinner at Mavis Anne's. She forgot about our lunch plans and ended up canceling."

"Well, that's not unusual for Isabelle," Iris said. "She can get quite wrapped up in her own life . . . to the exclusion of others."

I really couldn't recall this happening very much during the years of my friendship with Isabelle, but then I realized that the few times she had grown quiet or drifted away, I was always the one who made the effort to get in touch. I wondered what would happen if I now chose not to.

I didn't have to wonder too long because the next evening Isabelle called, gushing with excitement about her shopping spree in the Big Apple.

"It sounds like it was a fun time," I said.

"Oh, it was. Listen, I want to get together with you for lunch. Are you free on Wednesday?"

The one day I had plans. "No, actually, I'm not. I'm committed to volunteer at the shelter from ten till two."

"The what?" she asked, and I remembered I hadn't even had a chance to tell her about my new work.

"I'm volunteering at the animal shelter," I explained. "Louise is involved and got me interested."

"Oh," she said, but just that one word led me to think she couldn't begin to understand why on earth I'd want to do something like this. I recalled how Haley had had to beg and cajole to bring her beloved Ginger home from the shelter. And in the end, it was really Iris who had made that happen for her granddaughter. "Well, okay. Are you free tomorrow? I think I could see my way clear to taking an hour or so. Why don't we say noon at Panera's? We'll be able to get in and out fast."

Obviously this wasn't going to be a chatty, leisurely, girlfriend lunch, catching up on all of our news, complete with wine.

"Sure. Fine," I said. "I'll meet you there tomorrow at twelve noon."

I hung up the phone and continued cleaning up the supper dishes. As I washed the plate and bowl from my soup and sandwich, for the first time since I'd been friends with Isabelle, it hit me that what we shared tended to be one-sided.

Various incidents popped into my head. Like our senior year in high school when we spent so much time shopping for the perfect prom gown for her that I was left with only a couple of days to make my own choice and settled for a gown I wasn't crazy about. Or the time in college when she begged me to nurse her through a hangover brought on by her drinking way too much at a frat party. And after being up all night with her, I showed up late the following morning for my final exam in economics, knocking my grade down a few points.

And of course during the grueling weeks and months after she discovered her husband, Roger, was gay, I was there every step of the way for her. If not always there in person, I was a text or phone call away. Even at three in the morning when she had drunk too much and would call me to cry and complain about the injustice of Roger and her life.

Yes, our friendship had pretty much always been one-sided. Yet I had always overlooked it, because I loved Isabelle like a sister, and when she wasn't totally wrapped up in herself, she could be a loving and compassionate friend.

I let out a sigh, and Lotte's head popped up from her paws. She looked at me expectantly, hoping for a treat.

I reached into the biscuit jar on the counter and said, "Here ya go. Mama's going on the patio to knit."

By the time I was ready for bed around eleven, my head was swimming with thoughts of not only Isabelle but also the young boy I had only met once. I couldn't seem to get Jonah out of my mind, and I wondered if he'd ever get the dog he longed for.

I woke around four in the morning from what I was sure had been a dream. I sat on the edge of the bed and shook my head. I had been staying at Koi House not quite two weeks and I hadn't given much thought to Emmalyn, the original occupant of my room. And yet she had been the focus of my dream.

She was exactly as Chloe and Isabelle had described her—with long, flowing auburn hair, wearing a beautiful red gown. And she had been seated on the sofa in my room.

"Sometimes your past isn't just your past," she had said. "Sometimes your past can be your future."

Even in the dream I didn't understand what she was saying.

"What does my past have to do with anything?" I had questioned.

"Probably everything," she replied.

And then I woke up.

As I headed to the bathroom I realized that since I had come to stay at Koi House I hadn't made one attempt to research or locate my father. Was that what she had been talking about? But even more important, how the hell could I now be having these dreams about Emmalyn just as Chloe and Isabelle had? It made no sense. No sense at all.

# Chapter 7

I had arrived at Panera Bread before Isabelle and ordered myself a bowl of soup. She came rushing into the restaurant a few minutes later, looked around, saw me waving from a table, and came over to place a kiss on my cheek before plunking down in the chair opposite me.

"You look frazzled," I said.

"Yeah, I'm about to close my first real estate deal. Well, technically Chadwick will close the deal as I haven't taken my exam yet. We're meeting with the clients at two. I'm pretty sure they're going to make an offer."

"That's wonderful. You seem to enjoy your new job."

"I do. I feel a sense of accomplishment, showing potential buyers a home, finding one that's perfect for them."

"Well, you need nourishment, so go get your lunch."

She nodded. "Be right back."

When she returned she only had a cup of coffee.

"Aren't you eating?" I asked.

"Too nervous to eat. So . . . catch me up. What's going on in your life since you got here? Do you like it? How's living at Koi House going for you?"

Before she'd arrived, it seemed I had a million things to tell her. About my volunteering at the shelter. About meeting a young boy named Jonah. About my dream of the night before. But sitting here across from her now, it all seemed foolish and unimportant. It certainly couldn't compare to selling your first house or flying to Manhattan for a weekend of Christmas shopping.

"Yeah," I said. "Everything's going really well. I love Koi House. Lotte and I are settling in. We're having a Christmas gathering there on the eighteenth for the customers at the yarn shop. The tree is all decorated and Marta will be making the pastries. You will come, won't you?"

I noticed her head had been bent over her cell phone as I talked, and I wondered if she had even heard what I'd said.

"Isabelle?"

Her head shot up. "Right. Yes, my mother mentioned the Christmas tea to me. I'll definitely be there. Anything I can bring?"

"No, I don't think so, but I'll let you know. So I take it married life is agreeing with you?"

She smiled and nodded. "Very much so. Chadwick has changed my whole life."

I had no doubt that she loved him. A lot. But I knew that his wealth made that love even sweeter. And I also knew that Isabelle had always been attracted to the material things in life. But I wouldn't let myself think that his bank account had led in any way to their recent marriage.

"So what's with working at the shelter?" she asked. "God, Petra, you're *not* going to rescue another dog, are you?"

I felt annoyed that she would even question my right to adopt another dog if I chose to do that. And the thought flitted through my mind that maybe that was how Jonah's father had felt when I took the liberty of mentioning the boy's mother.

"I'm not *working* there. I'm volunteering. They need help so I assisted for a few hours on Saturday at Petco for the adoptions. I'll be doing a few hours a week at the shelter, answering the phone and helping out there."

Isabelle shook her head and laughed. "You know . . . you would have made some kid a great mom. I still don't understand why you don't like kids."

Her frankness bothered me. We had had this conversation a few times over the years, and she knew it wasn't that I didn't *like* kids. I just had no experience with them. I was an only child, had never done any babysitting or been exposed to small children. I recalled how uneasy I'd been with Haley when she was a baby, but by the time she reached four or five, she had become a little person I quite enjoyed—in small doses.

"You know that's not true," I told her. "It isn't that I *dislike* kids. They're just foreign to me."

She waved a hand in the air. "I know. I know. I'm just giving you a hard time. But I do think you take all of your maternal instincts and focus them on your dogs."

Now I was definitely annoyed. "And what's wrong with that?" I demanded.

"Hey, nothing," she said, holding up her palm in defeat. She glanced at her watch. "I'm really sorry, Pet, but I have to go."

She got up and hugged me to her chest. "We're okay, right?"

I nodded and felt the kiss she placed on the top of my head.

"Good. I promise to call you and we'll have a nice long lunch. But I have to run. Love you," she said, and with that she was gone, and I sat staring at my bowl of cold soup.

Isabelle might have been in a rush, but I decided to prolong my lunch. I got up and went to the counter and ordered a cookie and a cup of coffee. Bringing it back to the table, I thought about what she had said. Maybe she was right. I had never been like a lot of other women, dying to get married and have children. It just wasn't anything that excited me. I had always been completely happy with my own company, doing things the way I liked, not having to compromise with another person. All of this was probably one of the major reasons why any relationships I had eventually fizzled out.

And children? I just never had a burning, all-consuming desire to get pregnant and spend the rest of my life raising that child. But dogs? Yeah, different story. I had loved dogs ever since I could remember. I seemed to resonate with them. Understand their sadness or happiness, their joy over the smallest things, and their love truly is unconditional. No matter what. They loved me. And I loved them back. There was nothing wrong with any of this. So what was nagging at me?

I knew exactly what it was. A scrawny young boy, with hair that flopped onto his forehead and who wore black-framed glasses. I had looked up, seen him standing there, and an emotion that was completely alien to me had emerged. And since Saturday afternoon I hadn't been able to get the boy out of my mind.

As if I had conjured him up, I took a sip of coffee and saw him enter the restaurant, not with his father but with a middle-aged woman. *Probably his grandmother*, I thought.

He saw me immediately and came running to my table.

"Hey, Petra. Do you remember me? I'm Jonah. From Petco."

I laughed and nodded. "I do remember you. How are you?"

The woman had followed him and put an arm around his shoulder. "Jonah, are you bothering this woman?"

"No," he said. "She's my friend. I met her at Petco on Saturday when I went there with Dad."

The woman laughed. "Oh, okay." She put her hand out to shake mine. "I'm Jonah's nanny."

"Yeah," Jonah said. "This is Miss Betsy. She watches me when my dad's at work."

I smiled and returned her greeting. So the boy was cared for by a nanny, not even a bona fide grandmother. I found this to be sad.

"Did Lucy and Ethel get adopted?" he asked.

I shook my head. "No, I'm afraid they didn't."

But instead of feeling bad, Jonah seemed delighted. "Oh, that's good. Then I still have a chance to get them. Are they still at the shelter?"

"They are. I'll see them tomorrow when I volunteer there. I'll be sure to say hello for you."

"Really? That would be great. Thanks."

"Okay, now come along, Jonah," his nanny said. "Let's get your cookie. We can't be late for your piano lesson."

"Bye, Petra," he said. "I'll see you again soon."

After they left the restaurant, I sat there pondering two things that had occurred—Jonah had said he'd see me again, and he'd said I was his friend.

I knew nothing about this boy named Jonah. But one thing I did know for certain. He was right. I *was* his friend.

# *Rhonda*
## *January 1969*

The days seemed to be sliding one into the other and before I knew it, we had been working at Broadglen's for two weeks. It was going really well, and the tips were even better than I'd hoped for. So I was able to begin saving some money.

But I had to admit that the highlight for me was getting assigned to the Maxwell family table on the weekends. They were totally out of my league. I knew that. But it didn't stop me from falling head over heels for the son who accompanied his father and two sisters to dinner.

The first night I waited on them, Franklin Maxwell introduced himself and then pointed to his three children. The younger sister seemed to be about sixteen and the older one probably in her late twenties. They both smiled when their father made the introductions. But it was the son I had difficulty taking my eyes off. I thought he was probably about six or seven years older than me. Wearing a sport jacket and tie, he reminded me of a successful businessman. His dark eyes locked with mine as he gave me a huge smile. By the time the evening was over, I was certain the only time I'd seen a fellow quite this good looking was when I skimmed through one of Cynthia's movie magazines.

On the second weekend of my employment I wasted no time checking the reservation book on Friday morning. There it was: the name *Maxwell* booked for seven o'clock. I smiled before returning to the dining room to assist with the breakfast clean-up.

Cynthia and I had a couple of hours before returning for our lunch shift, so we went back to our cabin to relax. This was our time to catch up with each other and gossip. I knew she had had her first date with Earle the night before and I was ready to hear the details.

"So how did your date go?" I asked.

She sat in the chair next to me on our porch and stretched her legs up to the railing before lighting a cigarette. Blowing out the smoke, she turned to me and smiled with a coy expression on her face.

"I'd say it went well. Very well."

I shifted in my seat to get a better look at her expression. "Really? Then you like him?"

"He's sweet and he's fun to be with. We saw *Cactus Flower* with Goldie Hawn and it was good. We went out for a burger after the movie, and we were still laughing. So yes, I do like him. Plus, Earle is a very skilled kisser."

I knew Cynthia had more experience than I did when it came to dating. Way more. As I'd discovered the year before, when she had confided to me that she had lost her virginity to Jack, the fellow she had dated through high school and broke up with the day before we graduated.

She wasn't what we referred to as loose or immoral. Cynthia just had a more relaxed attitude toward sex than I did.

"But you . . . didn't . . ."

She waved a hand in the air and interrupted me. "No, I didn't have sex with him on the *first* date, Rhonda. Geez, I'm not a slut."

I wasn't aware there was an appropriate time frame for when a man and woman had sex for the first time. Sometimes I felt much younger than Cynthia, and this was one of those times.

"So you're going to see him again?"

She nodded. "Yes, he asked me to another movie Sunday evening." She took a drag off her cigarette. "Hey, aren't you the lucky one."

"What do you mean?"

"You got assigned to the Maxwell table for the weekends. With that dreamy son who all of us are drooling over. I got Mr. and Mrs. Webb—a stodgy couple in their eighties."

I laughed. "Yeah, he is pretty good looking, but not to worry. I don't even know his name."

"Oh, it's Peter."

"How do you know that?"

"The local servers who have worked here for a while know him. Let's see"—she held up her hand and began extending a finger at a time—"he's single, graduated college and works with his father at the manufacturing company they own. His mother passed away a couple of years ago. Oh, and in case you didn't notice, he couldn't keep his eyes off you all last weekend."

"Yeah, right," I said, jabbing Cynthia in the arm before I went inside the cabin.

I would be lying if I said I didn't take extra time with my hair and makeup before work later that evening.

By the time the Maxwell family arrived just before seven, my other three tables were having dessert and coffee, which would allow me to spend extra time catering to them. I headed to the bar immediately, and within a few minutes of their being seated I placed a Chivas Regal on the rocks in front of Mr. Maxwell, white wine for the older sister, Pepsi for the younger one, and Wild Turkey and water for the son.

All four nodded their thanks, but I noticed Peter's smile seemed to linger on my face a bit longer than necessary. I told them to enjoy their drinks while they looked over the menu.

By the time they had finished their dinner and I had completed my cleaning up chores, it was after ten and Cynthia had already returned to our cabin. On my way out, I noticed that Peter Maxwell was sitting at the bar alone, nursing a drink.

I had just gotten outside when I heard somebody call, "Rhonda?"

Turning around, I saw Peter walking toward me, smiling.

"Hi," I said, pretty sure that he had purposely lingered at the bar until I left. "Something wrong?"

"No. Not at all. I just wanted a chance to talk to you. Alone."

"Oh. Okay." Now I was confused. Why would he want to talk to me? "About what?"

He laughed. "I'd like to get to know you better." He pointed toward the parking lot. "It's a beautiful evening. Feel like going for a drive?"

I was off duty, so my time was my own. But I didn't really know him. I debated his offer for a few moments before realizing that was the purpose of the ride—to get to know each other better. I also briefly wondered what we could possibly have in common, but I ended up saying, "Sure. Just for a little while."

"Great," he said, placing his hand at the small of my back and leading me to a late-model convertible.

I slid onto the leather upholstery and smiled. I certainly hadn't expected this when I began my shift hours earlier.

He got in, shot me a smile, started the ignition, and said, "We'll drive to the beach and park there so we can talk."

I nodded as I luxuriated in the comfort of his car.

"So where are you from?" he asked and turned the car toward A1A.

"Pennsylvania. A small mining town in the west."

"I bet you're enjoying the winter here. Gets pretty cold in Pennsylvania this time of year."

"It does. And yes, I love the Florida winter."

A few minutes later he pulled into a parking lot overlooking the beach and ocean.

"Have you gotten to the beach very much since you arrived?" he asked, shutting off the ignition and shifting to face me.

"No, I'm afraid not. My only day off is Monday, and I've only been here a couple of weeks."

"Well, we'll have to do something about that," he said, giving me his killer smile. "Do you like working at Broadglen's?"

"I do. I came here with my best friend, Cynthia. We both worked in a small restaurant back home but the money is much better here. I'm hoping to save up to attend secretarial school."

"Good for you. My older sister attended accounting school and she works at my father's company with me. I majored in business in college."

"Did you go to college in Florida?" I asked.

He shook his head. "No. Harvard Business School. I suffered through four brutally cold winters in the Boston area."

I laughed. "But I'm sure it was worth it for the education you got."

"It was. Tell me more about yourself. What kind of music do you like? What do you like to read?"

This was the first time a fellow had asked what I was interested in, which made me wonder how old he was. He was definitely much more mature than the guys I'd dated in high school. He has spent four years in college and was now a successful businessman who displayed a sophisticated demeanor.

After I finished sharing my music and book preferences with him, I said, "Can I ask you something?"

He smiled and nodded. "Sure."

"How old are you?"

He threw his head back, laughing. "Why? How old do you think I am?"

"Twenty-five?"

"Close. I'm twenty-six. How old are you?"

"Nineteen."

"Hmm. Too much of an age difference?"

"That depends."

"On what?"

"If you think I'm too young."

He edged closer and placed an arm over the back of the seat. "No, I don't think you're too young at all. Actually, I think you're much more mature than many girls my age."

I felt a smile forming on my face just as he leaned closer and brushed my lips with his. Reaching for my hand, he said, "Is there any chance you'd like to go for a boat ride with me on Monday?"

"You mean like a sightseeing boat?"

He paused a moment before answering. "Um, no. My family has a boat and I thought we could go up the coast toward Jacksonville. I'll bring a picnic lunch. It'll be fun."

Could this really be happening? This super good looking, wealthy guy was asking *me* for a date? I could tell by the serious expression on his face that he wasn't joking with me.

I nodded and smiled. "I'd love to," I said. "I'd really love to."

"Good. I was hoping you'd say yes."

He leaned toward me, pulled me closer and kissed me—making me very sure that I wasn't with a high school boy any longer.

# Chapter 8

I told Lotte to be a good girl before I headed out the door the following morning to staff the front desk at the shelter. Thoughts of Jonah had occupied my mind since I'd seen him at Panera's the day before, so being busy answering a phone and greeting potential adoptive doggie parents would be good for me.

Just before I was due to leave the shelter, I glanced up from the counter to see the object of my thoughts walk in carrying a small bouquet of flowers. He was followed by his nanny, who remained near the door as Jonah extended his hand to give me the flowers.

"Hi," he said. "These are from my dad."

"Your dad?" I was confused.

He shifted from one foot to the other and nodded. "Yeah. He felt bad about the way he spoke to you on Saturday at Petco." He adjusted his eyeglasses and nodded again. "So he wanted to say he was sorry."

I looked at the flowers wrapped in cellophane and smiled. These weren't florist shop quality, more likely from Publix, but the message was touching.

"Thank you so much," I said. "This is very nice of him. Be sure to thank him for me."

"I will," he replied as he looked around the room. "Are Lucy and Ethel still here?"

"They are. They're in their crate in the back. Did you want to say hi to them?"

He hesitated for a second and then shook his head. "No. I can't today. I have to get to my piano lesson. But would it be okay if I come back?"

I smiled. "Sure. That would be fine," I said, but wondered if the dogs would still be at the shelter.

"Good," he said, reaching into his pocket. "Here's my phone number. You know . . . just in case you wanted to call me."

I took the scrap of paper and saw his hand-printed name and phone number. "Okay. Thanks."

"Do you think . . . um . . . maybe I could have your number? You know, just in case I wanted to call first to make sure the dogs are still here before I come by?"

I smiled again and reached into my handbag for my business card. "Sure. Here you go."

"Great. Thanks, Petra. I'll talk to you soon."

Miss Betsy sent me a smile and a wave, then put her hand on Jonah's shoulder and they were gone.

I was still pondering what had just happened when Suzanne came into the room from the kennel area.

"A secret admirer?" she asked, pointing at the flowers.

I laughed. "Oh. No, I don't think so. Just a small gesture of apology."

When I got home, I let Lotte out in the garden area before making myself a cup of herbal tea. I filled a crystal vase and arranged the flowers Jonah had given me before placing them on the breakfast nook table. This was when I realized I longed for some contact with Isabelle. I wanted to discuss the flower episode with her. But I knew that she was normally out showing houses with Chadwick in the afternoon. She had mentioned he was training her while she studied for the real estate exam and, hopefully, once she passed the test she would be able to show a few houses on her own.

Lotte wandered back inside from the garden and I said, "Come on, girl. We need some female company."

I went to get my knitting tote and we headed across the garden to the yarn shop.

"Hey, Petra. We were just talking about you," Chloe said.

"Yes." Mavis Anne put the pullover sweater she was working on in her lap. "How did it go volunteering at the shelter?"

I sat down and smiled before removing the baby blanket from my tote. "It went very well. I saw a few dogs go to their forever homes and that's always heartwarming. Suzanne is very pleasant to work with. And I even got a surprise bouquet of flowers."

Iris laughed. "Really? How nice. From a grateful adoptive parent?"

I shook my head. "Actually, no. Do you remember I told you that I'd met that boy, Jonah, on Saturday at Petco? And his father was upset when I mentioned maybe the mother would allow the boy to have a dog?"

Mavis Anne, Iris, and Yarrow had stopped knitting and all three stared at me.

"Right," Yarrow said. "Keep going."

"Well, I guess he felt bad for speaking harshly to me, because Jonah showed up today at the shelter with his nanny. And he presented me with the flowers. He said they were from his dad and his dad wanted to say he was sorry."

"Well, now that's what I call a true gentleman," Mavis Anne said. "That was a very kind gesture."

"It was," Iris agreed.

"What's this dad look like? I wonder how long his wife has been gone," Yarrow asked, making me laugh.

I shrugged and realized I had given barely any thought to the father. It was the boy who had stirred emotion in me. However, when I recalled the father I had to admit he was rather sexy in that nerdy sort of way.

"The dad is good looking," I told her. "But I have no idea how long his wife has been gone. Jonah hasn't said anything. The only things I really know are that this boy takes piano lessons, loves dogs, and has a nanny."

"Hmm," Mavis Anne said. "Well, you never know what can develop."

"Yeah, right," I retorted. "The father thinks I'm a busybody. Not much chance of a romantic involvement there. Besides which, I'm definitely not looking for a relationship."

Iris laughed. "Famous last words."

"Have you made any further attempt to get information on your father?" Mavis Anne asked.

I shook my head. "No. I keep saying I will . . . but . . . I did have a dream the other night. A rather crazy dream."

Chloe's head popped up from her knitting. "A dream?"

I nodded and we locked eyes.

"Emmalyn?" she asked in a soft voice and I nodded again.

Mavis Anne clapped her hands together, and an expression of pure joy crossed her face.

"My sister is back," she said.

"What was the dream about?" Chloe questioned.

"Not very much, actually. She looked exactly as you and Isabelle have described her from your dreams. She was sitting on the sofa in my room, and she said something about the past could be my future."

Everyone remained silent for a few moments.

"Do you think she was referring to your father?" Yarrow asked.

"I have no idea. I'm not even sure I believe this silly stuff about dreams having to do with Emmalyn."

I saw the knowing look that passed between Mavis Anne and Chloe.

Iris let out a deep sigh. "Well, maybe it's time you begin to do some research about your father."

And I knew Iris was right.


Later that evening after I did my supper clean-up, I got out my laptop and sat at the kitchen counter. I stared at the blank screen for a few minutes and then got up to pour myself a glass of wine.

Lotte followed my movements around the kitchen with her eyes.

Fortified with Pinot Grigio, I settled myself back on the stool and clicked Google. After a moment, I typed in "Peter Maxwell." A few seconds later, a page appeared. I did a quick scan and saw that the only item that seemed relevant was a website for a manufacturing company, so I clicked the link.

The page told me that the company was owned by somebody named Peter Maxwell. It seemed the business was no longer in existence, and it didn't look as if the site had been updated in quite a while. I scanned the page and saw that the headquarters was located in Jacksonville, Florida, and the company specialized in diesel backup pumps, which replaced generators. The unit continued pumping despite power loss or primary pump failure.

It sounded like a good business to have in Florida, especially during hurricanes, but beyond this, there was no personal information about the owner.

I scanned to the bottom of the page, where there was a black-and-white photo of the outside of the company building but no picture of the owner.

Was the man in the photo with my mother on the beach the same Peter Maxwell who owned this company? I had no way of knowing.

And from the lack of any further Internet information, it didn't seem likely that I would find out.

# Rhonda
## February 1969

The boat trip and picnic with Peter were like something out of my romance novels. He was good looking, fun to be with, and a perfect gentleman. He was also very intelligent, and I loved hearing him speak and learning new things from him.

He had picked me up at eight on Monday morning at the hotel. We drove to the local marina, where his boat was waiting for us. As we pulled away from the dock and he expertly steered the boat north, I had to pinch myself to make sure I wasn't dreaming.

And now two weeks later, I was certain none of it had been a dream—the laughter, the picnic on the beach, or the kisses we'd exchanged. I had seen Peter twice since then, and each time was more fun than the last. We had gone to a movie one evening, and the night before we had driven to Jacksonville for dinner at a restaurant I knew cost a fortune.

On the drive back to Amelia Island, he had pulled the car into the parking lot overlooking the ocean.

I felt super sensitive since I had met him. Soaking up sounds and smells and colors and everything that surrounded me. Experiences that at one time had seemed ordinary now seemed enhanced. I found myself paying more attention to the small things while I discovered that Peter Maxwell consumed my thoughts.

"Wake up, daydreamer," I heard Sally say as she jabbed me playfully in the ribs. "Your party at table seven would like their check."

"Right. Okay, thanks," I said, going to retrieve the bill.

My lunch shift was almost over, and I spent the remaining time doing the required tasks as I contemplated again the fact that tonight would be the first time I would be seeing Peter two nights in a row.

"Has he invited you to his house yet?" Cynthia asked as I removed rollers from my hair.

I shook my head and picked up my brush. "No. Why?"

She was stretched out on her bed, leafing through her current issue of *Photoplay*.

"Well, you have had a few dates. And this week two nights in a row. I just thought he might suggest you meet his dad."

I laughed. "I *have* met his dad. And his two sisters. Every weekend at the restaurant."

"Right. I know that. I mean in a casual atmosphere. Not while you're working."

I hadn't really given this any thought. I shrugged. "He hasn't said anything."

"Have you met any of his friends yet?"

I stopped brushing my hair to look at her. "No. Am I supposed to?"

Cynthia laughed. "Well, it's not mandatory. But Earle has introduced me to some of his friends outside of the restaurant." She waved a hand in the air. "Hey, maybe Peter just wants to keep you all to himself."

"Maybe," was all I said.

Peter had decided we should take advantage of the beautiful weather and drive south along A1A to have dinner at a restaurant he knew in Ormond Beach.

When we arrived, it was obvious that the staff knew who he was.

An older man came forward, pulled Peter into a bear hug, and clapped him on the back.

"It's been a while," he said, a smile covering his face. "Marion was just saying the other day it's been much too long since we've heard from you."

Peter laughed and nodded. "Busy. The business is keeping me tied up at the moment."

"Ah, but not too busy to escort a beautiful young lady to dinner? Good, good. Come this way. We have a nice table on the deck overlooking the water."

When we were seated, Peter said, "I know the legal drinking age is twenty-one, however, if you'd like a glass of wine or a cocktail, I think that could be arranged."

Up until now, I'd only ever had a few sips of wine or beer that Cynthia or a boyfriend had managed to get.

"Really?" I said, suddenly feeling more mature than my nineteen years. "What do you suggest?"

"Daiquiris are very popular right now. Rum and lime juice."

"Sounds good. I'll try one."

Peter gave the waitress the drink order and sure enough, she never questioned my age.

When she returned, I took a small sip and nodded. "Very good. I like it." The tart, citrus flavor was refreshing and very different from the bitterness of beer or sweetness of the wine I had tried.

He took a sip of his bourbon and water and nodded back. "I thought you might. That drink seems to be the rage with my sister and her friends."

"So how do you know the man who greeted us?" I asked.

"Milo? Oh, he's the owner and has been a friend of my family since before I was born."

I felt flattered that he'd chosen to take me to the restaurant of an old family friend. I would be sure to let Cynthia know this.

"So how is your job going?" he asked.

"Very well. I enjoy working at the hotel. Everybody is friendly, and Joyce—she's the one we report to—really looks out for us."

"Did you have to sign an agreement to stay a certain amount of time?"

I nodded. "Yes. We agreed to stay until the end of May and Memorial Day weekend. We were told that some of us might be asked to stay on through the summer. But I guess that will depend on how busy they think they might be with reservations."

He took a sip of his drink and nodded thoughtfully, before saying, "If there's no further work for you at the hotel, what are your plans?"

I hadn't really thought that far ahead. May was still three months away.

"I mean, will you return home?" he asked. "Go back to Pennsylvania?"

"When I applied to come here to work, I was hoping to be able to stay in the area. Make enough money to attend a local secretarial school here and then find a job. But I'll have to wait and see what happens in a few months."

The waitress returned with the menus and flashed a huge smile at Peter. "Milo said to tell you that he got a shipment of Maine lobster this morning."

"Ah, well, that settles it then. Lobster it is!" He looked across the table at me. "You do like lobster, don't you?"

Although I had never tried it in my life, I nodded and smiled. "Yes. Absolutely."

We continued talking as I soaked up the ocean waves rolling in to shore, Peter's handsome face, and the tart taste of my drink. This was certainly a far cry from my previous winters spent in Pennsylvania.

When the waitress returned and placed a platter of boiled lobster in front of me, I think a nervous expression crossed my face, because Peter said, "I've always found the easiest way to eat these things is to just crack them open with this and dig out the delicious meat with this one."

He held up unfamiliar utensils in the air.

I nodded and mumbled, "Right." And then proceeded to watch his every move.

Within a few minutes, I found I was getting the hang of it and even dipping the succulent pieces of lobster into the small bowl containing drawn butter, just as Peter was doing.

I didn't think I had ever tasted anything quite so good. I was focused on the culinary feast I was enjoying when I heard Peter laugh.

I looked up to see a smile on his face. "Enjoying it?"

"Oh, my God! I can't believe how good this is. I've never had . . ." I started to say and then realized what I was about to admit.

But Peter brushed it aside and said, "Yeah, lobster is special," before he reached for my hand and gave it a squeeze. "Just like you are."

The drink was tasty. The lobster, delicious. But being special in Peter's eyes made me feel on top of the world.

By the time we left the restaurant and headed back to Amelia Island, I knew I had never been happier.

As had become our ritual at the end of an evening, Peter pulled into a parking lot along the ocean. But instead of staying in the car, this time he got out, reached into the backseat for a blanket, and then opened my door, saying, "Come on. Let's go sit on the beach for a little while."

It was after ten and the beach was deserted when he spread the blanket and we sat down. I felt his arm encircle me before he lifted my face for his kiss. This time our kisses became more intense. More passionate. After a few minutes, it was Peter who pulled away, breathing heavily.

He reached for my hand. "I like you, Rhonda. I like you a lot."

"I like you too," I whispered.

He let out a deep sigh and nodded.

We sat there for a while longer in silence, each of us lost in our thoughts.

I heard the tide lapping the shore, and I saw a sliver of the moon hovering over the ocean. I wondered where we were headed, where whatever it was we shared would end up, and I shivered.

"Cold?" he asked, pulling me closer.

I shook my head. "No. I'm fine."

"I'd like to take you to my house sometime," he said. "To meet my father outside of the restaurant."

"That would be nice," I replied as I smiled up at him.

And I knew that Cynthia had been needlessly concerned.

# Chapter 9

There had been no further word or visits from Jonah the following week. But this didn't prevent him from occupying my thoughts

I had been kept busy knitting away making spa cloths to give at our Christmas tea. And I had managed to volunteer on Monday and Wednesday at the shelter. Both times the first thing I did was to check to make sure Lucy and Ethel were still with us. They were. On the one hand, I felt sad that they still hadn't been adopted, but on the other hand I was happy that perhaps Jonah might still have a chance to take them home.

I awoke Thursday morning and remembered I had an appointment for Lotte with the vet in the afternoon. I wanted to get her registered at the local practice and she was due for her annual checkup.

My phone rang mid-morning and I was surprised to hear Isabelle's voice.

"I promised I'd call," she said. "How are you?"

"I'm doing well. And you?"

"Busy. Things have slowed down a little at work. People aren't interested in house hunting a couple weeks before Christmas, but I've been busy shopping and decorating. I was wondering if you'd be free tomorrow for lunch?"

"I am," I told her. "Yes. That'll work for me."

"Great. Why don't we meet at LuLu's at noon?"

I hung up with a smile on my face. Damn Isabelle. I could be so annoyed with her, but I had to admit that I missed her company. Maybe tomorrow we could recapture some of what I felt we'd lost these past few months.

\* \* \*

Lotte and I pulled into the parking lot of the veterinarian's office about fifteen minutes before our appointment. I figured there would be some paperwork to do.

I reached into the backseat and picked her up. "Come on, sweetie. You're going to meet your new vet today."

I put her down near some shrubbery so she could pee before going inside. Today she was sporting a red-and-green Christmas beret on her head, but I'd passed on an outfit because of her exam.

I glanced up and saw that the sign outside the office read "Wellington Veterinary Clinic." Below this, was printed "Ben Wellington, DVM."

Walking inside with Lotte in my arms, I was greeted by a smiling young woman behind the desk.

"Aren't you a cutie," she said, reaching out her hand for Lotte to sniff. "Petra Garfield with Lotte, right?"

I nodded and returned her smile.

She passed me a clipboard with papers and said, "If you'll fill these out, Dr. Wellington will be with you shortly."

Lotte curled up beside me on the sofa while I completed the forms and then returned them.

A few minutes later the door opened, and another young woman called, "Petra Garfield and Lotte?"

"Yes," I said, getting up and carrying Lotte down the corridor behind her.

"Right here," she said, indicating a door on the left.

I placed Lotte on the exam table.

"I'm Cathy, the tech. Any problems going on that the doctor needs to know about?"

I shook my head. "No. She's doing very well."

"If you could put her on the scale there, we'll get her weight."

I did as instructed and heard her say, "Very good. Ten pounds, two ounces." She went to the computer and entered some information. "Does she need her annual injections? Heartworm test?"

I nodded. "Yes. She's due for that."

"Appetite good?"

I nodded again. "Yup. No problems."

"Great. Dr. Wellington will be in shortly."

She came over to ruffle the top of Lotte's head. "She's so cute. Love the Christmas beret."

"Thanks," I said and smiled.

I had my back to the door and was leaning over the exam table talking to Lotte when I heard it open.

I turned around at the same time the vet looked up from his clipboard, and our eyes met.

"It's *you*?" I said. "You've *got* to be kidding me!"

Because standing in front me, looking as surprised as I, was Jonah's father. Jonah's father was a vet?

"Yes. It would appear that it *is* me," he replied. He adjusted his glasses in the same manner that Jonah did, looking as uncomfortable as I felt. "Do you still want me to do the exam? It's up to you."

God! Talk about awkward. And why was Lotte acting like a traitor, wagging her tail and attempting to get the vet to pat her?

I shrugged. "Yes. Sure. Okay. We're here now."

He walked to the other side of the table, and the tech came back into the room to assist. Which allowed me to step back and slink into the corner.

"Hey, there, pretty girl," he said, addressing Lotte.

She placed her front paws on his chest and began lapping his cheek. Oh, yeah, definitely a traitor.

"We're just going to check you over," he said, completely ignoring me.

He proceeded to remove the stethoscope from around his neck and listened to her heart and lungs. "Very good," he said.

He then palpated her back and ribs, checked her ears, looked into her eyes, maneuvered each leg and nodded.

"She's obviously very well cared for."

This was said without looking at me.

"Okay, ready for your injections?" he said, before giving her the shots. "And now we'll take a little blood for the heartworm test."

He passed the vial to Cathy, who left the room.

"It'll just take a few minutes for the results," he told me, briefly glancing in my direction.

"Thanks," I mumbled, going to the table to cradle Lotte in my arms. "Good girl," I whispered to her.

He busied himself at the computer, entering information. It was obvious that Lotte was taken with him. And I couldn't help but recall that dogs are excellent judges of character. He had been very nice to her and certainly seemed to be a caring vet. And that was when I recalled he had attempted to make amends to me with the flowers.

Cathy came back into the room and said the heartworm test was negative.

"Okay, then," he said. "She's in very good health. Continue with her heartworm pills. Do you need a refill?"

I nodded. "Yes. A one-year supply, please."

Cathy left to get them.

"You know," I said, "I wanted to . . . ah . . . thank you for the flowers. It wasn't necessary, but it was a nice gesture."

His head swung around to stare at me and I could see by the expression on his face he had no idea what the hell I was talking about.

"The what?" he said as Cathy returned and passed me the packet.

I realized in a heartbeat exactly what had happened and thought I might die of embarrassment right there where I was standing.

"Oh . . . um . . ." I had no words and knew the best thing was to get out of there. Fast.

I scooped Lotte into my arms, stopped at the front desk, paid the bill in cash because it was quicker, and all but sprinted to the car.

I placed Lotte in the backseat, slid into the driver's seat, and blew out a huge puff of air. My head dropped onto the steering wheel as I let out a groan.

Throwing back my head, I said, "Oh, my God! It was Jonah! It was Jonah who got the flowers, brought them to me and then pretended they were from his father." Why in the world would a ten-year-old kid do something like that?

I pushed the keyless ignition, backed out of the parking lot, and headed straight up Granada. To Koi House. Where I could hide in my shame.

I was so upset by what had happened, I changed my mind about going to the yarn shop as I had planned. Walking into the house, I headed straight to the fridge, poured myself a glass of Pinot Grigio, and took a big gulp.

Settling myself on the counter stool, I shook my head. What had just occurred was like something from a romantic film. I took another sip of wine. After a few minutes, I got up to check the chicken dish I was cooking in the Crock-Pot.

An hour later I wasn't feeling much better, but it did occur to me that I never had to see Ben Wellington again. I could just find another vet for Lotte. Right. There were plenty of vets in the area. And if I never told anybody what had happened, then nobody would ever know the extent of my humiliation.

There was no doubt about it—I had never been this mortified in my entire life.

# Chapter 10

I almost choked on the bite of my salad tomato. "You think it's funny?" I hissed at Isabelle. "Why are you laughing?"

I should have stuck to my original plan and not mentioned one word of my encounter the day before. But over a glass of wine and a girlfriend lunch, I was feeling mellow and missing the sharing that Isabelle and I used to do. So I decided to bring her up to date on Jonah, his father, and the humiliating vet visit.

"Well, you have to admit," she said, "it is a bit humorous. You meet this guy, he tells you off, and then you find out he's your vet."

I took a sip of wine. "I'm not so sure he's going to remain my vet."

"How was he with Lotte?"

"Good." I neglected to tell her that he was in fact very good and that Lotte had been way too friendly.

"I would think that's all that matters."

"Yeah, well, it was very awkward. Bad enough that it was the guy who put me in my place at Petco, but then I thank him for flowers he didn't even send."

Isabelle nodded. "Yeah. What was that all about? Why would his kid do that?"

"I have no idea."

She waved a hand in the air in her usual dismissive way. "Well, don't let it bother you. I'm sure he's forgotten all about it." She took a bite of salad before saying, "Unless . . . unless you might be attracted to him?"

"Are you crazy?"

She shrugged. "It's just that you'd normally brush off something like this. Why is it bothering you so much?"

She did have a point. I had innocently mentioned the boy's mother.

And then I was merely being polite thanking him for the flowers. How was I to know *he* had not sent them? There was really no reason to dwell on the embarrassment of the situation.

"Well?" she questioned when I refrained from saying anything. "What's he look like?"

"I'm not sure what that has to do with anything." I took another sip of wine. "But he's . . . kind of preppy looking . . . in a sort of . . . sexy way."

"Hmm. Interesting."

I didn't bother to question her definition of *interesting*. "So how's Chadwick?" I asked, wanting to change the subject.

A smile covered her face. "He's great. Meeting him was the best thing that ever happened to me. Well, after having Haley, that is. But yes, he's fine. As a matter of fact, he's booked a holiday for the three of us to the French Alps to go skiing. We leave the day after Christmas and Haley is beside herself with excitement."

"Oh, my gosh, Isabelle. That *is* exciting! You've never gone skiing, have you?"

She shook her head. "No. Never. But he's arranged for Haley and me to have lessons. I think it'll be a lot of fun."

"It certainly will. I'm really happy for you, Isabelle. How long will you be gone?"

"Ten days. My mother said she'd take Ginger for us. Haley was worried about her dog, but she's happy her grandmother will keep her at her house."

"That's great. Your life has certainly turned around in the past year."

She nodded. "Don't I know it. Yeah, a year ago I had made the decision to move to Ormond Beach, but I had no clue what the results would be."

The next hour was consumed with Isabelle talking about her favorite topic: herself.

It wasn't until I was driving home that I realized I hadn't had a chance to tell her about my attempt to search for my father or about my dream.

Lotte did her usual happy dance when I walked in the door and I smiled. No matter what, she was always there for me.

"Did you miss me, sweetie? Come on, Mama will let you out in the yard."

After she sniffed, squatted, and made sure the yard was safe, she followed me back into the kitchen. I saw that it was only three o'clock and decided to spend some time at the yarn shop.

Mavis Anne was arranging a new delivery of baby alpaca on a shelf and Chloe was waiting on a customer.

Mavis Anne turned around and smiled. "Have a seat, Petra. I'm almost finished and I'll join you."

I sat at the table and began finishing up another spa cloth.

"Very pretty," she said, a few minutes later when she sat down. "Those will make nice gifts for the customers. Fay has also made quite a few. The French soap we'll include with the facecloths arrived yesterday. So we're going to get together here tomorrow afternoon to put everything together. Can you join us?"

"Definitely," I said. "I'll be here. Marta said she'll be over tomorrow morning to finish up the pastries for Sunday."

"Very good." Mavis Anne smiled. "Everything is right on schedule."

Both Chloe and Yarrow joined us a few minutes later.

"It's Friday afternoon," Mavis Anne said. "Why don't you open a bottle of wine, Yarrow?"

We looked up as Louise walked in.

"Hey," I said. "Feeling better? I haven't seen you for a while."

She sat down and nodded. "Oh, yes, thanks. Much better." She reached into her knitting bag and removed a brightly colored scarf.

"That's so pretty," I said, leaning forward for a better look. "Is that pattern called mosaic knitting?"

"Yes, it is. It's fun to work with."

"I've been meaning to ask you, Louise, if you would do a class on that pattern?" Mavis Anne asked.

"Oh, I'd love to. Sure. I could do just a basic mosaic brick pattern."

"That's great. We'll put out a sign-up sheet and schedule it for after the holidays. I've had a fair number of customers ask about how it's done."

"Are we all set for the tea on Sunday?" Louise asked.

Mavis Anne nodded. "Yes, I think we are. We're gathering here tomorrow around three to put together the gift items and finalize everything."

"Wonderful. I'll be here too," Louise said before turning toward me. "So it's going well for you at the shelter?"

"Yes. I really enjoy it there. Suzanne is very nice and it's rewarding to work with the adoptive parents and animals."

"It certainly is," she said. "I'm glad you offered to volunteer. Extra hands are always welcome."

"Oh," Yarrow said, as she passed a glass of red wine to each of us. "Didn't you take Lotte to Dr. Wellington yesterday? How did that go?"

I took a sip of wine and nodded. I wasn't sure how much to tell them. "Yeah, I did. Lotte seemed to like him a lot."

"What's not to like?" Yarrow said, causing the others to laugh.

I nodded again. "Right. Well . . . the funniest thing is . . . remember that story I told all of you about what happened at Petco with the boy and his father?"

"Oh, I heard about that," Louise said, making me realize that the yarn shop did more than just sell yarn. It was a source of news and gossip that traveled at a good speed.

"What's that incident have to do with the vet?" Chloe asked.

"Well . . . it seems the man who berated me for not minding my own business is in fact . . . Dr. Wellington."

"No," Yarrow gasped.

"Are you sure?" Louise questioned.

"Very sure," I said. "Yeah, it was a bit awkward when he walked into the exam room and we recognized each other."

"Oh, my goodness," Mavis Anne said, as she stopped knitting. "But did he apologize?"

I shook my head. "No. He did not." I decided it best to avoid the subject of the flowers.

"Wow," Yarrow said. "That's quite a coincidence."

"You could call it that," I mumbled.

"Oh." Yarrow drew out the word before taking a sip of wine and then nodded. "That's right. I'd heard that his wife had died and he had a young son. So that was his son who wanted the dogs?"

"Yup. And I interfered by telling him to ask his mother."

"I'm surprised that Dr. Wellington would react in such a negative manner," Chloe said. "But of course we've only seen him under professional circumstances."

"Does anybody know what happened to his wife? Is he from this area originally?"

Louise shook her head. "No, he's not. He's only been here about two years. From what I heard, his wife was killed in a car accident in upstate New York, which was where they lived. Apparently, his brother and family live in the Jacksonville area, and Dr. Wellington relocated here with his son to open his practice."

"Well, it still doesn't excuse his rudeness," Mavis Anne said. "My goodness, Petra was only trying to be nice to the boy."

I nodded. "Yeah, I was." I thought of Jonah, and realized I probably wouldn't be seeing him again, and that caused me to feel a sadness I wasn't familiar with.

I went back to Koi House, had supper, cleaned up, and then settled down with my knitting. Lotte was curled up beside me on the sofa. Knitting had a way of soothing the soul, and I hoped it would soothe mine after the week I had had.

A little while later my cell phone rang, and I heard a male voice say, "Ah, yes, hi. This is Ben. Ben Wellington. *Dr.* Wellington. Is this Petra?"

I detected anxiety in his tone and said, "Yes. Yes, it is."

"Listen . . . I think we got off on the wrong foot. You know . . . at Petco last week. And then I'm afraid I made matters worse at my office. About the flowers."

I had no idea where this was going. "Okay," was all I said.

"I'm afraid the flowers were Jonah's idea, and he took it upon himself to fix things. I think we both owe you an apology."

"Okay," I said again. "Thank you."

"Right." There was a pause before he said, "So we were wondering if you'd like to come to dinner. You know . . . so we could make it up to you."

He'd taken me completely by surprise. I found myself stupidly asking, "At your house?"

I heard a chuckle come across the line before he said, "Yeah. Maybe next Wednesday evening. If you're free. I don't even know if you have a husband, but he's certainly invited too."

"Oh. No. I don't have a husband."

"Okay. Well, Jonah and I would like you to come. Nothing special. I was just going to grill hot dogs and hamburgers, if that's okay with you."

"Sure. That's fine. What time, and can I bring anything?"

"Six would be good. I have a request from Jonah . . . ah . . . if you could bring your dog; he'd really enjoy that and would like to see her again."

Lotte was invited too? "Sure," I said again. "Yes, that sounds good. We'd both like to come. I just need your address."

I reached for a pen and paper and jotted down what he told me.

"Okay. Thank you," I told him. "We'll see you next Wednesday at six."

I disconnected the call and shook my head. I certainly had not expected that to happen. A dinner invitation to apologize? I couldn't help but wonder how much of it had been due to Jonah. Maybe Ben had gotten my phone number from the business card I had given to his son.

# *Rhonda*
# *March 1969*

Peter and I continued dating, but it was a few weeks before he again brought up the subject of my visiting his home.

We had been to the movies to see *Hello, Dolly!* with Barbra Streisand and Walter Matthau. Both of us loved the movie and had been discussing how great it was. Peter pulled into our spot overlooking the ocean.

"Want to sit on the beach for a while?" he asked.

"Sure," I said.

We sat on the blanket with his arm around my shoulders, staring at the sky and the ocean. Spring had arrived and the evenings were getting warmer. I recalled the recent letter from my mother telling me they had received a spring snowstorm dumping fourteen inches. All the more reason I loved Florida.

"A penny for your thoughts," Peter said.

I smiled. "I was just remembering my mother's letter. They got fourteen inches of snow at home last week."

He nodded. "That does make Florida extra nice, doesn't it? Have you made any plans yet? Will you stay down here or return back home?"

"I've been able to save quite a bit of money in the eight weeks I've been here. So I'm going to start inquiring about a secretarial program, and if I get accepted, then I'm definitely staying here."

"Good," he said and pulled me closer.

I felt his fingers on the sides of my face as he kissed me. This time I was the one who ended the kiss and exhaled. I knew each time

I was with him what we shared became more passionate, and for the first time in my life I understood the meaning of the word *desire*.

Peter also let out a deep breath and ran his hand through my hair. "I've never met anyone like you, Rhonda. You're different."

"In what way?" I questioned. I wasn't sure if this was good or bad.

"You're interested in just having a good time. I don't think it matters to you exactly what we do. You seem to enjoy everything."

He was right and I nodded. "I do," I told him. I wasn't sure I should admit it but I went on to say, "I just enjoy being with *you*."

"I can tell," he said and kissed the top of my head, squeezing me tighter. "Have you dated many fellows?"

I realized I had not. "Just a few. In high school. Nothing serious." I paused for a second before asking, "How about you?"

He laughed and gave my hand a squeeze. "Well, I do have seven years on you. So yes, I dated quite a few different girls throughout college. I guess that's how I'm so certain that you're different. There's no drama with you. You're a pleasure to be with." He paused for a second before saying, "Easy. You're *easy* to be with."

He turned to place his lips on mine, and this time I felt not only my own desire, but his as well. He guided me down on the blanket as he repositioned himself so his body was stretched out on top of me.

I felt his hand slip under my blouse and caress my breast. A groan filled the night air and I wasn't sure if it was mine or his.

"Oh, God," I heard him say, his voice husky. He sat up and shook his head. "We have to stop. Or . . . I might not be able to."

I nodded and rearranged my blouse. What I felt with Peter Maxwell wasn't anything like what I'd ever felt before. This wasn't high school petting. This was serious adult foreplay. This was how two people in love felt. And while the unknown frightened me, I also knew that had Peter not stopped, I would not have pulled away.

He stood up and reached for my hand. "Let's head back," he said.

A few minutes later he pulled into the hotel parking lot. We had remained silent on the drive back from the beach.

He leaned over and brushed his lips on mine. "I love being with you, Rhonda. Can I see you again tomorrow night?"

I smiled and nodded. For a brief second on the beach, when he suggested we leave, I was afraid maybe he didn't want to see me again.

"Yes," I said. "Yes. I'd like that."

"Good. You have the breakfast and lunch shifts tomorrow?"

"Yes."

"I'll pick you up at six. I'd like you to come to my house for dinner."

"Okay. I'll see you tomorrow," I said, turning to get out of the car. But Peter reached for me and kissed me again. He buried his face in my neck and sighed. "I think I'm falling in love with you."

Because I had no idea how to respond, I opened the door and walked slowly back to the cabin.

I smelled it as soon as I got to the porch. Cynthia had recently begun smoking marijuana, courtesy of Earle. I had quickly come to see that he was a really nice guy, but he was also a hippie at heart. His hair had grown in the time since we'd arrived, and he was now wearing it a bit longer than was conventional. On duty at the hotel he secured it at the nape of his neck in a ponytail but off duty, his waves were chin length. He wore tie-dyed T-shirts with bell-bottom jeans and sandals. He also enjoyed playing his guitar and singing, and Cynthia had been joining him at local clubs in the evening, where he sometimes joined the band playing popular Creedence Clearwater Revival music. The group had a top song that played constantly on the radio. "Fortunate Son" was music with a message—against the war, against politics, and against the establishment of our day.

"Hey," she said, lifting her joint in the air. "Want a hit?"

"No, thanks," I told her as I walked inside to grab a can of Tab. It wasn't that I was a prude about smoking pot. I just had no desire to achieve a high with hand-rolled leaves. I took a gulp of the overly sweet soft drink and joined Cynthia back on the porch.

"So what's going on?" I asked her. We had had opposite shifts at the hotel for the past few days, and I hadn't seen much of her.

"Well . . . let's see." She took another drag off the joint. "I'm sleeping with Earle now."

I shifted in my seat. "Okay."

She laughed. "He's hot. Different from the other guys I've been with. But we're being careful. I sure don't want a kid right now. So Earle is using rubbers but I'm trying to get the pill. It's pretty difficult for unmarried girls, though."

I nodded. Although things were changing for women, we still had a long way to go.

"And . . ." she said. "Do you know yet what you'll be doing in May when the season ends here?"

I shrugged. "I'm still not sure. I need to see if I'll have enough money saved by then for secretarial school. Why?"

"Well . . . Earle is talking about heading out to California."

This was a surprise and the first I was hearing about it. "Really? California? Why way out there?"

"Earle's plan has always been to do this, I guess. Hook up with a band and play the clubs in San Francisco. In the music business, it's the place to be."

I knew about the Summer of Love two years before and had heard about the crowds of teenagers flocking to the Haight-Ashbury district, claiming they had turned their backs on society, protesting the Vietnam War and believing in free love. But the scene had fallen apart by the end of the summer and had become a haven for dropouts.

"So it's still a popular place to be?" I asked.

She nodded. "Yup, it is. And have you heard about the Woodstock Music and Art Fair that's being held in New York in August?"

I shook my head.

"Well, Earle would like for us to go there, and maybe from there, we can hook up with some people to get to San Francisco."

All of a sudden Cynthia's life seemed to be going in a completely different direction from mine. I wasn't at all sure where I was headed with Peter, but I was grateful that maybe we would be taking the first step the next evening when I visited his home.

# Chapter 11

A little after three the Sunday before Christmas, Koi House was filled with happy, chattering women. The Christmas tea was proving to be a huge success with a good turnout.

I headed to the kitchen to refill a pitcher of sweet tea and saw Mavis Anne arranging more cookies on a platter.

"Everyone seems to be having a good time," she said.

"I think they are. And the house looks so festive."

In addition to the tree, we had placed red and green candles on the tables along with other Christmas decorations.

By the time the party ended a few hours later, everyone was in the Christmas mood. Yarrow had even played Christmas carols on the upright piano and we had a sing-along.

"That was fun," she said, as we all begin to pitch in for the cleanup.

"It was," I agreed.

Mavis Anne was wrapping some leftover pastries. "Oh, Petra, I wanted to talk to you about Christmas day. We were thinking maybe all of us could spend it together here at Koi House. David and Clive have offered to cook a turkey and ham. The rest of us can make side dishes and I'm sure Marta will do the desserts for us. Do you have any plans for Christmas?"

I shook my head. "No. None at all." I really hadn't given it much thought. "But I think that's a great idea."

"Oh, good. We'll have a buffet and I think it'll be nice to spend the day together. Now, I was thinking, rather than do a gift exchange, maybe we could donate money to the animal shelter."

"I love that idea," Louise said as she filled the dishwasher with plates.

"I do too. Yes, let's do that. Who will be coming?"

"Well," Mavis Anne said. "Yarrow, David, Clive, and me. Chloe? Can you and Henry make it?"

Chloe looked up from washing wineglasses in the sink. "Yes. Absolutely. We have no other plans. That'll be fun."

"We leave the next day for our ski trip," Isabelle said. "So it would be nice to celebrate Christmas here. Count Chadwick, Haley, and me in."

"And I'll definitely be here," Iris agreed.

"Louise?" Mavis Anne questioned. "Can you make it?"

"Yes. My nephew is going to his wife's family for Christmas. They did invite me, but I'd much rather spend it here with all of you."

"Then it's settled," Mavis Anne said. "Let's see . . ." She counted on her fingers. "That will be twelve of us. Perfect."

After the cleanup was completed, I opened a bottle of wine, poured each one a glass, and we took it outside to the patio.

"What a gorgeous evening," Iris said. "It's hard to believe that Christmas is a week from today. I'm really enjoying this mild weather in December."

"Yeah," Yarrow said. "I grew up in this area but I have no desire to experience snow and cold."

Isabelle laughed. "I'm sure skiing in Switzerland will make me appreciate the south even more."

"Did you pack all your warm knitted hats and mittens?" Louise asked. "Because you'll certainly need them."

Isabelle nodded. "Yes, we'll definitely have the proper attire, but I'm not sure that will make me any warmer."

After a few minutes, I said, "Well . . . I have some news."

Everyone looked in my direction, waiting for me to continue.

"I got a phone call Friday evening. From Ben. Dr. Wellington."

Everyone remained silent.

"He wanted to apologize for his behavior at Petco. And . . . I neglected to tell you, but Jonah showed up at the shelter with a small bouquet of flowers last week. He said they were from his dad, who wanted to say he was sorry."

Iris started laughing. "Oh! No! Let me guess . . . they were *not* from Dr. Wellington."

"Correct. So I compounded the problem by thanking him for the flowers at his office."

Yarrow chuckled. "And I'm sure he was wondering what the hell you were talking about."

I nodded. "Exactly. It was a very awkward situation."

"So Jonah took it upon himself to bring you the flowers?" Mavis Anne said.

"Yup. And when Ben . . . Dr. Wellington . . . figured out what had happened, he called to apologize."

"Well, I'd say that was very gentlemanly of him."

"It was. It really was," I said. "And . . . he invited me to dinner Wednesday evening. You know . . . to make it up to me."

"Hmm," Mavis Anne said. "That's a very nice way to apologize."

"So are you going?" Yarrow asked.

"I am," I told her, and I realized that I hadn't considered saying no when he invited me. "No big deal. Just a barbeque at his house. And he requested that I bring Lotte. Jonah would like to see her again."

"Sounds like a big deal to me," Yarrow said.

I began to stammer, "No . . . it's really not . . . it's just an informal dinner . . ." I looked up and saw the grin on her face and could feel heat radiating up my neck as I realized she was teasing me.

"Well, from what I know of him, he seems like a very nice guy," Iris said. "I'm glad you're going. You need to meet some male friends in the area."

I brushed her off. "Oh, I'll probably never see him again. Well, except for taking Lotte in for her exams."

"Don't be too sure of that," Mavis Anne said as she sent me a wink.

After everyone left, I spent the evening knitting. The yarn shop did charity knitting and I had finished a baby blanket and now wanted to make a matching sweater. I casted on my required stitches and knew I'd enjoy working with the Plymouth DK yarn again. It was soft, with a white background and just a hint of pink for a baby girl. This made me think of Jonah. And the fact that he'd lost his mother. At eight years old. That must have been difficult for him, but he seemed like a well-rounded and personable boy. It also led me to think about the devastation that Ben must have felt losing his wife. I wondered if she had been driving the car. If she had been killed instantly and how he had managed to get through the days and weeks that had followed. Maybe he had had family and friends to help him.

I might be alone in my life, but unlike Ben and Jonah, I had never had such a shattering loss. When my mother passed away, it had been expected. She had been diagnosed a few years before with cancer. And my father . . . it's true that what you don't have, you don't miss.

But this made me wonder again if he was alive and if so, where he might be. I also had begun to wonder if he even knew of my existence. My mother said he had died—but had he? She had been married to Jim Garfield. So who was the man in the photo? With the name Peter Maxwell written on the back?

It was looking more doubtful that I would ever find out.

I woke at three in the morning to use the bathroom and realized that I had had another dream. About Emmalyn. This time we were outside by the fishpond. She looked exactly the same as in the first dream—wearing that red formal gown. Although it was out of place, in the dream I never questioned it. She was sitting on the bench, looking down at a photograph in her hand. I couldn't see what it was, but I heard her say, "Sometimes things aren't always as they seem."

"What do you mean?" I questioned.

When she lifted her face to look at me, I saw sadness in her eyes. She let out a sigh. "Just because something isn't what we thought, it doesn't mean that it isn't good."

"Yes," I agreed, but even in the dream I had no idea what she was talking about.

"Sometimes we have to take a chance. Trust our instincts."

"Okay," I said. "But how?"

A smile covered her face. "You'll figure it out. When the time is right, you'll figure it out."

I got back into bed, pulled up the sheet, and stared at the ceiling. Why was I having these unexplainable dreams? What did they mean? And how could it even be possible that I would dream of Emmalyn Overby just as Chloe and Isabelle had?

I had no answers.

# Rhonda
## March 1969

I didn't have a vast wardrobe to choose from, so I was nervous about finding the proper attire for dinner at Peter's home.

I finally decided on a red-and-black plaid skirt, matching jacket, white blouse, and black flats.

I took a final look in the mirror before walking out to the parking lot to meet Peter.

He was already there, leaning against his car waiting for me.

"Hi," he said, a smile covering his face. He pulled me into an embrace and kissed my cheek. "You look beautiful."

"Thanks," I said. I felt relieved that my choice of clothes was probably okay. He was wearing chino slacks and an open-collar shirt.

"Nervous?" he asked as he put the key in the ignition.

I nodded. "A little bit."

He reached over and touched my hand. "Don't be. My father can be a bit gruff, but he's okay."

I hadn't seen a gruff side of him in the restaurant, so I was surprised by this information.

"Will your sisters be there too?" I asked.

"Just Sheila. My older sister is off to Miami for the week with her friends."

Peter drove a little north on A1A and then pulled into a long driveway. At the end was a black wrought-iron fence with an elaborately carved gate in the center. A stone post held a metal box, which Peter unlocked with a key. He opened it to reveal a telephone. Removing the receiver, he dialed a few numbers and a smile crossed his face as

I heard him say, "Sadie. It's Peter. I'm at the gate." A moment later the double gate swung open, allowing him to drive inside to a circular driveway. And there sat the Maxwell home: a two-story redbrick structure with black shutters. The house itself had been hidden from the road due to large oak trees that formed a canopy of privacy.

I let out a gasp. "Oh, wow. This looks like a mansion," I said.

Peter laughed. "No. It's far from a mansion."

He got out of the car as I continued to stare at the house, opened the passenger side door, and led me up the few steps to the front door.

We walked inside to a large foyer with white tiled floor, butter yellow walls, and white crown molding. A cherrywood table held a Tiffany lamp and a crystal vase of pink and white mums.

I tried to avoid gushing but it wasn't easy. And this was only the foyer.

"It's beautiful," I whispered.

Peter took my hand and led me to the right into what I assumed was a den or sitting room. I glanced at leather furniture, dark wood tables, more fresh flowers, and paintings on the wall. French doors at the far end of the room were open, and I followed Peter through the doors and outside to a brick terrace patio area.

The view in front of me took my breath away: a garden area that began at the patio and stretched straight down the slope to the Atlantic Ocean.

"This is just gorgeous," I said.

"I'm glad you think so," I heard a male voice on my left say.

I looked to see Mr. Maxwell standing near a barbeque grill, a long silver fork in his hand.

"How are you, Rhonda?" he asked, but even with those few words I detected that the friendliness he normally displayed at the restaurant was missing.

"Very well, Mr. Maxwell. And you?"

He reached for a rocks glass on the round patio table, took a sip, and nodded. "I'm fine. Peter, get your friend a drink."

"What would you like?" Peter asked. "A glass of wine, soft drink?"

"A soft drink is good," I said, unsure which one I should accept.

"Have a seat." Peter gestured toward the patio chairs before walking to a refrigerator on the patio, opening it, and removing a can of Sprite. He added ice to a glass and passed me the drink.

I now saw that a small bar area had been built on the patio. Walking behind it, Peter reached for a bottle of wine and uncorked it.

"This is a nice red," he told me. "Maybe you'll try a little with dinner."

I nodded.

"Yes. We're having steaks," Mr. Maxwell informed me. "Do you like steak?"

I nodded again. "Yes, I do."

I was beginning to feel a little awkward being with somebody who had been my customer at the restaurant. I normally waited on *him*. And here he was cooking me a steak for dinner. So I was grateful when Peter's sister breezed onto the patio.

"Hi, Rhonda," she said, putting me more at ease. "How are you?"

"I'm good. Thanks. How are you doing?"

She was wearing a very pretty blue-and-white-striped dress. Her dark hair was pulled back into a ponytail, and I noticed she had on a pair of trendy sandals that showed off her red painted toenails.

"I'm doing great. But I'd be doing even better if I could convince my father to let me go to Woodstock in August."

"Oh, my friend Cynthia might be going with her boyfriend."

"Really?" Sheila sat up straighter in her chair. "See, Dad. Everybody's going."

Mr. Maxwell took a gulp of his drink, finishing it off before flipping one of the steaks on the grill. "Everybody is *not* going. So no more discussion about this tonight. You're only sixteen and I'm not about to let my daughter go traipsing to some farm in New York with hippies and musicians."

Sheila shrugged, looked at me and rolled her eyes.

I gave her a smile and took a sip of my soft drink. My eyes kept going to the view of the ocean and sky. This had to be one of the most beautiful houses I'd ever seen. It was hard to picture growing up in a place like this, but Peter and Sheila seemed to take it for granted as if it wasn't anything beyond the ordinary.

The table outside had been set when we arrived, but a few minutes later I helped Sheila bring out a large bowl of potato salad and hot dinner rolls that Peter had removed from the oven.

"I think we're all set," Mr. Maxwell said.

At dinner, Sheila chatted about an event that was coming up at school. I was grateful for her presence. I was seeing a different side of Mr. Maxwell from what I saw at the restaurant. I guess being in his own home caused him to be more like the lord of the manor. Because that's how he was coming across to me. He had an air about him I couldn't define. But then again, I had never been exposed to a man as wealthy as Mr. Maxwell.

I was sorry when Sheila stopped chatting because it allowed him to now focus on me.

"So, Rhonda," he said, before taking a sip of his freshened drink, "Peter tells me you're going to be attending secretarial school?"

I wiped my lips with the linen napkin and nodded. "Yes. I hope so. I . . . ah . . . I'm saving money to attend. I hope to begin this summer."

He nodded. "Does that mean you're not considering college?"

Was he being condescending? College? I had never considered this. I knew from a young age that I'd never be able to afford it. It had never been an option for me, and my grades weren't high enough to earn a scholarship.

"Dad," Peter interrupted before I could answer. "Give her a break. Not everybody has to attend college today."

We had finished eating, and Mr. Maxwell now lit up a cigar and nodded. "No. No, of course not. I was simply inquiring."

Peter mentioned something work-related—I'm sure to keep the conversation away from me—and the two of them got into a discussion having to do with the company.

A little while later a middle-aged black lady walked out to the patio.

"Evening, Mr. Maxwell," she said and nodded to the rest of us. "Are you ready for me to clear away the plates?"

I wondered where she had been while we were eating but got no explanation.

He waved a hand in the air. "Yes, Sadie. That would be good, and you can bring out dessert."

They had a maid? I'm not sure why this surprised me, but it did. Being alone with Peter was way different from being here in his home with his father.

A few minutes later Sadie brought out a tray carrying dishes of key lime pie and cups of coffee.

She placed mine in front of me, and I looked up at her and smiled. "Thank you," I said.

"You're welcome, honey," she replied. I loved the drawl of her accent.

We were just finishing up dessert when I heard the telephone inside the house ringing. A minute later, Sadie appeared.

"It's for you, Mr. Maxwell." She looked at Peter's father.

"Thank you," he said, getting up. "Excuse me."

"I'm going to listen to my records," Sheila said, also getting up. "I'm glad you could join us for dinner, Rhonda. I hope you'll come again."

I gave her a smile and thanked her. I liked this girl. She was like Peter—down-to-earth and friendly. I wasn't sure I could say that about their father.

Peter also stood up and reached for my hand. "Come on," he said. "I'd like to show you the boathouse. Take your glass of wine with you."

We walked along a flagstone path leading away from the house. Beautiful hibiscus bloomed in colors of red, white, and yellow. There was a breeze coming off the ocean and a hint of salt in the air. Oak trees formed a canopy and lampposts lighted the path as the sun had now set in the western sky.

Peter reached for my hand and gave it a squeeze. I looked up at him and smiled.

A few moments later we came out into a clearing. The ocean and beach were to my right and ahead of me was a medium sized structure. I had always pictured a boathouse more like a ramshackle shed used to store a boat. But this was much more upscale. Red brick, like the house, it had windows and French doors with a perfect view of the ocean. And from the front another flagstone path led to a dock area where the boat Peter had taken me on was moored.

He gestured with his hand. "Here we are," he said. He reached into his pocket for keys and unlocked the door.

We stepped inside and I was surprised that not only were there no boats, but the room reminded me more of a retreat. A day bed took up the entire back wall, providing a good vantage point to enjoy the ocean view. Tables held lamps, and paintings of seascapes covered the walls. An easel had been set up, and I saw a palette of paint and brushes in a ceramic jug on another table.

"This is a *boathouse*?" I asked, and Peter laughed.

"Well, that's what my family has always called it. But it was my mother's favorite spot. She loved to paint and would spend a lot of time here. It doesn't get used much anymore. Sheila sometimes comes here with her friends or by herself to read."

"It's beautiful," I said. "It's a lovely spot. You don't use it?"

He shook his head. "No. I have to say I really don't. Maybe I should."

"How long ago did your mother pass away?"

"It's been five years now. I think it was the hardest on Sheila. She was only eleven. It was a heart attack and very sudden, which made it more difficult."

I nodded. "I'm sorry," I said.

I felt Peter's arms around me as he pulled me close. "I do love you, Rhonda. I need you to know that."

"I love you too," I whispered.

I felt him easing me back toward the day bed as we kissed, and I found myself lying down. His body stretched out beside me as our kisses grew more passionate. I felt his hand under my blouse gently teasing my breast before he slid his hand across my stomach and reached under my skirt to trace his finger along my thigh.

We were both breathing heavily when he pulled away and groaned. He sat up, running a hand through his hair.

Shaking his head, he whispered, "I'm sorry."

I sat up and rested my chin on his shoulder. "Don't be," I whispered in reply.

And I knew with those two words there was no turning back.

I had never known that making love could be so frenzied. That a person loses track of time and space and anything else except two bodies coming together in a passion that fills their very souls. I didn't realize that a hunger could be fulfilled with a connection that made everything else pale in comparison. But that was how it was with Peter. And when we finished, we lay beside each other, holding tight to what we had just shared—our naked bodies still tingling with desire.

We were both silent, absorbing the moments and acknowledging our choice to make those moments happen.

Peter was the first to speak. "I love you, Rhonda. I love you."

There was no doubt in my mind about my feelings or taking that love to culmination. "I love you too. So very much."

He shifted to better see my face and looped a strand of hair behind my ear before letting his finger trace my profile as he exhaled. "You had never done this before, had you?" he asked.

I shook my head.

"I am so sorry," I heard him say, but I had no idea why.

I was afraid to ask.

He went on to say, "I'm not sorry we made love. Not at all. But I'm sorry I didn't give more thought to protection."

All of a sudden I knew exactly what he was saying, and I felt dread in the pit of my stomach. We had not used a rubber. In the ecstasy of the moment—we hadn't even given it a thought.

I reached for his hand and gave it a squeeze. "We'll be okay," I whispered. "We'll be okay."

# Chapter 12

I had been raised to know that it was good manners to bring a gift of some sort to the hostess when invited for dinner. It didn't have to be elaborate. Flowers, chocolate, or a bottle of wine. However, when I thought of bringing any of these things to Ben Wellington, I felt it might be another *faux pas*.

Flowers might be misconstrued as snarky because of the flowers Ben had *not* sent to me. For all I knew, he could be a diabetic—so chocolate was out. And even wine. How did I know he might not be a recovering alcoholic? Which all proved to me that I knew absolutely nothing about Ben Wellington—except that he was a vet and had a really sweet son.

This made me decide to go to Barnes and Noble and get the hostess gift for Jonah rather than his father. It was probably at Jonah's request I was being invited. I found three age-appropriate books that all had dog stories. I knew Jonah adored dogs, so I hoped he might enjoy them.

I followed the directions that Ben had given me—north on Nova and west into the development. I drove past a few homes that were Tudor style; some were ranch style or colonials and looked like they had been built in the late sixties. All of them were well maintained with landscaping and sweeping front lawns that led to circular driveways or brick walks. I found Ben's house at the end overlooking the river, a two-story brick that looked cozy and welcoming.

I pulled into the driveway, and as I got out of the car two things struck me: The house seemed a bit spacious for just a man and his son, and there appeared to be a large yard in the back, which would be ideal for a dog. Or two. Reaching into the backseat, I lifted Lotte into my arms.

"Here we are," I told her.

I walked to the front door and rang the bell. I wasn't surprised that it was Jonah who swung the door wide open, a huge smile on his face.

"Hey, Petra," he said, extending his hand for Lotte to smell. "Hi, Lotte. Come on in."

Ben appeared from the back of the house. "You found us okay. Yes, come on in. It's nice to see both of you."

I had Lotte still on her leash and put her down on the tile floor as I passed the tote bag to Jonah. "This is for you. I hope you'll like it."

He peeked inside and removed one of the books. "Oh, thank you. Yes. I love to read. Especially dog books."

"That was nice of you," Ben said. "How about a glass of wine?"

I nodded. "Yes. Sounds good."

I followed the two of them through the foyer to a family room that opened to a large screened pool area.

"You have a very pretty spot here," I said, noticing the river to my left. The large yard with mature oak trees was enclosed by a black wrought-iron fence.

"Thanks," Ben said as he uncorked a bottle of red wine.

"Could I take Lotte to play in the yard?" Jonah asked.

"Sure," I said, bending over to unclip her leash. "I think she'd like that."

Jonah opened the screen door and they both ran out to the yard.

Ben passed me a wineglass. "Here you go."

"Thanks," I said and nodded. I took a sip and said, "Have you lived here very long?"

"Two years. My wife passed away, and I knew that staying in New York wasn't good for Jonah or me. My brother and his family live in Jacksonville so I thought it might be good to live closer to them. He has a boy Jonah's age."

"That's nice. Do you get to see them often?"

"Well, probably not as much as we should. Between my work schedule and Zak's, we try to get together about once every month or so." He took a sip of wine. "How about you? Do you have family here?"

I saw Jonah tossing a ball to Lotte and smiled. "No. I'm an only child, and my mother passed away a few years ago. I grew up in Pennsylvania but after college and some traveling, I settled in the Jacksonville area before coming to Ormond Beach about a month ago."

"What brought you to this area?"

"Friends. I had been coming here last year to visit my best friend, Isabelle. Actually, her daughter and mother come to you for their dogs. Iris and Haley, and their dogs are Fred and Ginger."

Ben nodded and laughed. "Yes, I know who they are. I always got a kick out of the dogs' names. So after visiting here, you decided to relocate?"

"Well, I'm not sure it's permanent. I still own my home in Jacksonville, but I thought it might be a nice change. I came for Isabelle's wedding in September and decided to stay on a trial basis. So I'm living at Koi House on Beach Avenue. Mavis Anne Overby owns the house. I met her through Isabelle."

"Sounds good. Are you working in the area?"

"I'm fortunate to work from home. I do work for a software company. So that made my decision to come here easy. It wasn't like I had to give up my job."

Ben nodded and was silent for a few moments, then said, "Before Jonah comes back inside, I just want to tell you again I'm sorry for what I said to you at Petco. That was rude of me."

"Apology accepted, but it was also presumptuous of me to interfere. So I'm also sorry."

I saw a slight smile cross his face and realized it was the first time I had seen him smile. His gaze met mine, and behind his black-framed glasses, I saw sadness in his eyes.

As if sensing my understanding, he said, "It's been a difficult couple of years. Losing Emily turned my life upside down." He took a sip of wine. "It was a car accident."

"I'm so sorry." I couldn't begin to understand such a loss.

He nodded. "A drunk driver hit us. We were on our way home from having dinner at a local restaurant. The one thing I'm so very grateful for is that Jonah wasn't with us in the car. He was home with the sitter." He took another sip of wine. "But I was driving the car."

I glanced at the faint scar along the side of his face and wondered if it was a result of the car accident. And I also wondered if he felt guilty for not being able to avoid the accident that had taken his wife's life.

He shook his head and gave me the hint of a smile. "Listen to me. Rambling on. I'm sorry. I very seldom discuss this with anyone," he said, standing up. "You do like burgers and hot dogs, right?"

"Absolutely. Can I help with something?"

"Maybe set the table? Betsy, Noah's nanny, prepared macaroni salad. It's in the fridge. So you can take that out to the table."

I followed him through a set of French doors to the kitchen. I was surprised. Though he was a man living alone with his son, the area looked spotless.

Ben pointed to the plates and silverware that had been set out on the counter. "Betsy got things ready for us. She's gone out for the evening but lives here with Jonah and me. Having a live-in nanny makes it nice for Jonah, and Betsy has no family, so it works for both of us."

"Oh, that *is* nice. You were fortunate to find her."

Ben nodded as he removed hot dogs and hamburger patties from the fridge. "Yeah, I was. Actually, she's my brother's wife's aunt. Betsy's husband passed away quite a few years ago and she had no children. She lived in the Jacksonville area also. When I made the decision to move here, Sue suggested I consider hiring her aunt as a nanny and housekeeper for me and Jonah. This house was ideal because Betsy has her own bedroom and sitting area upstairs so she has her privacy, yet she's here for Jonah. She takes him to school and picks him up. Cooks our meals and looks after the house. She's a real godsend."

"She certainly is," I agreed.

I took the plates and began setting the table as Jonah ran back inside with Lotte.

"She's so much fun," he said. "I really like her."

I laughed. "I think she likes you too."

"I'm starved," he said. "Is supper ready?"

"Go wash your hands," Ben told him. "Not much longer."

After we finished eating, I helped Ben to clear the table and clean up the kitchen.

"How about some coffee?" he asked.

"Definitely."

"Mugs are in the cabinet at the end," he said, pointing.

I got them out as he removed the cover from a cake plate on the counter. "Courtesy of Betsy. She makes the best carrot cake."

"That does look good," I said. As I reached into the drawer for forks and spoons, I realized how comfortable I felt in Ben's kitchen.

"Oh, Betsy's carrot cake," Jonah said as we came back outside.

Without being asked, I sliced three pieces and passed plates to Ben and Jonah.

Taking a bite of mine, I nodded. "You're right. This is exceptional."

"Do you bake?" Jonah asked.

"Ah . . . well . . . I know how to bake, but I guess I don't very often."

"Why?" Jonah questioned.

I laughed. "Well . . . it's not so much fun to bake just for me."

"Oh, you can bake for me anytime. I love dessert," Jonah informed me, causing me to laugh again.

I saw Ben shake his head and a grin covered his face. It struck me that he was a very serious sort of guy. He didn't laugh or smile easily. If not for Jonah, I wondered if he'd ever smile at all. *Uptight* was the word that came to mind.

After we finished the cake, Ben said, "More coffee?"

"Yes, please."

He refilled our mugs from the French press on the table.

"Can Lotte and I go back in the yard to play?" Jonah asked.

"Well . . . actually," Ben said, "I have something to tell you. Both of you."

"What? What is it?" Jonah rocked from side to side in his chair. "A surprise?"

Ben nodded. "Yes. A surprise. I've given some thought to those two dogs. Lucy and Ethel. And . . ."

Before he could finish his sentence, Jonah had jumped up and run to his father. "Can I have them? Can I have Lucy and Ethel?"

This time Ben's laugh was loud and genuine as he nodded. "Yes. We're going to adopt them."

I could hardly believe what I was hearing.

Jonah began jumping up and down and threw his arms around his father's neck. "Really, Dad? Really? When? When can we get them?"

"Okay, calm down," Ben said, returning his son's hug. "I called the shelter and we're going to bring them home tomorrow. So they'll have a home for Christmas."

"Oh, wow," I said.

"I'm so excited." Jonah leaned down and scooped Lotte into his arms. "Did you hear that? Lucy and Ethel will be coming to live with me."

Ben laughed again and I felt moisture stinging my eyes. Not only were those two lovely dogs going to get a wonderful home but one little boy was filled with joy.

"That is so great," I said.

"Well, I think we can thank *you*, Petra. For suggesting that Jonah give Lucy and Ethel a home."

This was certainly proof that Ben Wellington had forgiven me for interfering.

"What time can we go?" Jonah questioned. "Can I skip school tomorrow?"

Ben shook his head and laughed. "Ah, no, you can't. And I have office visits in the morning, so I told the shelter we'd be there to get them around three. We'll go shopping first at Petco for food and some toys. And I want to get a crate. It's good to have them crated when we're not home and that will give them a sense of security until they settle in."

"Wow," Jonah said, still clearly excited. "This is going to be the best Christmas ever. Even if we *are* alone. At least now we'll have Lucy and Ethel."

I picked up on what he'd said and looked at Ben. "Oh, you're not going to your brother's for Christmas?"

"Not this year. They're taking the kids and going to visit Sue's parents in Georgia."

"Betsy won't be here either," Jonah said. "She's going to visit a friend in Tampa."

A father and his ten-year-old son alone on Christmas? That was just plain sad.

"Oh, gosh," I said. "Nobody should be alone on Christmas. We're having a gathering at Koi House. Nothing fancy. Just a buffet dinner, but it will be festive." Before I gave it a second's thought, the words were out. "Why don't you and Jonah come too?"

"Oh, I don't know," Ben began to say.

But Jonah cut in. "Could we, Dad? Could we go? Please?"

Ben looked at me and shrugged. "Are you sure?"

For the first time in a long time, I knew I had never been so sure about something.

# Rhonda
## April 1969

Over the next couple of weeks Peter and I continued to see each other for dinners, movies, and a couple of times we went out on his boat. The boat afforded us complete privacy and when we made love in the cabin, he was adamant about using protection.

However, by mid-April I had no idea where our relationship might be going. If anywhere at all. We acknowledged our love for each other. And I truly believed Peter loved me. But I wasn't at all certain that I saw a future for the two of us as a couple. We came from very different worlds and although Peter tried to assure me this didn't matter, I knew that it did.

And that was proved to me when I reported to the hotel for my dinner shift.

"Hey," Sally said when I walked in. "It's getting warmer out there, isn't it?"

I nodded. "It doesn't feel like April in Pennsylvania, that's for sure."

"Are you going back home for the summer?" she asked.

"I don't know. I might have enough money to stay here and take a secretarial course."

"That would be great. I think I'm going back, though. I miss being home."

I was ashamed to admit that I didn't miss Pennsylvania. I wrote to my mother faithfully and according to her letters, nothing at all had changed in the three months I had been gone. As much as she missed me, she agreed that I had many more opportunities here.

"Well, my first table has arrived," she said, heading toward the dining room.

I served my early diners and just before seven I was totaling a check when Sally nudged me as she giggled and said, "Looks like the son brought his girlfriend tonight."

I looked up from tallying the check. "What?"

She nodded in the direction of the dining room. "The Maxwells. They have an extra person with them tonight. Looks like she could be the son's girlfriend."

A wave of dizziness came over me, and I gripped the counter as I turned around. Peter was pulling out a chair for an extremely beautiful woman who seemed to be about his age. Her blond hair was styled in the popular French twist. I saw the sparkle of a jeweled necklace around her neck, and she was wearing a fashionable black dress. Who *was* this person?

I went to the reservation book and sure enough—rather than the usual four, five people had been booked for this evening.

I inhaled a deep breath and knew that I had no choice but to walk to the table and take the newcomer's drink order.

"Good evening," I said, avoiding eye contact with Peter and focusing on the woman beside him. I noticed her makeup was flawless. "What may I get you to drink?"

"Oh." She waved a manicured hand in the air. "A daiquiri would be nice."

The drink that Peter had suggested to me. I glanced at him and saw a very uncomfortable man. If this woman was his date, he didn't look happy.

"Ah, Rhonda," Mr. Maxwell said. "Yes, this is Marion . . . Peter's girlfriend. We thought it would be nice if she joined us for dinner this evening."

"Dad," I heard Peter say, annoyance tingeing the word. "Marion and I are just friends."

"Yes . . . well . . . I believe I just said that. Now . . . may we have our drinks, please?"

Without another word, I headed to the bar and realized that my hands were trembling. Girlfriend? Peter had a *girlfriend*? How stupid could I have been? But, no. Peter *did* love me. I was certain of that. But was love enough?

Somehow I managed to get through the next couple of hours. I brought out the appetizers, entrees, and then dessert and coffee. Each time I glanced at Peter, he looked extremely uneasy.

I brought their check and passed it to Mr. Maxwell. I normally got a thank you, but this evening he remained silent and continued talking across the table to Peter.

I headed to the ladies' room, and when I returned to the dining room I was surprised to see the Maxwells had left. So until I heard from Peter I would have no idea who Marion was or why she was with them at dinner.

I reported for my lunch shift the following day and was surprised to see Mr. Maxwell sitting at the bar having a Bloody Mary. He very seldom frequented the restaurant for lunch, and when he did it was with other businessmen. I had not heard from Peter, but that wasn't unusual. We had plans to see each other that evening for dinner.

I walked past the bar and heard my name called. I knew it was Mr. Maxwell and turned around.

"Yes?"

He motioned me closer.

"Rhonda, I was wondering if we might have a word before you begin working."

"Oh. Well . . . yes. I guess so."

He stood up, threw some bills on the bar and said, "Good. Let's go outside for a few minutes."

I followed him out to the parking lot.

"Is something wrong?" I asked, having no idea why he would want to speak with me.

He shook his head. "No. No. Not at all. I just wanted to discuss something with you." When I remained silent, he continued. "I know you like Peter and he has a fondness for you. But . . . in all honesty, I just don't think something like that would ever work out. If you know what I mean."

A combination of fear and anger surged through me. "No. I don't think I do."

"Well, honey, let's be honest. You and Peter are very different. Those kinds of flings never work out. And besides, Marion has been in Peter's life since they were born. Her father and I have been friends since college. It's always been assumed that Peter and Marion would end up together."

"Oh," was all I could manage to say. Fling? He considered me merely a *fling*? Was that what Peter really thought too?

"So, look," he said, reaching into his shirt pocket and removing a piece of paper, which he passed to me. "I know you want to attend secretarial school and I think that's a very good idea. But it would be much better if you returned to Pennsylvania and went to school up there. This will help to make that happen."

I felt the paper burning my fingers and looked down to see it was a check. For ten thousand dollars. A wave of dizziness came over me at the same time nausea creeped up my chest. I wasn't sure if I was going to pass out or throw up, but I had the presence of mind to shove the check toward him before running in the direction of my cabin, where I promptly threw up in the azalea bushes.

# Chapter 13

Mavis Anne was thrilled that I had invited Ben and Jonah for Christmas day, and I had to admit it had been fun. She kept saying that Koi House was jubilant to have so many happy people filling its rooms.

I sat at the kitchen counter a week later sipping my coffee before going to the yarn shop. Thoughts of Ben were running through my mind. The relationships I had been involved with over the years had all started with an attraction. Ben certainly had not attracted me at our first meeting. Quite the opposite. He had been rude and upset with me. And yet, after a few weeks of getting to know him, I felt drawn to him. I loved watching the interaction between him and Jonah. The love they shared was obvious, and Ben's consenting to rescue Lucy and Ethel proved it. He was a nice man and a good father. We'd met because of Jonah, so initially it never crossed my mind that we could share a romantic interest.

But when he'd called me the evening before, I began to wonder. He'd extended an invitation to have dinner at their home again. He thought I might like to see how Lucy and Ethel were settling in. This was far from a romantic reason, but I still wondered.

I finished my last sip of coffee and looked at Lotte curled up asleep in a patch of sunshine on the kitchen floor.

"You be a good girl," I told her. "I won't be gone long to the yarn shop."

I walked in to find only Mavis Anne and Chloe sitting at the table knitting.

"Where is everybody?" I asked.

"Yarrow had to run to Walmart for some things," Mavis Anne

said. "And it's a quiet morning here in the shop. I'm glad you came over."

"Yeah," Chloe said. "It gives us a chance to catch up. So what's going on with you? I haven't seen you since Christmas day."

I removed a cowl from my knitting bag and nodded. "I know. I had some work that had piled up. After taking a month off to move and then Christmas, I thought I should devote some time to catching up. My clients understand but I don't like to get too behind in my work. So there isn't much going on with me. How about you?"

"Quiet at the moment," Chloe said. "And that's not always a bad thing."

I laughed and nodded again.

"I've been wondering," Mavis Anne said, "did you ever find out any information about your father? I know you wanted to pursue that."

I let out a sigh. "No. I'm afraid not. I hit a dead end before I really even started. I found someone named Peter Maxwell who lived in Jacksonville, but there's hardly anything about him online."

"So you don't think the man your mother married was your father? The man named Garfield," Chloe said.

"I honestly don't know what to think. Jim Garfield died before I was a year old. I didn't even know him. I was really raised by a single mother."

"Whose name is on your birth certificate?" Mavis Anne asked.

"Jim Garfield. But a woman can put any name on a birth certificate, can't she? I have no proof that she even married him. No photos. Nothing."

"And your mother never told you about him or his family or where he was from?" Chloe stopped knitting and stared at me.

I shook my head. "Nope. I used to badger her with questions. She would say his family was all gone. He had nobody. And she said he was from out west. The only other thing she would tell me was that she met him while working in Jacksonville, it was a brief romance, they married, and then he died. When I'd try to ask more questions, she'd refuse to answer. By the time I was a teenager I had stopped asking."

Mavis Anne nodded. "Believe me, I know about family secrets. They might stay hidden for a while, but eventually . . . they do have a way of coming to the surface. So after your mother died, you found this photo of you, her, and a strange man?"

"Right. And I'm assuming that this man is my father. But the mystery is why did she write 'Peter Maxwell' on the back of the photo, if Jim Garfield is my father?"

"Hmm," Chloe said. "Because maybe he's not?"

"I'm thinking the same thing," I said. "That's why I'm trying to find something related to Peter Maxwell, but I've pretty much hit a dead end. I did find somebody by that name on the Internet, though. He owned a manufacturing company in Jacksonville, so there's a connection there. But it seems the company is no longer in existence and there was no photo of the owner."

"I'm hearing about these stories more and more," Mavis Anne said. "Family finding family. Do you remember the story last year about the twins born in Korea who were separated at birth? They were each adopted into different families. One grew up in Paris, France, and one in New Jersey. And twenty-five years later, they found each other through Facebook."

I nodded. "I do recall hearing about that. Well, I guess there's always hope."

"Of course there is," Chloe said. "Look at my friend Sydney in Cedar Key. She went there to start over and ended up finding Sybile, her biological mother. So it's certainly possible."

We moved on to discuss some new knitting patterns and yarn.

"Oh, I wanted to tell you," Mavis Anne said. "I put in an order for the Toshstrology Collection for 2016."

My head snapped up from my knitting. There's nothing like new yarns and patterns to make a woman's heart beat a little faster. "Is that collection the Madelinetosh yarns done with patterns for the zodiac?"

"Yes," Mavis Anne said. "The patterns came out through Marinade Designs on Ravelry. One was released each month, and the colorways for each zodiac sign are amazing. I'll be carrying all the yarn here at the shop."

"My birthday is later this month," I said. "So I will definitely purchase some yarn along with the pattern."

I placed my knitting in my bag and stood up. "Time to go home for lunch. I'm invited to Jonah's house for dinner tonight, so I thought I'd bake some cookies to take with me."

"Oh, really?" Mavis Anne said, a grin covering her face. "Don't you mean *Ben's* house?"

"Well, yes, but I'm sure it was Jonah's idea to invite me. He wants me to come over to see how Lucy and Ethel are settling in."

"Hmm, right," she replied. "But don't be too sure it was all Jonah's idea."

I waved a hand in the air and laughed. "Oh, Mavis Anne, you're too much of a romantic. Ben and I are just friends."

"Famous last words," I heard Chloe say as I walked out the door.

Jonah answered the doorbell the moment I pushed it, making me think he'd been watching for me out the window. Skidding on the tile right behind him were Lucy and Ethel.

I bent down to pat them while juggling a plate of cookies in my other hand. One of the dogs must have smelled them, because the next thing I knew the plate flew out of my hands, cookies landed on the floor, and both dogs were trying to gobble up as many as they could.

"Oh, no!" I exclaimed, while trying to hold the dogs back with Jonah's help.

I heard deep laughter and looked up to see Ben rushing toward us. The fact that my cookies were ruined wasn't my first thought. I realized that this was the first time I'd heard a genuine belly laugh from Ben Wellington. I shook my head and joined his laughter as he reached for both dogs by their collars and held them back as Jonah and I scooped up cookies.

"I am *so* sorry," I said.

"Not a problem," I heard Ben say. "Jonah, go get the broom and dustpan."

I continued to push the cookies together and was grateful I'd used a plastic plate. At least we didn't also have glass to contend with.

Jonah returned, and we worked together to sweep up my cookies before placing them in the trash.

"I think this proves these girls need obedience training," Ben said. "I'm really sorry about that. After you went to the trouble to make cookies."

His words were sincere, but I couldn't help noticing a slight grin on his face.

"Ah, well," I said. "Dogs will be dogs. That's why we love them. I just feel bad we don't have the cookies."

"It's okay," Jonah said. "Betsy baked us a blueberry pie this morning."

I laughed and knelt down again to pat the dogs. "Come here, you naughty girls," I said.

Ben released their collars and both dogs ran to me, covering my face in kisses.

"They're just beautiful," I said, standing up. "I think they're very happy to be living with you, Jonah."

"I love them so much, Petra. I really do."

"Okay, now why don't you take them in the yard for a little while so Petra and I can enjoy a glass of wine before dinner."

I followed Ben to the kitchen, where the aroma of Italian food filled the air.

"Smells good," I said.

"Betsy made a pan of lasagna for us, and we'll have salad and garlic bread with it."

I watched as he uncorked a bottle of red wine, filled two glasses, and passed me one.

"That sounds great," I said. "Thanks." I took a sip and nodded. "Very nice."

"Let's sit out on the patio. The weather has been mild for January."

"Yes. Once I left Pennsylvania, I never looked back. I got spoiled by winters in the south."

"I feel the same way. You had mentioned your mother passed away. How about your father? Is he still in Pennsylvania?"

I shook my head. "I never really knew who my father was."

I saw the look of interest that crossed Ben's face. "Was that difficult for you?"

"I didn't think so while I was growing up. But lately I've been giving thought to who my father was."

Before I knew it, I was sharing my story with Ben. When I finished, I wasn't sure whether I was more surprised that I had opened up to a person I didn't know that well or that he seemed completely interested in what I had told him.

He took a sip of wine and nodded. "Yes, that has to be difficult not having any answers. So do you intend to keep searching?"

"Well, I think I've hit a dead end. But yes, I was thinking about joining Ancestry.com to see if I might be able to track down this Maxwell family."

"I think you should. I feel it's important to know where we come from. Most of us take it for granted because we have all the answers. But for people who don't, I think there's a need to find the pieces to the puzzle." He paused for a second before saying, "If there's anything I can do to help, just let me know."

By the time I left Ben and Jonah's home, I knew two things for sure. Even if we never progressed beyond friendship, I felt fortunate to have Ben Wellington as a friend. And after spending another enjoyable evening with him, I had to question if perhaps my feelings might be progressing beyond friendship.

# Rhonda
## May 1969

When I'd returned to work the morning after my encounter with Mr. Maxwell, I'd found an envelope from Peter in my box. I had asked Cynthia to tell Peter I wasn't feeling well and had to cancel my date with him the evening before.

I walked outside to read his letter in private.

> *My dear Rhonda,*
> *I'm so terribly sorry you're sick and I will miss seeing you this evening. We need to talk, but please do not be concerned about Marion. Give me a chance to explain. Unfortunately, my father has insisted I leave in the morning to tour some of our offices out of state. It looks like I could be gone about two weeks. I'll miss you a lot and I can't wait to see you when I return. I love you, Rhonda. And I always will.*
> *My love forever,*
> *Peter*

And here I was two weeks later waiting for Peter to return and unsure what to do.

I turned over in bed as a wave of nausea gripped me. I made it to the toilet bowl just in time. Sitting on the floor with my face in my hands, I heard Cynthia say, "Rhonda? Are you okay?"

I nodded and swiped my hand across my clammy forehead. "Yeah."

She reached out her hand to help me up. "Come on. Let's sit outside. Some fresh air might help."

I followed her to the porch and sat down, gulping in the scent of salt air.

"You're pregnant, aren't you?" she said.

I felt the tears stinging my eyes. "I think so," I whispered.

"Holy shit. I thought you were using protection."

"We are. We did. But . . . that very first time . . . we didn't."

"Oh, God," she groaned. "And the timing is right. That was late March, wasn't it?"

I nodded as I made an attempt to push away another wave of nausea.

"Does Peter know?"

I shook my head slowly. "No. He's been out of town on business." I took some slow, deep breaths to quell the nausea. "Besides, I'm not sure I want him to know."

She reached out and gripped my arm. "Are you nuts? Why not? He loves you like crazy. He'd marry you in a second."

I had never told Cynthia about the money Mr. Maxwell had tried to force on me. I was too embarrassed. The thought of that money made me feel dirty. I knew Peter's family would never accept me. And no matter what Peter had written, I questioned whether two people from such different backgrounds could ever build a successful marriage.

I took a deep breath. "Because I'm just not sure that would be the right thing to do. That's why. And . . ." I shifted to look her in the eyes. "You have to promise me, and I mean *promise*, that if I choose not to tell him, you will support me and never say a word."

"But, Rhonda . . ."

"Promise," I said, raising my voice. "It's my choice. Not yours. As my best friend, you have to promise." Before I knew it, I felt tears coursing down my cheeks.

Cynthia patted my hand. "Okay. Okay. I promise. Of course I do. But I don't agree with you."

"You don't have to. I just want your word. If I don't tell him, you never will and you'll never tell anyone."

After a second, I heard her say, "Yes. I do promise. But Rhonda, you can't get through this alone. What the hell are you going to do? Are you going to tell your mother and go back to Pennsylvania?"

I let out a sarcastic chuckle. "Go back home as an unwed mother? No, I don't think so."

"This is what I mean. Then we have to *do* something."

My head snapped up. "What do you mean by that?"

"Well . . . I know abortion isn't legal, but . . . I also know there are some safe places you can get the procedure done. I can help you."

I couldn't believe this was my best friend talking. My entire life was falling apart, but one thing I knew for certain—I could *not* get rid of this baby. It was a part of Peter and me.

"No," I said emphatically. "Absolutely not. I won't even consider an abortion. Or adoption. I want this baby. It's not the best circumstances, but I don't care. I *want* this baby."

Cynthia blew out a breath and nodded. "Okay. Then I'll support you. But we have to find somebody who can help us. Who can tell you what you should do. You're supposed to be working here another month. Do you plan to avoid Peter when he returns? I don't think he'll let you go that easily, Rhonda."

She was right. I knew that. I also knew in that moment that my mind was made up. I would not tell Peter about the baby. I couldn't.

When I remained silent, she said, "How about Joyce?"

"Joyce?"

"Yeah, she's like our supervisor here and has looked after us. She's a great person. I think she could give you some advice."

"Maybe," I said, doubtfully.

Cynthia jumped up. "Okay. That's it. You talk to her today. You're going to have to confide in her. We both know she can be trusted."

I had made an appointment to meet with Joyce in her office later that afternoon.

Sitting across from her at her desk, I clasped and unclasped my sweaty hands.

"What can I do for you, Rhonda?" A sincere smile crossed her face. "Is everything okay?"

The gentle tone of her voice and her compassion caused another flood of tears.

She jumped up and passed me a tissue. "Gosh, are you ill?"

I shook my head and then blew my nose. "No. Not ill."

"What is it then?"

"I need your help. I'm . . . I'm pretty sure . . . I'm . . . pregnant."

I heard the gasp as she stood beside me and put a hand on my shoulder.

"Oh," she said and walked back to her chair. She was silent for a few moments. Then she folded her hands on the desk, leaned forward, and nodded. "Okay. And how can I help you?"

"I don't know." I felt the start of tears again.

"Let's start at the beginning. I happen to know that you're seeing Peter Maxwell. Is he the father?"

"Yes."

"Have you told him?"

"No."

"Do you plan to?"

I hesitated only briefly before saying, "No."

"Can I ask why?"

I blew out a breath. "Because . . . as much as we love each other . . . and we do, it would never work. We're from two different worlds. I know that. I knew that when I met him and first started dating him, but . . ."

"But you can't control love, can you?"

I shook my head. She might only be about ten years older than me, but I had no doubt that she was a wise woman.

"Okay. I understand," she said. "Do you plan to keep the baby?"

On that question, I didn't hesitate. "Yes. Definitely."

"And I'm thinking you don't want to return home to your mother?"

"Yes," I said again.

She let out a sigh. "Okay. Then we need to figure out a plan for you. You've said that you want to take secretarial classes to get a decent paying job, right?"

"Yes, I do. I have quite a bit of money already saved."

Joyce smiled and nodded. "Good. Okay, I think I have an idea. It will involve your leaving this area, but not too far. Are you willing to go to Jacksonville?"

I nodded.

"Okay. Let me work on this. I'll meet with you tomorrow morning at ten, okay?"

I nodded again.

"There's only one thing I insist that you do."

When I remained silent, she said, "You must see Peter one last time. If you're not going to tell him about the baby, then you have to break up with him. You can't disappear without at least giving him that information. It would be cruel not to tell him face to face and give him closure. Can you agree to that?"

I had been hoping to avoid facing Peter, but Joyce was right. I knew she was. And I also knew it would be the hardest thing I would ever have to do.

But I nodded and said quietly, "Yes. I will. I will break up with him."

Peter returned to Amelia Island two days later. I had a letter in my box when I reported for my breakfast shift, telling me he would pick me up that evening at six.

I wasn't sure how I got through my work hours. I found it difficult to focus on anything but Peter and what, exactly, I would say to him.

By the time I walked out to the parking lot at six and saw him leaning against his car waiting for me, I prayed that I'd have the strength to do what I had planned. But seeing him standing there, looking so handsome, seeing the love on his face, made me waver. And when he pulled me into his arms and kissed me, weakness washed over me.

"I've missed you so much," he said, opening the passenger door.

I got in and remained silent. He then slid into the driver's seat, started the engine, and headed north along A1A.

Reaching across the seat, Peter grabbed my hand. "I thought we'd park at the beach so we can talk," he said, and I nodded.

A few minutes later he pulled into the area overlooking the ocean. The radio played softly, and if I weren't breaking up with him, it would have been another romantic evening. But I couldn't let that happen.

He shifted in his seat and took my hand. "Rhonda, I'm so sorry about that episode with Marion at the restaurant. She is *not* my girlfriend. She never has been. That's always been wishful thinking on my father's part. I need you to know that."

I nodded but said nothing.

"It's *you* who I love, Rhonda. I always will. Do you believe me?"

I nodded again.

"I see a future for us. I want to be with you forever. But I need to know that you feel the same."

My hands had grown clammy, and I prayed that nausea wouldn't betray me.

I took a deep breath and finally spoke. "I love you too, Peter. I want you to know that. What I'm about to say has nothing to do with love."

I saw anxiety on his face.

"As much as I love you . . . as much as we love each other . . . we can't be together."

He attempted to say something, but I put my fingers over his lips. "Let me finish," I said. "It just won't work, Peter. We're from two different worlds. We could never have a life together. You might think right now that we could, but you're wrong. In the years to come I think you'll see that. I'm breaking up with you, Peter, because neither one of us deserves regrets in the future."

He pulled me into his arms, and I felt his lips against my ear as I heard him say, "No. No, Rhonda, please. Don't do this. You're wrong. Our lifestyles have nothing to do with how we feel about each other. And if you leave me, *I'll* have the regret of losing you for the rest of my life."

Tears slid down my face as I pulled away and saw Peter was also crying.

"Please, Rhonda," he begged. "Please don't do this to us."

For one brief second I thought I might relent. I wanted to. With my entire heart and soul. But I couldn't.

I shook my head. "Take me home, Peter. I'm sorry. But please take me home."

As soon as I said the words, I heard the Righteous Brothers' popular song come on the radio, "Unchained Melody."

Peter reached for my hand, exhaled, and shook his head. "This can't be happening," he whispered.

Part of me was sorry when he did as I asked, drove on to A1A and headed south. And part of me knew that despite the anguish I saw on his face, I had done the right thing.

But I also knew that like the words in the song—we would always hunger for each other's touch.

# Chapter 14

I hadn't heard from Ben since the previous week, when I'd had dinner at his home. I had been thinking that perhaps our relationship would remain simple friendship and was surprised to discover during this time that I was disappointed.

Although I had never been a woman who felt she needed a man in her life, I did welcome the company of a male now and then. My mother had raised me to be an independent female, so I had never depended on a man for security, but I had enjoyed the few serious relationships I'd had over the years. Still, they weren't destined to be permanent, and by the time we arrived at the end, both of us had been ready to call it quits.

At age forty-six I now wondered if I would eventually end my days as my mother had. Alone. Growing up, I used to question why she didn't even date. From the little she ever said about Jim Garfield, it didn't appear she'd shared a great love with him, which might have prevented her from loving again. So this was always a mystery to me.

When I thought about Ben I realized that I also thought about Jonah. In my mind, they were a package deal. This also surprised me because by the time I was thirty, I was pretty sure I had been given an extra low dose of maternal feeling. And I was always fine with that. I certainly didn't feel empty or like I was missing something. That was, until the day I met Jonah. From the moment I met him, I felt we shared an unexplained connection. And although he didn't voice it, I had a feeling Jonah felt the same way.

So I began to realize that I was missing both father and son.

The ringing of the phone interrupted my thoughts. I answered to hear Suzanne from the shelter.

"Petra," she said, "I was wondering if you could do me a favor tomorrow."

"Sure. What's up?"

"We have a benefactor who kindly donates items for us to sell. Elaine Talbot called and said she's cleared out some closets and has a few boxes to be picked up. Do you think you might be able to get those for us tomorrow?"

"Not a problem. Give me her address and I'll be happy to do that."

"She lives in a condo at Daytona Beach Shores," she said and went on to give me the details. "She asked if you could stop by around one?"

"Yes. That will work for me. I'll pick up the stuff and then bring it to the shelter."

"Thanks so much. I'll see you tomorrow."

I hung up the phone and headed to the computer, where I was still catching up on business.

By lunchtime I felt I had put in a good morning of work and deserved a few hours at the yarn shop.

I entered through the tea shop and found Yarrow behind the counter.

"Hey," she said. "How's it going?"

"Good. I've been working all morning and needed a break. I'll have a cup of jasmine tea and . . ." I looked into the pastry display case. "Give me two of your peanut butter cookies."

Yarrow laughed. "Your lunch?"

I nodded. "Yup. Sometimes a woman has to give in to her basic instincts."

"I'll bring it over to you."

"Thanks," I said and headed into the yarn shop to find Mavis Anne, Chloe, Iris, and Louise.

"We were hoping you'd stop by today," Mavis Anne said.

"Really? Why?" I sat down and pulled out the baby sweater I had been working on to donate to charity.

"Because we want an update on Ben, that's why." Mavis Anne stopped knitting to fix me with a stare.

I felt heat creeping up my neck. "An update? There's nothing to report."

"Well, I saw the way he was looking at you on Christmas day."

"Looking at me? Mavis Anne, you're way too much of a romantic," I said, brushing off her statement.

"I never claimed to be an expert, but I will tell you that the chemistry between the two of you is difficult to dismiss. Didn't you go to dinner at his home last week?"

"Yeah . . . but . . ."

Now Louise leaned forward. "So what happened? Any mention of a date?"

"No. Not at all. I was only invited so I could meet the new dogs. Jonah wanted me to come."

"Ah, so it was all Jonah's idea?"

I looked up to see the grin that covered Iris's face.

"Well, yes. Probably."

"Probably not," Mavis Anne stated. "You have to admit that Dr. Wellington is mighty nice eye candy."

There was no denying that. Despite being a cross between a nerd and a preppie, he definitely possessed a good amount of sex appeal.

I refused to admit this and said, "You women need to get a life. Stop focusing on mine."

Chloe patted me on the back. "Oh, honey, you'd better get used to it. Groups of women are notorious for matchmaking. But Mavis Anne is right. I was there Christmas day, and even Henry remarked that Ben certainly seemed interested in you."

What was I missing?

"Well, I think all of you are wrong."

"Oh, by the way," Chloe said, "we want to do another knit-along here in the shop, and I was thinking of designing something for you, Petra."

"For me?"

"Yeah. I know you've been giving a lot of thought to finding your father. And it will involve some unraveling of information. So I thought I'd design maybe a scarf or a shrug, and I want to name it Petra's Past."

"Really? For *me*?" I was touched by Chloe's explanation. "That would be very meaningful. Thank you."

"Wonderful idea," Louise said.

"Yes, I agree." Iris smiled. "I thought the scarf you designed for Isabelle was just beautiful."

"Thank you," Chloe said. "Yes, I've sold quite a few patterns for Isabelle's Challenge. And all of us enjoyed working on the scarf here in the shop."

"I also loved the shawl you designed for Chloe's Dream," Mavis Anne said. "I think you have another great idea."

"Okay. Well, I'll give it a little more thought and then decide if it will be a scarf or a shrug."

"Have you been to the shelter this week?" Louise asked me.

"Yes, I was there on Monday, and Suzanne called earlier. She asked if I could pick up some items somebody is donating. A woman named Elaine Talbot."

"Oh, Elaine is a wonderful person. She's one of our top supporters for the shelter. You'll just love her. But be prepared to stay awhile visiting with her."

I laughed. "Why is that?"

"Her husband died many years ago, she has no children, and I think she gets lonely. Although she's in very good health and is quite active with various groups, she always welcomes the chance for company. I went there once to pick up a few things for the shelter and ended up staying for four hours."

"That's good to know, but she does sound nice."

Louise nodded. "Yup, she is. Comes from money. From what I hear, scads of it, but you'd never know it to talk to her. Her condo is simply stunning, though. It's a penthouse on the top floor overlooking the ocean. Way too large for just one person . . . oh, and her three dogs . . . but she loves it there. Moved in with her husband and never left. Wait until you see her decorating and paintings. You'll think you're stepping into the pages of *Architectural Digest*."

I laughed. "It sounds very interesting."

Louise nodded. "Be sure to tell her I said hello."

After skimping on lunch, I decided to have a healthy supper. I placed lemon herb chicken breasts in the oven and was making a salad when my phone rang.

I was surprised to hear Ben's voice when I answered.

"Have you got a minute?" he asked.

"Yes. How are you?"

"I'm good. And you?"

"Yes. I'm fine," I said and was glad he couldn't see the smile that crossed my face.

"Good. Good."

Was that nervousness I detected in his voice?

"Well . . . I was wondering . . . if maybe you'd like to have dinner with me?"

Did he mean *just* him? Or, as in the past, both him and Jonah? Either way would work for me.

"Oh, sure," I said, feeling awkward. "That would be nice."

"Great. Are you free Saturday evening?"

"I am."

"I'm pretty sure you like Italian food?"

"Yes. One of my favorites."

"Good. I was going to make a reservation at Mario's. Have you been there?"

"No, but I've heard it's good."

"Yes, it is. They've been there since 1956. It's a family-run restaurant on South Yonge. I think you'll like it."

"Sounds great."

"Okay. I'll pick you up at six-thirty. Will that work for you?"

"That'll be fine. I look forward to seeing you."

"Same here, Petra," he said, before hanging up.

I disconnected the call and looked down at Lotte, who had been sitting by my feet.

"Well, what do you think of that, girl?" I asked.

Her ears perked up, and she wagged her tail.

"I do believe Ben Wellington just called me for a bona fide date. Imagine that."

I smiled as I continued preparing my salad and heard one of my mother's favorite songs come on the radio. "Unchained Melody" by the Righteous Brothers.

I let out a sigh as I recalled how that one song always moved her. And I felt a twinge of sorrow for the love she probably never had in her life.

# *Rhonda*
# *May 1969*

I had tossed and turned all night and finally cried myself to sleep. Cynthia had already left to do her breakfast shift by the time I got up at eight. I showered, dressed, and then attempted to have some coffee. But after two sips I was running for the toilet again.

Sitting outside on the porch and breathing in deep gulps of ocean air helped. I was meeting with Joyce at ten and I wondered where on earth my life would end up. What she might have in mind for me. No matter what it was, it would be better than returning home and causing embarrassment for my mother. I couldn't do that to her.

And then my thoughts went to Peter. Peter. Who I knew without a doubt would always be the one great love of my life—and yet we were not destined to be together. Was I wrong? To deny him the knowledge of his child? No. I truly felt I would cause him more harm if I had told him. He led a privileged life, and without me as part of it, he was certain to continue with that life.

At promptly ten o'clock, Joyce ushered me into her office.

A reassuring smile crossed her face. "How are you this morning, Rhonda?"

I blew out a breath and nodded. "I'm okay." I paused for a second. "I met Peter last night and . . . I broke up with him."

She put her head down and then looked up and said, "I'm sure that was terribly difficult."

I nodded again. "It was. But he finally seemed to accept what I told him. That our lives are completely different and our relationship has no chance. I'm not sure he believed it, but he honored my request and took me home."

"Before I explain how I might help you, I want you to know how very sorry I am that this happened to you. It shouldn't matter about your different lifestyles, but sometimes it does. Unfortunately. I just want to be sure that you don't want to give Peter a chance to decide that. To make the choice."

I shook my head. "No. It's not fair he should have to. So I'm making the decision for both of us."

Joyce nodded. "Okay. Well, I have a sister who lives in Jacksonville. Sebine is a bit of a free spirit." She grinned. "And I don't mean this in a negative way. But she willingly admits that she's a feminist. Very independent. Makes her own choices. Lives her own lifestyle."

"She sounds interesting," I said, and I meant it. I wasn't sure I'd met a woman like her before, but it was the late sixties and society was changing.

"She is. And she's quite brilliant and extremely compassionate. Sebine is an artist and does quite well with her paintings. Her studio and gallery are on the same property, detached from the house. She has a large home and shares it with . . . her companion. Lillian is a doctor and has a practice in town. They met in Paris about twenty years ago. Sebine is now forty-two and a truly wonderful human being."

"Oh," was all I said, still pondering the part about her companion. Did she mean a girlfriend?

When Joyce remained silent, I said, "And she's willing to let me stay with her?"

"With her and Lillian, yes. She knows your story, she knows you're pregnant, and she knows the circumstances. She would like to help you."

"I think that's great, but . . . why would a complete stranger want to help me?"

"Oh, you'll come to see that's just how Sebine is. It's her nature to help those who need it. They recently had two fellows staying with them who were avoiding the draft. I can't say she agreed with what they were doing, but she wholeheartedly supported their right to choose not to go to Vietnam. So the fellows stayed for a while to work and get money to relocate to Canada."

"Wow, she does sound like an amazing person."

"She is. I'm very fortunate to have her as my sister. So the plan would be for you to live there and get some type of work until your pregnancy prevents your working. Actually, Lillian has said she could use you in her office. You could do filing, answer the phone, that kind of thing, and you could take classes in the evening for secretarial courses."

I felt the tears stinging my eyes. Such generosity from strangers? "I can't believe they'd be willing to help me like that. That's so kind of them. I definitely accept. Is there anything I can do to pay them back? I'll pay them rent, and I can cook."

Joyce shook her head and put a hand in the air. "I don't think that will be necessary. They will not accept rent from you, but I know they'd be happy if you just pitch in a little around the house. The main thing is they want you to take those classes and complete the secretarial program. They both feel very strongly about education for women."

"Of course. Absolutely. I'll do that."

"Okay. Let's just go over something one more time. I want you to be positive you want to go there. Sebine and Lillian are partners."

When I gave Joyce a blank stare, she said, "More to the point, they're lesbians."

"Okay," I said, unsure what else to say. I really had no experience with homosexuals.

"Does this bother you?" she asked.

I thought about it a few moments before answering and shook my head. "No. Although I've never known any lesbians, I don't have a problem with it. Isn't it supposed to be about who we are *inside*?"

Joyce smiled. "I think you'll do just fine there."

"When will I go? How will I get there?" All of a sudden I had a million questions.

"I'm thinking you'd probably like to leave as soon as possible so you don't bump into Peter again?"

I nodded.

"Tomorrow's Wednesday, and there's a bus to Jacksonville at two tomorrow afternoon. Would that be too soon for you to go?"

"No. All I have to do is explain to Cynthia what I'm doing and pack my bag."

"That's another thing we need to discuss. Cynthia knows you're pregnant?"

"Yes, but we had a discussion about her not ever telling Peter, and I trust her. She's leaving here with Earle at the end of the month anyway. They're heading north to go to Woodstock in August."

"Okay. He might question the other servers and workers here as to your whereabouts, but probably not. If so, they don't know a thing and of course, if he ever approached me, I would simply say you gave notice and left. I don't know where you went."

I nodded. "Yes. That will work. So there's no chance he can find me."

Joyce stood up and came around the desk to give me a hug. "I'll drive you to the bus station in town tomorrow. And Sebine will meet you at the station in Jacksonville. You're going to do just fine. I have no doubt about that."

Amid hugs and tears on my part, I boarded the bus in Amelia Island and headed south to Jacksonville, knowing that in less than an hour my entire life was about to change.

I sat down and stared out the window, thinking of my good-bye with Cynthia that morning. Although she'd been against my plan when I had first told her, she relented and agreed it was for the best. She also agreed that I was very fortunate to have the assistance I'd be getting from Sebine and Lillian. Cynthia didn't question their relationship, and I didn't tell her. I truly had no problem with living with two lesbians, but I also knew homosexuals were not accepted by many people.

Cynthia had promised to keep in touch with phone calls and letters. She even assured me that she and Earle would stop for a short visit before leaving for Woodstock in August.

I let out a sigh as I watched the landscape of palm trees out the window. By August I would be four months pregnant. And shortly after the New Year bringing in 1970, I would be a mother. Peter Maxwell would never know that he was a father. I felt tears stinging my eyes again.

I hadn't been in touch with my mother, but I planned to write her once I got settled in and give her my new address. My plan was to tell her I had saved enough money and was now living in Jacksonville to attend secretarial school.

I dozed off for about twenty minutes and woke to see the Jacksonville sign along A1A. I stretched and yawned as I looked out the window at a commercial area with shops, banks, and restaurants. This seemed to be a larger and busier area than Amelia Island.

A few minutes later we pulled into the bus station and I gathered up my two bags to join the other passengers leaving the bus.

I stepped outside to bright sunshine and an ocean breeze. Joyce had given me a description of Sebine; it appeared that the woman walking toward me might be her. She was tall and slim with long, straight, brunette hair parted in the middle. Wearing bell-bottom jeans and a white T-shirt, she smiled, and said, "Are you Rhonda Bradley?"

When I nodded, she said, "I'm Sebine LeBlanc. Welcome to Jacksonville." Then she pulled me into an embrace.

"Thank you," I said and I knew in that split second that I liked her. She had a friendly glow about her, and although I had been concerned about feeling awkward meeting a stranger, I knew my anxiety had been unfounded.

"The car is right over here," she said, pointing to the parking lot and reaching for one of my bags. "Did you have a good trip down here?"

"Yes, I did. It didn't even take an hour."

"Good. We live about seven miles from here, in the Riverside area of the city."

I followed her to the car and we got in, as she said, "Lillian has appointments until five, so supper will be around six, if that's okay with you."

"Oh, yes, fine. I can't thank you enough for allowing me to stay with you. I appreciate it so much."

She reached over and patted my hand before starting up the car. "It's our pleasure. When Joyce told me your story, both Lillian and I wanted to help you. I'm just sorry you have to go through such a difficult time."

Sebine drove onto A1A and I nodded. "I still can't believe I'm in this situation." I felt comfortable in her company and went on to say, "The one time we didn't use protection . . . and I find myself pregnant."

"All it takes is once. But your life is far from over. It won't be easy for a while, but you'll get through it and be all the stronger."

She sounded so positive it was hard to disagree with her.

A little while later Sebine had cut off A1A and we were driving through a beautiful, older residential area. The houses and landscaping were well maintained. There were a lot of huge oak trees providing shade and a cozy feel to the neighborhood. Both the street and sidewalks were cobblestone. I saw a man walking his dog on a leash and a young mother pushing a toddler in a stroller. We drove to the end of a cul-de-sac and Sebine pulled into a driveway.

A gray brick two-story home with black shutters sat back from the street with two brick steps and a brick walkway leading to the front porch. Along the walkway were beautiful green bushes. In front of us to the right of the house was a smaller detached building, and I saw a sign hanging from the stained glass door: "Sabine LeBlanc ~ Artist."

"Oh, my goodness," I exclaimed. "This is just beautiful."

Sebine rested her hands on the steering wheel and leaned forward, staring at the house and studio. "Thank you. Yes, we love it here. Actually, the house used to belong to Lillian's grandparents. Her grandfather was the doctor in town for many years. When he and her grandmother passed away, they left the house to Lillian, and she also inherited his medical practice."

"How nice to keep it in the family," I said, wondering if when the time came someday I'd have anything of value to leave to my child.

"Come on," she said. "Let's go inside so you can settle in."

As we walked onto the porch, I heard barking from inside the house.

"You have dogs?" I asked.

She paused before putting her key in the lock. "Oh, gosh, yes. Joyce didn't tell you?"

"No. But I love dogs. So it's not a problem."

Sebine blew out a breath of air. "Oh, good. Because Sonny and Cher are our babies."

I laughed at the names and followed her into a beautiful foyer as a black lab and a golden retriever came running from the back of the house.

Tails and butts were frantically moving from side to side, but Sebine held up her palm and said, "Okay, kids. Sit and behave. I'd like you to meet our house guest, Rhonda."

Both dogs automatically extended a paw for me to shake.

"It's so nice to meet you," I said, taking each paw and smiling. "My goodness, you're better behaved than a lot of children."

"Thank you," Sebine said. "Leave your bags here and let me show you around the downstairs."

I nodded and followed her into the room on the right, a cozy and beautifully furnished family room. Two cushy leather loveseats were facing each other in front of a fieldstone fireplace. Two club chairs in a chintz fabric of bright orange, tan, and yellow were placed in the corners of the room, with an entire wall behind the chairs covered with bookshelves from ceiling to floor. A sliding ladder was attached at one end. Cherrywood tables and ginger jar lamps completed the décor. Antique casement windows along the front and side of the house brightened the entire room with sunlight.

"This is so beautiful," I said. "Such a cozy room."

"It is. We spend the majority of our time here. Lillian's grandfather had his practice here at the house, and this was the waiting room. When he retired, they remodeled the downstairs so the family room and the dining room across the hall were updated at that time."

I followed her to the back of the house, where a large eat-in kitchen overlooked a brick patio area and beautiful garden.

"And over here," she said, opening a door off the kitchen that led into a small hallway, "is your bedroom and bath area."

She opened another door and we stepped into a large room that overlooked the back of the house and garden.

I gasped as I looked around. "This is just beautiful." My eyes took in the double bed with a puffy floral comforter and matching pillows. The drapes were a pale yellow, and a wingback chair was in the corner with a floor lamp behind it. French doors looked out to the patio, bringing more light into the room. I noticed that the small television on the tall bureau was the first I'd seen in the house.

"I hope you'll like it," Sebine said. She opened a door and pointed. "And this is your bathroom."

I could hardly believe I'd be staying here in this room. It was the nicest bedroom I'd ever had.

"Oh, my gosh," I gushed. "I will love it here. Thank you so much."

"You're very welcome. Oh, and you probably noticed we don't have a television in the family room. Lillian and I normally listen to the radio and read or do needlework or knitting in the evening. But you have a small television here to use. However, we don't want you to feel you must seclude yourself in the evening. We'd love for you to join us in the family room."

"Thank you," I said and once again, I felt tears in my eyes.

"Okay," she said. "Let me show you the dining room and the up-stairs, and then you might want to have a rest before Lillian gets home and we have supper."

I followed Sebine and realized how fortunate I was to be given this chance for both myself and my child.

# Chapter 15

I woke and knew right away that I'd dreamed again of Emmalyn the night before. I pulled on the cobwebs of my memory, trying to recall what it was about and then remembered that Emmalyn had been standing by the French doors in my bedroom. She was slowly shaking her head from side to side.

"What's wrong?" I asked.

"You have to pay attention," she said. "Pay attention to the clues."

"What clues?"

"The clues that will give you the answers," she said.

And that was it. I sat up in bed and said, "What the hell!" Did these dreams have any meaning? And if they did, what were they about? It made no sense to even dream of a person that I had never met. And what she said in the dreams only confused me.

I looked at the clock and saw it was just after seven. I was scheduled to meet with Elaine Talbot at one o'clock to pick up the items for the shelter, so I had the entire morning to myself. I decided that a long walk on the beach with Lotte after breakfast might be what I needed.

When Lotte and I arrived at Andy Romano Park, I was happy to see the beach was mostly empty. There were a few walkers and a few people were already soaking up the rays in beach chairs.

We headed to the shore, and I took a deep breath of the salt air as we began walking. I let my mind wander and found myself thinking of my mother. We had always had a good relationship, but the older I got, the more I felt she had kept a part of her life secret from me. I knew that she'd left Pennsylvania at age nineteen with her best friend,

Cynthia, to work at a hotel resort on Amelia Island. She had told me that she'd rented a room from a woman in Jacksonville, worked at a doctor's office while she attended secretarial classes in the evening, and it was during this time that she met my father, Jim Garfield. She never volunteered any information about him except that they had married shortly after meeting, she became pregnant and he was sent to Vietnam, where he was killed. When I would question her about aunts, uncles, or cousins on my father's side, she claimed that he had no family. My mother remained in Jacksonville working and raising me until I was almost three years old. Then her mother had become ill in Pennsylvania and she'd returned home to take care of my grandmother. She had secured a good secretarial position at the university and passed away at age sixty-three, two years before she was due to retire. End of story.

Looking at my mother's life in retrospect caused me to feel sad. She was a good mother, raised me well, worked hard—but had she ever been truly happy? As far as I knew, she had never been deeply, passionately in love. Jim Garfield might have been my father, but I tended to doubt that any great love had existed between them.

I gazed toward the horizon and realized that when it came to love, I wasn't very different from my mother. Could any of my romantic relationships possibly have progressed to something more meaningful? I didn't know—because I *did* know in my heart that I had never given any of them a chance.

Lotte and I returned home after our walk. I made myself a grilled cheese sandwich for lunch before leaving to meet with Elaine Talbot.

"Now you be a good girl, Lotte," I told her as I headed to the door. "I shouldn't be gone too long."

I easily found the condo building in Daytona Beach Shores and pulled into the parking lot. The front door had an intercom pad and I pressed the button marked "Talbot."

"Yes?" I heard an older woman say.

"Yes, hello. I'm here to pick up your items for the dog shelter."

"Wonderful," I heard her reply at the same time the door buzzed. "Come on up."

I walked into the lobby and headed to the elevator, where I pressed the button for the seventh floor. I noted that it was the top floor, so maybe Louise hadn't been kidding about it being the penthouse.

When I exited the elevator, I saw there was only one door on this floor. I knocked.

I heard a chorus of barking before the door was opened by a tall, slim woman. Her white hair was styled in a becoming French twist and she wore beige linen slacks with a pale yellow top that set off her mahogany eyes. I guessed her age to be early seventies. I saw the look of surprise on her face when she opened the door and saw me. When she remained silent, I wondered if perhaps I had the wrong person.

"Are you Elaine Talbot?" I questioned.

She blinked her eyes and nodded, seeming to recover her composure.

"Yes. Yes, I am. And you are?"

"I'm with the animal shelter. I had called about coming to pick up the items that you're donating." I began to wonder if maybe she had episodes of forgetfulness.

"And your name?" she asked.

A sense of uneasiness came over me, but I replied, "Petra. Petra Garfield."

I didn't miss the raised eyebrows or the deep swallow she took before saying, "That's a lovely name. Petra. Now, children," she said, shooing the dogs away from the door, "quiet down and show your manners." She extended her hand. "It's so nice to meet you. Please come in."

I stepped into a large foyer, and the first thing I noticed was the paintings that covered both walls. Then my eyes were drawn straight back to a wall of glass doors behind a balcony that showed the sky and the ocean below.

"Thank you," I said, following her into a large open space I assumed was the family room. "You have a gorgeous place here, and what a view!"

"Yes, I do enjoy watching the ocean and the sky. Sometimes it can change from hour to hour."

I felt her staring at me as I continued to gaze outside.

"Please forgive me," she said. "Have a seat." She gestured to the sofa.

I looked up to see a black woman walk into the room holding a tray, which she placed on the coffee table in front of me.

"Oh, Cordelia, thank you," Elaine said and began to pour tea into two china cups. "I do hope you enjoy tea."

"Yes. Very much," I told her, but not before I saw both women exchange a glance. I was beginning to feel a bit like Alice in Wonderland and wondered if I'd fallen down the rabbit hole.

Elaine passed me a cup. The three small dogs sat at attention watching her every move. I noticed there was also a plate of cookies on the tray, and if these dogs were anything like Lotte, I knew they were hoping for a few crumbs.

"Your dogs are so cute," I said. I was pretty sure one of them was a King Charles spaniel, one had a lot of schnauzer, and the third one appeared to have a lot of terrier in his heritage.

"Oh, thank you. Obviously, they are my babies. All three are rescues, and I adore them. Do you have any dogs?"

I took a sip of tea and nodded. "Yes, I have a Yorkie named Lotte, and I know what you mean about them being your children."

She looked at me from her chair, and there was no doubt her stare was intense as she took in my features. But instead of asking if we'd met before, which I thought she might be thinking, she said, "Oh, you have no children either?"

I shook my head. "No. No children and never married."

"I was married," she said. "Happily married for many years, but I lost Michael about five years ago. Are you from this area?"

"No. Not originally. I was born in Jacksonville but my mother . . ."

"You were born in Jacksonville?" she questioned.

I wasn't sure why she considered this important, but I nodded. "Yes. My mother lived and worked there for a while. Then my father passed away, my grandmother in Pennsylvania got ill, and my mom went back home to care for her."

"Oh, I see. So you grew up there?"

"Yes. I went to college there and traveled quite a bit before settling in Jacksonville. I still own a home there."

"So what brought you to this area?"

"My best friend. She lived in Atlanta but relocated to Ormond Beach after her marriage broke up. I came to visit last year and made more friends here. So two months ago I decided to come for an extended stay. I'm fortunate that I work from home and can live anywhere."

She nodded. "Yes, that is convenient. You mentioned your father passed away. I'm sorry to hear that. You must have been young when you lost him."

"Actually, he died right before I was born. He died in Vietnam and I never knew him."

"That *is* sad," she said. She remained silent for a few minutes before saying, "So . . . you must be in your mid-forties?"

I laughed. "Hard for me to believe, but I'll turn forty-seven at the end of the month."

She reached for a cookie, broke it into three pieces, and passed a bite to each dog.

"Right," she said, thoughtfully. "January, 1970."

I recalled that Louise had said Elaine Talbot loved company, but her strong interest in me was beginning to feel a bit weird.

"So," I said, wanting to get the conversation off me, "are you originally from this area?"

"No, not Daytona, but not too far from here. Amelia Island. I was born and raised there."

"Oh, just north of Jacksonville. I've never been there. I always wanted to visit but never got around to it."

"It's a beautiful town. Much more crowded now than when I grew up, but still nice all the same."

I took the last sip of my tea and glanced at my watch. "I've really enjoyed talking to you, Mrs. Talbot, but . . ."

"Oh, please. Call me Elaine."

"Elaine," I repeated and smiled. "I really should take the boxes and get going."

She nodded but didn't get up. "I've also enjoyed talking to you. I hope you won't think me odd, but I don't get a lot of company, and I'd love for you to return for lunch sometime. Would that be possible?"

I found that even though Elaine Talbot did seem a bit odd with her questions, I liked her. She was friendly and had an open quality about her.

"That would be great," I said. "I'd enjoy seeing you again."

She stood up and gave me a huge smile. "Wonderful. Are you free any day next week?"

I hadn't expected the invitation to be quite so soon but said, "Let me think a minute." The only plan I had for the following week was my volunteer time at the shelter. "Next Wednesday or Thursday would work for me."

"Why don't we say Wednesday? You can come around eleven-thirty if that's okay. Oh, and please, bring your Lotte. We'd all love to meet her."

"Are you sure?"

"I'm positive. My dogs would be delighted to have some company. Now if you'll follow me to the foyer, I have the boxes for you in the closet. There are only two and they're light. Mostly jewelry and a few items of clothing."

I followed behind her but paused to stare at some of the paintings on the walls. I saw one in a dark frame and shivered. I had seen this particular painting before, but I didn't know where. There was something about it that caused a sense of nostalgia to rush over me. It was the back of a gray brick house with black shutters. A brick patio was in the foreground with tubs of red azaleas along the perimeter and three brightly painted blue Adirondack chairs in the center.

"Something wrong?" Elaine asked as she turned from the closet.

I swallowed and shook my head. "No. Not at all. I was just admiring your paintings."

"Thank you. Yes. They've been in my family for many years."

I reached for the boxes she passed me.

"Thanks so much for your donations. The shelter really appreciates your generosity."

"It's my pleasure. I look forward to seeing you and Lotte next Wednesday."

I drove home thinking about what an unusual meeting I'd just had with Elaine Talbot. I wasn't even sure where to begin questioning why it was so unusual. It was just a sense of déjà vu I had. And seeing that painting had enhanced the feeling. If only I could remember where I had seen it before.

# Rhonda
## June 1969

I had been living with Sebine and Lillian almost a month and had felt at home from the beginning. Lillian, or Dr. Fletcher, as I referred to her during working hours, was every bit as friendly and kind as Sebine.

Both of them had gone out of their way to make me feel welcome in their home. The first weekend I was there, Lillian had left after breakfast and returned with a third Adirondack chair for the patio. They each had one and wanted me to have one also. Both she and Sebine had set to work that afternoon and painted it a bright blue to match the other two.

My morning sickness was beginning to ease up and I found my appetite slowly returning. But not one day had passed that I didn't think of Peter. Cynthia had called the Monday after I had left and said Peter had been at the restaurant on Friday evening with his family but not Marion. And he had cornered her to find out where I was and why I was no longer working there. She assured me she had told him she couldn't divulge my private information. I knew from her following phone calls that he had continued to question her over the past month.

The ringing phone brought my thoughts back to my work. I was pleased with how professional I sounded when I said, "Good morning, Dr. Fletcher's office. How may I help you?"

Lillian had taken me under her wing, explaining how to answer the phone, file the patients' charts, and tend to the mail. She was a general practitioner and seemed to be well regarded in the community. Her practice was busy, and I welcomed the hours that my job consumed. It gave me less time to think about Peter.

I scheduled the appointment with the caller and looked up to see Lillian walk into the waiting room from the exam room. She was about the same age as Sebine, but shorter, and she wore her sandy colored hair in a pixie style that suited her. She seemed to always have a smile on her face, but I thought she had a more serious demeanor than Sebine did.

"Rhonda, Mrs. Jacobs needs to be scheduled for blood work at the lab. Is Darlene in the back room?"

I nodded. Darlene was the main secretary and had done the bulk of my training. I was grateful that she didn't make me feel like an intruder and had willingly taught me how the office was run. "Yes, she is."

"Okay. Have her schedule that when she finishes lunch, but let her show you how it's done."

"Yes, Dr. Fletcher," I said, getting up to go to the back room.

Darlene had just finished lunch. She was smoking a cigarette and flipping through a bridal magazine. She looked up and smiled. "What's up?" she asked.

I explained Lillian's request, and she looked at her watch. "Okay. I have about another ten minutes and then we'll do that. So how's it going? Do you like it here?"

"I do. Very much. And I want to thank you again for all your help training me."

She waved a hand in the air, and I admired the bright red polish on her nails. From the first time I'd met Darlene, she struck me as a top New York City secretary. Her gorgeous red hair was a cloud of loose curls around her face. Her makeup was expertly applied, and she had a wonderful sense of style. Today she wore a navy blue corduroy skirt about two inches above her knee, navy tights, navy pumps, and a white silk blouse. And the gorgeous diamond engagement ring on her left hand sparkled in the sunlight coming through the window.

"It was my pleasure. You're doing *me* a favor. I felt bad about taking time off at the end of the month when I get married. But now I know I'll be leaving the office in good hands."

I smiled. "You must be getting excited. A few more weeks and you'll be a bride."

She nodded. "It is a bit exciting. I just pray that Ron won't get drafted for Vietnam. He's graduated college now . . . so who knows what will happen."

"Well, think happy thoughts," I told her. "And aren't you going to the Poconos for your honeymoon?"

She sent me a wink and nodded again. "Yes. Ron said they have heart-shaped beds there. That should be interesting." She stamped out her cigarette. "Okay. Let's get Mrs. Jacobs booked for that lab work."

When five o'clock came and the last patient had left, Lillian came out of her office.

"That should do it for today." She looked around. "Has Darlene left?"

"Yes. Just a few minutes ago. She had another fitting for her gown."

Lillian nodded. "Right." Rather than saying we could leave, she pulled up a chair to the desk and sat down. "Rhonda, I wanted to talk to you about your prenatal care. You'll be three months along soon and should think about seeing an obstetrician."

I had recently been giving that some thought. "Yes. I know. Do you have any suggestions?"

"I do," she said and passed me a piece of paper. "This is the name of a colleague of mine. Frank Doyle. I've already spoken to him and explained your circumstances. He's more than happy to have you as a patient and he said you can make payments for the delivery. So just call his office and get an appointment scheduled."

I was beginning to hate the way I had no control over my emotions lately, as I felt tears stinging my eyes as I reached for the paper. "Thank you so much, Lillian. I honestly don't know what I'd do without you and Sebine. You've both been so kind to me."

She patted my hand and stood up. "We're happy to do it. Come on or we'll upset Sebine by being late for dinner."

We drove home as I thought about Darlene and her upcoming wedding and the new life that lay ahead for her. She was involved with wedding gowns and honeymoons, and I was focusing on becoming a mother. Without the benefit of marriage.

After dinner the three of us settled into the family room. Sonny and Cher were curled up next to each other in front of the fireplace.

Lillian sat in one of the club chairs, legs tucked under her, reading a medical magazine. A Mozart symphony played softly on the radio. And Sebine had a sketch pad on her lap but kept glancing up at me as I knitted a white baby sweater. I had attempted knitting as a child but had lost interest. However, when I discovered that Sebine was an expert knitter, I asked if she could help me. She wasted no time getting me downtown to the local yarn shop to choose yarn, needles, and a pattern. I had never worked on circular needles before, but with Sebine's assistance, the sweater was working up nicely.

I thought about the three of us sitting there enjoying the evening together, and the word *family* came to mind. A family could be comprised of many different people. I felt like we were becoming a family and the knowledge warmed my heart.

"Something wrong?" I asked, when I saw her look up again.

She pushed a strand of hair behind her ear and laughed. "No. I was hoping you wouldn't catch me."

"What are you doing?"

"Sketching you knitting. I'd like to turn it into a painting."

"Me?" I was surprised to hear she'd want to paint me.

"Yeah. Come look," she said.

I got up, looked over her shoulder, and gasped. The likeness to me was uncanny.

"Oh, Sebine. You *are* good. Gosh, that looks more like a photograph than a sketch."

"I'm glad you think so. You're easy to sketch. You have beautiful features. Would you mind if I work on it some more each evening?"

I laughed. "No. Not at all. I'm flattered."

"How would you feel about me selling it if we're both happy with the final result?"

"Sell a painting of me? For money? I can't think why anyone would want to buy it. Oh, not because it's not a good painting," I hastened to add. "It's just that . . . I'm so ordinary."

"Give yourself more credit. You're not ordinary at all. Let's see how it turns out."

"Watch out," Lillian said. "She'll have you posing all the time if you're not careful."

I heard the humor in her tone and smiled as I sat back down to resume knitting. I hadn't been sure at first what it would be like living with two lesbians. I wondered if it would be awkward. Or I'd be witnessing open displays of affection that would make me feel uneasy. It had not been any of that.

I had caught a kiss on the cheek between them a few times. The touching of a hand on an arm or lower back. A lot of bantering exchanged. But all of it had felt *right*. Never did I feel uncomfortable or out of place.

I thought of Peter and what we had shared. How I loved being with him, talking to him, hearing him talk. I should have known from the beginning it would not work out for us. But as Joyce had said, you can't control love.

I glanced at Lillian and Sebine and felt a smile cross my face. They were so right together.

"So you two met in Paris?" I asked.

"We did," Lillian said, putting down her magazine. "It was four years after the war ended. Nineteen-forty-nine was a good time to be in France. Americans were flocking there. The exchange rate on the dollar and the franc was very good."

Sebine had stopped sketching and nodded. "Yes. Lillian's right. I wanted to study art in Paris and that was a good time to go there. I had just graduated college that summer, was just twenty-two years old and the world was my oyster." She laughed. "I was fortunate that both of my parents were a bit bohemian and they encouraged me to go and helped me out financially. My father's family was originally from France, so it also helped that he had an aunt there who allowed me to stay with her."

"I was taking some time off before beginning medical school," Lillian said. "Sebine and I met one evening at *La Rotonde*. The café in Montparnasse that Hemingway and his crowd had frequented in the thirties." She took a sip of wine and nodded as a faraway look crossed her face. "I had gone with some friends I'd made, and Sebine was also there with a group. Cafés in Paris are the place to meet people and socialize. Both of our groups got to talking and debating issues and trying to solve all the world's problems."

Sebine laughed. "As I recall, we were there till the early morning hours. I liked what Lillian had to say. When she debated an issue, she had the intelligence and knowledge to back it up. I knew she was well read and well educated. That's what first drew me to her. And then, of course, her attractiveness didn't hurt."

I saw the smile that crossed Lillian's face and the look of love that passed between them when they glanced at each other across the room. *And that's what it's all about*, I thought. It didn't matter what gender you were, who you were, where you came from, or even where you were going. Love was simply *love*. The most powerful human emotion.

At least, that's the way it should be.

# Chapter 16

I woke on Saturday morning, and the moment I opened my eyes I knew where I had seen Elaine Talbot's painting before. My mother had one just like it. I rolled over and pulled the pillow to my chest as I tugged on my memory.

I recalled that it had hung in our living room for a while, but by the time I was a teenager it was gone. She had replaced it with one of my school photos. But when my mother passed away and I had to clean out her house before putting it up for sale, I had found the painting stashed in the back of her closet, along with a few other paintings I had never seen. I was busy with my work, had a lot going on in my life as I grieved the loss of my mother and had not paid a lot of attention at the time. I now remember debating whether to keep the paintings or get rid of them. In the end, I couldn't part with them. And they were now at my house in Jacksonville—stashed in my own closet.

I headed downstairs to brew my coffee and knew there was an eerie connection between those paintings, Elaine Talbot, and my mother. What could it be? I wondered about the significance of the house and patio. I couldn't recall ever questioning my mother about it. I thought perhaps she had purchased the painting simply because she liked it. But maybe not. Maybe there was more to it than that.

Tonight was my date with Ben, and I had to admit I was looking forward to it. Behind his serious exterior, I felt there was a warm and compassionate man, and I was looking forward to getting to know him better.

After my coffee, I showered, dressed, and decided to spend a couple of hours at the yarn shop.

Both Chloe and Mavis Anne were waiting on customers, so I headed to the back to get a cup of coffee.

"Hey," Yarrow said. "How're you this morning? What are your plans for today?"

"I'm good. And actually... I have a date tonight. With Ben Wellington."

Yarrow's head snapped up, and she stopped pouring coffee into a cup to place both hands on the counter and lean toward me. "Really? When did this happen?"

"He called me Thursday evening and asked me to dinner."

A huge smile covered her face as she raised her hand in the air to give me a high five. "Well, you go, girl! That's great."

I laughed and shook my head. "This yarn shop is more like a romance club."

"Hmm, you're right. And since I can't remember the last time romance came my way, I'll live vicariously through you."

She passed me the mug of coffee. "Thanks. Are you just not looking or not interested?"

"I have to admit, I'm not actively looking. Running the shop here takes up a lot of my time, but I'm not averse to some knight on a white horse charging in here and whisking me away to a land of fantasy and romance."

I laughed. "Hey, you never know. Well, I'm going to go knit for a while."

"Have a great time tonight, Petra. And remember, we'll all want the details next week."

"Right," I said over my shoulder as I walked into the yarn shop.

Chloe had finished with the customer and was arranging a new delivery of yarn on the display table.

"Oh, that looks yummy," I said, reaching to finger the soft fiber. "Is it Debbie Bliss?"

"Yes, it's the Baby Cashmerino Tonals. Isn't it gorgeous? Look at the colors. I'm planning to make a sweater for Eliza using this." She reached for a pattern on the table. "It's called the Rainbow Sweater and I just love it."

I nodded at the beautiful blend of lime, blue, grape and yellow in the sweater photo. "It's gorgeous and I love the soft pastels. How's Eliza doing?" I asked.

Chloe had become a first-time grandmother seven months before, and she was over the moon with happiness. And making her even happier was the fact that her son and his wife had relocated from the Boston area to live in Jacksonville, only a ninety-minute drive away.

"She's doing great. She has two teeth now and Treva said she thinks another one is on the way. Eli called last night and he's on vacation next week, so Henry and I are going to drive up there tomorrow to visit for a few days."

"Oh, that's great, Chloe. You be sure to bring back loads of photos of Eliza."

Chloe laughed. "Right. As if I wouldn't."

"How are you this morning, Petra?" Mavis Anne asked as she joined us.

"Good. I thought I'd knit for a little while."

"Oh, before I forget, Petra," Chloe said, rushing to get her knitting bag, "I've decided the new design for the knit-along will be a shrug. What do you think?"

She passed me a sketch of a very stylish shrug, shorter in the back and falling to two points in the front. Across the top of the page was written *Petra's Past*.

"Oh, Chloe. I just love it! I'm so flattered that you designed this for me."

"Good. I'm glad you like it. And here's a swatch so you can see how it will work up."

"Very nice," I said, fingering the soft yarn in subtle shades of blue, purple, and a hint of green.

"It's Malabrigo yarn, which is quite popular with knitters. Okay, now that I know you like it, I'll begin to test knit it before I release the pattern for our knit-along."

"The color is gorgeous. It reminds me of the ocean."

Chloe nodded. "I thought so too. It's called Azules. It's a DK weight yarn and a superwash, which knitters love."

"You did a beautiful job with the design," Mavis Anne said.

I sat down to begin working on the baby sweater. I loved doing top-down sweaters because they seemed to go much faster. I was already on the sleeves.

I looked up as Yarrow joined us and I heard her say, "So. Did you tell them your news, Petra?"

"What news?" Mavis Anne asked.

"Oh . . . well . . . Ben called the other evening and he asked me to dinner tonight."

Mavis Anne pointed a finger at me. "See! I told you he was interested."

"That's wonderful," Chloe said. "Where are you going?"

"To Mario's."

"Oh, a very nice choice. I think you'll like it." Mavis Anne nodded.

"I'm sure I will," I said, and realized that I was excited about going.

"I'm very happy for you," Mavis Anne said. "And of course you'll give us all the details next week."

I laughed. "Right. Of course I will."

"How did it go the other day picking up the donation from Elaine Talbot?" she asked.

I let out a sigh. "It was interesting." I went on to explain how I got the feeling that she knew me. And then I mentioned the painting and how she'd invited me back for lunch.

"That *is* interesting," Mavis Anne said. "Do you mean she acted like she'd met you before?"

I nodded. "Yeah. Sort of. It was the way she stared at me when she opened the door and first saw me. It wasn't anything she said, but more a feeling I got."

"Yet she didn't look familiar to you?" Chloe asked.

"No. Not really. But the painting did look familiar, and it finally hit me this morning that my mother had one that was almost identical."

"Hmm," Chloe said. "Well, it could be a copy and not an original by the artist. Where did your mother get it?"

"I have no idea, but it's at my house in Jacksonville now. I'm thinking about driving up there tomorrow to get the paintings."

"That's a good idea," Mavis Anne said. "It might be signed, and you can question Elaine about it when you go to lunch."

"That's my plan," I said. I recalled my recent dream about paying attention to the clues, and I wondered if this painting just might be a clue of some sort.

I was waiting and ready when Ben pulled up in my driveway at precisely six-thirty.

He rang the bell, and Lotte raced to the living room. I scooped her up as I opened the door.

"Hi," I said. "Come on in. I just have to get my bag."

He reached over to give Lotte a pat before I put her down. He looked very nice in gray dress slacks and a navy cashmere pullover sweater. I had chosen black slacks with a white silk blouse and a swingy black cotton cardigan I had knitted.

"You look great," he said. I saw the expression of approval on his face.

"Thanks." I reached for my bag. "I think we're all set. Now you be a good girl and watch the house," I told Lotte.

"This is a gorgeous place," he said as we walked to the car.

"It is. I'm fortunate to be able to stay here."

As he headed west on Granada, I asked how Jonah was.

I saw the smile that covered Ben's face. "He's fine. He said to be sure to say hello from him."

"He's quite a special boy. Is he still enjoying the dogs?"

Ben nodded. "Oh, yeah. Getting those dogs for him was the best thing I ever did. I imagine it can be lonely at times being an only child, so I'm glad he has them for company. And I want to thank you again. You said you were an only child. Did you have a dog growing up?"

"I did. We had a cocker spaniel we got when I was about eight. She passed away right before I left for college. Being away from the house made the loss a little bit easier."

"Yeah, that's the tough part. When we lose them. But they certainly make all the years together worthwhile."

"I take it you also grew up with a dog?"

"Yes. My brother and I always had a dog. That's why I feel bad about not giving in sooner to Jonah. I'm really not sure what accounted for my reluctance, to be honest."

We had turned onto South Yonge and a little farther along Ben pulled into the parking lot of the restaurant.

"Well, everything in life is timing," I said.

Minutes later we were seated at an intimate booth for two. The waitress came to take our drink order and Ben asked if I'd like red wine.

"Sounds good," I said, and he ordered a bottle of red from Tuscany.

I looked around and liked how a partition separated the diners, creating a sense of privacy for conversing.

"This is a nice restaurant."

He nodded. "It's not elaborate or fancy but has a nice atmosphere and the food is excellent. So what have you been up to? Keeping busy?"

"Yes. I spent some time this week catching up on my work. I volunteered at the shelter on Monday, and on Thursday I went to pick up some donations from a woman named Elaine Talbot. She donates a lot to the shelter."

"I know Elaine. She brings her three dogs to me. Very nice woman."

"She was delightful. As a matter of fact, she invited me back for lunch next week. I think she's lonely."

"Yeah, it's not always easy being alone," he said, and I wondered if he was also referring to himself. "Well, it sounds like you two might become friends. I'm sure Elaine would welcome that."

The waitress brought the wine, uncorked it, poured a bit for Ben to test, and then filled my glass.

When she walked away, he lifted his glass to mine and said, "Here's to what I hope will be a new friendship for you and me."

"To friendship." I took a sip and nodded. "Very nice." I'm not sure why, but I felt the need to tell Ben about Elaine's reaction to meeting me and about the painting. He had a quality that made me feel I wanted to share things with him, and I realized that as a vet his clients probably felt the same way.

When I finished telling him about the visit, he said, "But she didn't look familiar to you?"

I shook my head. "Not really. And now the painting has me curious. If it was painted by the same artist, how did my mother get one just like it? It's not like we had money or my mother was an art collector."

"Hmm, I see what you're saying. So you're planning to drive to Jacksonville tomorrow to get the ones you have?"

"Yes. I thought I'd bring my painting with me to lunch on Wednesday and maybe Elaine and I can figure it out."

He laughed. "Okay. I admit it. I'm a huge mystery buff. You have me intrigued." He took a sip of wine. "This might be a bit presumptuous, but would you mind if I drove to Jacksonville with you tomorrow?"

It took me by surprise that he would even be interested in my story, but his question appeared to be genuine. "Really?"

He shook his head and I detected an expression of embarrassment cross his face. "I apologize if I'm being too forward. It's just that . . . well . . . I like you, Petra." He adjusted his glasses on the bridge of his nose, a gesture I was coming to find endearing. "And I guess it was my way of asking to spend some more time with you. I understand if you'd rather go alone. But I really am interested in your story."

I reached across the table to touch his hand. "Oh, no. It wasn't forward of you at all," I hastened to say as I gave him a smile. "As a matter of fact, I think it's very nice of you to offer. I would love you to go with me. Will Jonah be coming too?"

The smile that now crossed his face was definitely flirty as he said, "Ah, no. I think Jonah's dad needs some time alone with his new friend."

And I most definitely agreed.

# Rhonda
## August 1969

My time in Jacksonville was racing past. It was hard to believe I'd been living with Sebine and Lillian for three months and I was already almost five months along in my pregnancy. My morning sickness had ended and I was now beginning to show. And not one day had passed that I hadn't thought of Peter.

My hand went to my stomach, and I smiled as I recalled my visit to Dr. Doyle the week before. He assured me that the flutters I had begun to feel were perfectly normal—it was my baby beginning to move. The baby that Peter and I had created together.

I let out a sigh as I finished the last of my coffee and walked to the sink to wash the cup. Today was the day that Cynthia was coming to visit with Earle. Part of me was excited about seeing her again but part of me wondered if seeing her would renew the pain of leaving Peter. She was no longer living at the hotel. When her job assignment ended at the end of May, she and Earle had rented an efficiency apartment. They had both been working at a burger place to make extra money for their trip to Woodstock and then San Francisco.

I looked up as Sebine walked into the kitchen.

"Doing okay?" she asked.

"Yeah. I'm fine. Cynthia will be here in about an hour."

She nodded. "Okay. The crabmeat salad is in the fridge for lunch and I made a new container of sweet tea for all of you. I'll be out in my studio if you need anything."

"Can I bring them out to meet you?"

Sebine smiled. "Of course you can. I'll see you later," she said, before walking out the back door.

\* \* \*

Cynthia and Earle arrived in a beat-up Volkswagen bus that caused me to chuckle. The word *Peace* was painted across the front. Huge psychedelic-colored flowers and peace signs were painted on the sides of the bus.

I walked out front to greet them, shaking my head. "Do you honestly think that thing will get you out to San Francisco?"

Cynthia came running toward me and pulled me into a bear hug. "Oh, Rhonda. I've missed you so much." She stood back and placed a hand on my abdomen. "And look at you. You're showing!"

I laughed as Earle came over and hugged me.

"And yes," he said. "The VW might not look roadworthy on the outside, but she's in very good condition to do a cross-country trip."

"Come on in," I told them.

Sonny and Cher greeted us at the door. Earle stooped down to pat them while Cynthia gushed about the house as her eyes darted everywhere.

"Oh, my gosh, Rhonda. This place is so nice. No wonder you love it here."

I nodded as they followed me to the kitchen. "I'm very fortunate. I couldn't ask for nicer people to live with than Sebine and Lillian. How about a crab salad sandwich and sweet tea?"

"Sounds great," Rhonda said. "I'm starved. Oh, look at the beautiful patio and garden out back." She pointed out the kitchen window as Earle pulled up a stool and joined us.

"So bring me up to date on your news," I said, as I began to prepare the sandwiches.

Cynthia launched into various stories about Earle playing in the band while I listened and marveled how things seemed so different between us now. Cynthia's hair had grown to her shoulders and she wore it straight in the hippie style. She was wearing cut-off jean shorts with a tie-dyed shirt of purple, red, orange, and yellow. I noticed a bracelet of beads around her ankle. Earle also looked much different from the waiter we had met in January at Broadglen's. His hair had grown to his shoulders and he now wore it loose and flowing. He had also grown a beard.

"So Earle is hoping to meet up with this guy, Brad, at Woodstock. He's very interested in hearing Earle play his guitar in person and might hire him to play his club in San Francisco."

"That would be great," I said as I realized neither one of them had to worry about responsibility or settling down. I suddenly felt much older than both of them, but at that moment I felt a kick in my stomach and knew I wouldn't trade places for anything.

I placed the sandwiches and tea on the table as Cynthia was still talking away.

"Here we go," I said. "Let's eat."

"So you like it here?" Earle asked.

"I do. And I love working for Dr. Fletcher and taking my secretarial classes at night."

"Right," Cynthia said. "From what you've said, that's also going well."

I nodded. I didn't want to brag, but my instructor said my speed and efficiency were at the top of the class. "It's going very well and I enjoy it. I love learning shorthand and my typing is good."

"Do you think you'll stay here after the baby is born?" Cynthia asked, before reaching for another sandwich.

"I'm not really sure what I'll do. Of course my mother doesn't know about the baby and I'm not ready to tell her yet. Sebine and Lillian said I can live here as long as I want."

"Well, that's good," Earle said. "I'm glad you're doing okay, Rhonda."

"Thanks, Earle."

There were a few moments of silence and I began to feel the elephant in the room was about to make an appearance.

"Do you still think you did the right thing not telling Peter?" Cynthia asked.

"I do. I wish it all could have been different. But it couldn't. So yes, I believe I did the right thing." I waited a second before asking, "Do you ever see him around?"

Cynthia shook her head. "No. Never. But then, we don't travel in the same circles, do we?"

*My point exactly*, I thought.

Cynthia helped me clean up after lunch as she continued telling me what it would be like in Woodstock, who would be there, what they would do, until I realized I had little interest in a gathering of rock musicians and their hippie followers.

"Why don't we go out to the studio so you can meet Sebine," I said.

I had a feeling Cynthia agreed so as not to offend me.

We walked inside and I made the introductions.

"I'm glad you could come to visit Rhonda," Sebine said.

"Yeah, I wanted to see her before we leave tomorrow for Woodstock. I'm not sure I'll ever be back in this area again."

Sebine was cleaning a paintbrush and looked up. "Oh, are you planning to settle out in San Francisco?"

Earle had remained silent, but I saw him shrug. "Who knows? Like Bob Dylan says, everything is blowin' in the wind. If I can get a good gig out there with a club, we'll stay. If not, we'll move on."

After a few more minutes we went back to the house and I made coffee.

As I sat on the patio listening to Cynthia and Earle talking, I knew that although she had been my friend since childhood, we would probably now drift apart. Her life was going in a completely different direction from mine. And that was okay.

Sebine, Lillian, and I were relaxing in the living room that evening after supper, and once again that sense of family and love came over me.

"So the visit with your friends went well today?" Lillian asked.

I was now working on a baby blanket. I had completed the sweater and was proud of the end result, so I had decided to continue making baby items.

I stopped knitting and nodded. "Yeah. It went okay. I think I was surprised at how quickly things seemed to have changed between me and Cynthia."

"Well, you're both at that age where you reach a turning point in your life. From the sounds of it, her path is much different from yours."

"Way different. She's carefree with nobody to think about but herself. And there's certainly nothing wrong with that, but . . ."

"But you're quite happy to be where you are in your life?" Sebine asked.

I nodded. "Yes. I really am. I won't lie. I wish it could have been different with Peter. But having the baby? I wouldn't change a thing."

"Good. I'm happy to hear that. Oh, by the way. I finished the painting of you knitting. I hope you'll like it. I think it's one of my best. Actually, now I'm not sure I can part with it."

I laughed. "Really? You're not going to sell it?"

"Maybe not. But if you don't mind, maybe I'll do another one that's similar."

"Sure. That would be fine."

"See," Lillian teased, "I told you if you weren't careful, you'd end up being Sebine's model."

When I got ready for bed, I went over the day's visit in my mind again. I was glad Cynthia had come to see me. Maybe we'd stay in touch with letters or postcards, but I had a feeling she'd never be returning to Pennsylvania and probably wouldn't be coming back to Florida either. So I was pretty sure we'd probably never see each other again.

As I got into bed and closed my eyes, I saw Peter's face. Smiling. Laughing. Looking at me in that very special way. I was just as certain that I'd never see Peter again either. I felt like there was a scab on my heart. Some days it seemed to be healing. And other times, like tonight, it was raw and open, and it hurt like hell.

I placed my hand on my stomach and was grateful that for the rest of my life I would at least always have a part of him with me.

# Chapter 17

Ben picked me up at ten Sunday morning and we headed north on I-95.

"Thanks for letting me tag along with you," he said.

I smiled. "It's nice that you offered. But what's Jonah doing today?" I felt bad that maybe he was spending the day alone without his father.

Ben laughed. "Oh, he's fine. He was invited to a barbeque at a friend's house this afternoon. He said to be sure to say hello to you, though."

"It's nice that the two of you are so close. He's a great kid."

Ben nodded. "He really is, and it wasn't easy at first when Emily died. But I think we're in a good place now." He paused a second before saying, "I pretty much isolated myself after the accident. It wasn't good for Jonah and it wasn't good for me. Having Betsy come to stay with us was a big help, though. She was excellent for both of us."

"The grieving process is different for everyone. Losing a spouse and somebody you shared a life and a love with has to be difficult."

"I'm afraid the love wasn't all that strong at the end," he said. "And that only added to my guilt feelings."

"Oh," was all I said.

"Emily resented the long hours I put into my work to grow the practice, so it created a lot of disagreements. And I have to admit I never took the steps to make it better. In retrospect, I'm not sure it would have helped. When Jonah was five or six, Emily wanted another child. Under the circumstances, I didn't think it was a good idea. I thought we should wait. Make sure our marriage was strong and that it would survive."

I remained silent, waiting for him to continue.

"She said she agreed with this decision only... obviously, she didn't. She never brought it up for further discussion, but when she was killed in the accident... I found out she was pregnant."

I reached over and touched his arm. This had been a double tragedy for him, and I could see it disturbed him to talk about it.

"I hope you don't mind... but I want you to know what happened. I've never discussed this with anyone... but I want to with you."

I nodded and squeezed his arm. "Go on," I said.

He cleared his throat. "As I said, we had not discussed anything about her getting pregnant, so when the medical examiner told me she was about eight weeks along, I was pretty surprised. I met with her obstetrician and was even more surprised to learn that he thought the pregnancy had been a mutual decision, because Emily had purposely stopped taking the birth control pill the year before."

I let out a sigh. Another example of a woman attempting to save a marriage with a child.

"I imagine that created a lot of different emotions for you," I said.

"Yeah, it certainly did. I was angry that she had deceived me. Hurt that she hadn't even discussed the pregnancy with me. And... now I was also grieving for a child I would never know."

"You were certainly justified in your feelings." I began to understand Ben Wellington a little better, and I admired the man that he was.

"Well, it took me a while to work through all of it, but I have. It reaches a point where we have to let go of the past or we have nothing for the future. And after two years... I've done that. This is why I wanted you to know. Nobody else does. I saw no point in telling Jonah or even my brother. It served no purpose."

And yet he felt it was serving a purpose to tell me. Knowing that this was important to him raised the friendship level a little more.

"Thank you for sharing this with me," I said.

He reached over and gave my hand a squeeze as a smile crossed his face. "Thank *you* for understanding. Now... I have something else to tell you, and if you'd rather not do it, that's fine."

I shifted in my seat, curious to hear what he had to say.

"What is it?" I asked.

"Well, as you know, my brother and his wife live in Jacksonville. So I gave him a call last night to tell him I was going to be there today. Zak and Sue have invited us to their home for dinner. If you don't want to go, I certainly understand."

Meeting his family? Call me silly, but a feeling of warmth came over me, and I felt special.

"I'd love to meet your brother and his wife. It was so nice of them to invite us. Of course we'll go."

"Oh, that's great. I think you'll like them."

"They have two boys, right?"

"Yes. Ian is thirteen and Sam just turned eleven."

"I look forward to meeting them."

Ben pulled into my driveway, and after being away for two months I was surprised at the lack of nostalgia I felt. I had wondered if perhaps when I saw my home again I'd be ready to come back. I hadn't even walked inside yet and already I knew I wasn't.

Ben leaned over to look out the passenger window. "What a lovely house."

"Thanks," I said, reaching for the keys in my bag.

"You have a caretaker for the house, right?" Ben asked as we walked inside.

"Yes, it's a property management company. They arranged for a cleaning service to come and somebody checks on the house frequently." I tapped the security pad inside the door. "And the house is protected with a security system."

"Would you like some coffee?" I asked, heading to the kitchen.

"Sure, that would be good."

Ben sat at the counter while I prepared the coffee machine.

"You're still not sure if you're staying in Ormond Beach or coming back here?"

I shook my head as I pushed the button for the coffee to brew. "No, but I love Ormond Beach, so I'm in no hurry to get back here. If ever."

I saw a smile cross his face. "If you decide to stay down there full-time, would you put this place on the market?"

I nodded. "Yeah. I think it would sell pretty easily. Come on," I said. "Let's go get those paintings out of my closet."

Ben helped me carry the four paintings out to the living room, where we leaned them against the sofa. They were approximately 22" x 28" in size and covered with padding.

"Have you seen these before?" he asked.

"I've seen one of them. The one that was similar to what Elaine has. But no. I don't think I've seen the others. When I moved them from my mother's house, I never bothered to take off the padding to look at them. I guess I didn't think they were that important."

I carefully removed the padding from the first one. Holding it on each side, I leaned it back against the sofa and gasped. It was the largest of the three and showed a woman sitting on a patio in a blue Adirondack chair holding a baby in her arms. There was no doubt that woman was my mother. And the baby had to be me.

"Oh, my God," I whispered. "That has to be my mother holding me."

Ben stepped back to get a better look. "It's really beautiful. The artist caught the tenderness of the moment."

I nodded. "She did," I said, as I picked it up and saw *SL* in small letters on the bottom left of the painting. "SL. That has to be the artist."

"Does that ring a bell at all?"

I slowly shook my head. "No. Not at all," I began to say, and then something occurred to me. "Wait. Sebine. Sebine is the name of the woman my mother lived with here in Jacksonville when I was born. Actually, my middle name is Sebine. My mom never mentioned her very often to me. She only said the woman had been very kind to her."

"Had they stayed in touch? Did you ever meet her?"

I shook my head. "I'm not sure, but I don't think they stayed in touch after my mother moved back to Pennsylvania. If they did, I wasn't aware of it."

"So do you think Sebine is the artist?" Ben asked.

"I don't know. It seems the more I find out, the less I know."

I removed padding from another painting. "This is the one that Elaine has," I said. I stared at the patio area with the three blue Adirondack chairs and felt a shiver go through me. I then took off the padding of the third painting and saw my mother sitting on a sofa, head bent, holding knitting needles and a small white sweater on her lap.

"This is also my mother," I said before uncovering the last painting. This one showed a toddler sitting on a carpet with two large dogs on either side. One was a black lab, the other a golden retriever. A feeling of déjà vu came over me.

"Something wrong?" Ben asked.

"I know this child is me. I'd say I was probably around two. And the dogs . . . they seem familiar to me. Like I know them."

"Maybe they belonged to Sebine, and you remember them from living at her house."

I nodded slowly as I struggled to untangle what all of this meant. We both stood there staring at the paintings for a few minutes.

"Let's have that coffee," I said, walking to the kitchen.

I filled two mugs and joined Ben at the counter.

"Are you okay?" he asked.

"Yeah. I am. Just confused. If the artist is Sebine and she's the same woman my mother lived with, I don't understand why she never showed me these paintings. I don't get it."

"Hmm, I understand what you're saying." Ben took a sip of coffee. "But maybe there's more to the story. Maybe it would have been too painful for your mother to discuss any of this with you."

"Well, she certainly was a private person. She never shared very much with me. Despite all my questions. All I know is that she worked at that hotel on Amelia Island, left there, went to live with a woman named Sebine in Jacksonville, attended secretarial school, supposedly married somebody named Jim Garfield, had me, and after my father died, she returned to Pennsylvania."

"I think many people were like that back then. People are much more open today. But years ago, almost all families had secrets of one kind or another. It's just the way society was. It certainly wasn't like today with social media and reality TV shows where everyone shares their dirty laundry."

I nodded. "Yeah. And I'm truly not sure which way is better."

"Probably somewhere in the middle," Ben said.

I let out a sigh. "You're probably right. Let's finish our coffee and go visit your brother."

# Rhonda
## March 1970

I had been in Florida fourteen months and my entire life had changed. Most of all it had turned into one huge lie.

After lying to my mother about my pregnancy, the next lie came when I put a false name for my baby's father on the birth certificate. I simply made up the name Jim Garfield. Then I compounded this lie by telling my mother I had gotten married the previous September. I fabricated a story based partly on truth and partly on fiction.

I had met a nice fellow the summer before. Cal Hampton was the son of the pharmacist who owned the local drug store. I would stop in for a vanilla coke at the soda fountain and Cal would wait on me. He was a few years older than I was and friendly. He could see that I was pregnant but it didn't seem to matter. We would chat about music and movies and current affairs. I'm not sure if there might have been more on his part, but for me, he was simply a friend. And I desperately longed for a friend. The girls in my secretarial class had formed a clique and I hadn't been included. That was fine with me—but I still yearned for a companion. And a friend had appeared with Cal.

So when I told my mother I had married Jim Garfield, I told her he was the son of the local pharmacist. As for her new granddaughter—I told her I was pregnant at Christmas, but she still didn't know I had given birth eight weeks before.

I looked at my daughter sleeping soundly in the carriage on the patio. I reached over to adjust the blanket covering her and smiled. Both the pregnancy and delivery had gone very well. The pain of labor had been intense, but all thought of it had been forgotten as soon as I saw my baby. Petra. I had known all through my pregnancy if I had a boy, he would be named Peter, and if a girl, Petra.

I let out a sigh and resumed working on the sweater I was making for my daughter. My daughter. And Peter's daughter. Yet he had no idea. And he never would.

"Did you have lunch?" Sebine asked as she walked to the patio from her studio.

"Yes, I did. It's so beautiful out I thought I'd sit here and knit for a while."

Sebine peeked into the carriage. "And our little angel is sleeping away. She's an excellent baby, isn't she?"

I laughed. "She really is, but I think you're a tad biased."

I had been surprised at how both Sebine and Lillian fussed over Petra. It was obvious they adored her.

"Nah, I'm just being honest." She looked down at Sonny and Cher curled up on either side of the carriage. "Well, she's certainly well protected, isn't she?"

I nodded. "They really take their job seriously. It's great that they like her so much. I was worried they might be a little jealous."

"I knew they'd be great with her. Dogs usually love babies. I'm going to get some sweet tea. Would you like some?"

"Yes, thanks."

Sebine joined me a few minutes later and sat beside me in the Adirondack chair tilting her neck from side to side, stretching out muscles.

"I'm working on the painting of you holding Petra. I think it's going to be beautiful."

"You're such an accomplished artist. It must be wonderful to do something you enjoy so much."

"It is. I've been fortunate to be able to pursue my career as an artist. But you're turning into quite the secretary as well."

I smiled. I would be resuming the last semester of my classes in a few weeks and by the fall I would have my certificates in typing, shorthand, and bookkeeping. Lillian's office manager Darlene was now pregnant. She planned to stay until August and then I would take over her position at Lillian's practice.

"I'm so grateful to be working for Lillian. You have no idea how comforting it is to be able to bring Petra to the office with me."

It was Lillian's idea to set up a portacrib in the break room where

I could keep an eye on her as I worked. We had decided when she got bigger and began crawling, I would hire a woman to stay with her at the house.

"Are you kidding? Lillian loves having Petra right there. Not to mention all the patients gushing over her."

I laughed. "Hmm, you're probably right."

"So how's Cal doing?"

"He's good, but I'm worried he might be enlisting in the army. He's been talking about it recently."

Sebine nodded. "Yeah, so many of the young guys have either been drafted or enlisted."

I thought of Earle, who had adamantly refused to go. I had gotten a few postcards from Cynthia when they got to San Francisco but the last one was from Vancouver. All she said was they would be staying there for a while, which led me to believe he was a draft dodger.

"He's a really nice guy," Sebine said. "No chance of anything developing between the two of you?"

I shook my head. "No. Not at all. I like him a lot as a friend. But . . . that's it."

Sebine blew out a breath. "You know, Rhonda, you're barely twenty. You have your whole life ahead of you. I know how you loved Peter, and you'll probably never love like that again. But it doesn't mean you can't have a relationship with somebody else."

I knew what I felt in my heart, but I said, "Yeah, maybe." I also knew that the soul was only capable of one great love in a lifetime—and Peter Maxwell would always be mine, leaving no room for anybody else.

# Chapter 18

The dinner at Zak and Sue's house had been a lot of fun. They were a happy couple who appeared well suited, and both had welcomed me into their home as if they'd known me forever. I enjoyed watching the sibling banter between Ben and his brother. Zak was two years older and kept joking that he was also the favorite of their parents. I had found out that their parents still resided in upstate New York but would be relocating to Fort Lauderdale in September.

Sue had been very chatty and I liked her immediately. Their sons were well mannered and friendly. By the time we left, with an invitation to be sure to come back, I felt like I'd made two new friends.

I rolled over in bed and saw it was going on seven. Today was my lunch with Elaine, and I was anxious to see how we might be connected through the paintings.

By the time I let Lotte out, had breakfast, showered, and dressed, I saw it was just after ten, and I decided to stop in at the yarn shop before driving to Daytona Beach.

"Good morning," Chloe said when I walked in. "What are you up to today?"

"I have that lunch with Elaine Talbot."

She looked up from putting price tags on skeins of Ella Rae yarn.

"Oh, that's right. And you got the painting on Sunday? Is it the same one that Elaine has?"

"It's almost identical except mine is smaller. I also found three others that belonged to my mother. I had never seen those before, and it's clear to see that my mother is the subject of two of them. In one she's knitting and another she's holding me. There's also one of me as a toddler with two dogs."

"Yet you don't know who the artist is?"

"Well, I'm now beginning to think it could have been Sebine, the woman she lived with in Jacksonville. Although my mother never mentioned she was an artist. That's not a surprise, though, because she told me very little about living in Jacksonville."

Chloe nodded. "This is turning into quite the mystery. I hope that Elaine will be able to provide some answers for you today."

"Yeah, me too," I said, as I fingered the soft lace yarn.

As I pulled into the parking area of Elaine Talbot's condo my eyes were drawn to the ocean. At the last minute I had decided to slip the photo of my mother and the unidentified man on the beach into my handbag. I thought that possibly Elaine might know who he was.

I had Lotte on her leash and was carrying the paintings in my other arm as I stepped off the elevator on Elaine's floor.

She was waiting for me outside her door, and all three dogs came scampering to greet Lotte. I let go of her leash to better handle the paintings and laughed.

"Hi," I said. "I think our dogs like each other."

Elaine laughed too and shook her head. "George, Philip, and Victoria are the official greeting committee here. My goodness, what do you have here?" she asked, reaching to take one of the paintings.

"Some paintings," I said. "I thought maybe we could discuss them."

"Come on in. Cordelia has some sweet tea waiting for us."

I followed her into the family room and propped the paintings against a side table.

"So this is Lotte," she said, bending over to pat her. "What a little cutie she is."

"Thank you. She's quite friendly and loves to visit."

I watched as Victoria ran to a basket of toys and deposited a stuffed animal in front of Lotte, who looked at it for one second, grabbed it, and took off running down the long hallway to the opposite side of the condo with the other three dogs in pursuit.

"They'll have a great time," Elaine said. "Plenty of room around here for them to run and play. Come sit down."

She filled a glass with sweet tea from a crystal pitcher and passed it to me.

"So what is it you wanted to discuss about the paintings?"

I took a sip of tea and tried to formulate my thoughts. "Well . . . when I saw your painting in the hallway last week . . . the gray brick

house with the patio . . . I knew I had seen a painting just like it before."

She sat up straighter in her chair, and a look of interest crossed
her face. "Where did you see it?"

"My mother owned it. She had it hanging in our living room for a
few years and then she put it away in her closet. She never explained
where she got it or who painted it."

Elaine nodded. "And have you now asked her about it?"

"My mother passed away three years ago."

"I'm so sorry."

"Thank you. I think the artist who painted yours was the same one
who painted my mother's. And I'm now thinking the artist could be
Sebine. My mother lived with a woman by this name in Jacksonville.
She even gave me the middle name of Sebine. But my mother was a
very private person. I don't know the woman's last name or even
who she was."

Elaine nodded again slowly before saying, "Her name was Sebine
LeBlanc. She was the artist and the same one who did both paintings."

I leaned forward. "You knew her?"

She shook her head. "No, I never met her. I only know of her.
What are the other paintings that you have there?"

I got up to remove the padding and held up the first one of me
with the dogs.

"This is me as a toddler." I then held up the second one. "This is
my mother knitting." Unwrapping the next one, I said, "And one of
her holding me as a baby."

Elaine stood up and walked toward the painting. "It's the same
patio as my painting."

"Yes, and here's the one of the back of the house with the patio."

"Come with me," she said, and led the way to the long hallway
leading to the other side of the condo.

More paintings filled the walls. Seascapes, mountains, some of
European scenes. She stopped in front of one and pointed.

"I'm pretty sure this is also your mother," she said softly.

I looked up to see a beautiful young woman sitting on a beach
with the ocean behind her. Her knees were clasped to her chest and
she was looking off into the distance, her long brown hair blowing in
the wind.

"It's absolutely my mother," I whispered. "*Where* did you get this?"

"From my brother. Peter Maxwell." She put a hand on my shoulder. "Let's go back and sit down."

My head was spinning as we walked back to the living room. Peter Maxwell was her brother? How was all of this connected? I wondered. But somewhere, deep in my soul, I was pretty sure that I knew.

"Peter Maxwell is your brother?" I asked when we sat down.

"Yes. And your mother was Rhonda, wasn't she?"

I nodded. "Rhonda Bradley. You knew her?"

Elaine let out a sigh. "Not nearly as well as I wish I had."

I reached in my handbag and passed the photo to her. "Is this your brother?"

She reached for reading glasses on the side table, put them on, and brought the photo closer. She then turned the photo over and saw my mother's handwriting spelling out the name Peter Maxwell.

"No. This is not Peter. But it's my brother's name on the back. She told you this was my brother?"

I shook my head. "No. Basically, my mother told me very little. She told me my father was Jim Garfield and that he died before we left Jacksonville. I never saw this photo until my mother passed away. It was hidden among some of her belongings. That's when I got really confused. I had never heard the name of Peter Maxwell growing up, so I wondered who this man in the photo was."

Elaine blew out a breath of air and nodded. "I have no idea who the man in the photo is, but I have every reason to believe my brother is your biological father."

A million different emotions ran through me. Anger, joy, relief, but most of all, a sense of loss. What Elaine said next confirmed the loss.

"I'm very sorry to say that my brother also passed away three years ago."

I felt an ache in the pit of my stomach. "So he's gone?"

She nodded again. "Yes. I'm afraid so. It was sudden. Peter had a massive coronary and was gone at age seventy."

I found myself mourning for a man I'd never met. A man who had given me life and passed on his genes to me. I felt tears stinging my eyes and reached for a tissue in my bag.

Elaine reached over and squeezed my hand. "I'm so very sorry. Peter would have adored you. Just like he adored your mother."

I swiped at my eyes and my head shot up. "So you knew about them?"

"Not until many years later." She let out a sigh as Cordelia entered the room. "Let's have lunch and I'll tell you what I know."

We sat down to a lunch of crab bisque and quiche, but I knew I'd have to force every bite down my throat. I had a million questions and didn't even know where to begin.

"Cordelia, I do believe this occasion calls for a nice glass of white wine," Elaine said.

Cordelia nodded, shot me a smile, and walked to the wine cooler. I watched her uncork the bottle, fill two flutes, and place them on the table before walking away.

Elaine lifted her glass. "Here's to family secrets," she said. "To the turmoil that they have a way of creating."

I nodded and took a sip of the dry wine.

Elaine and I both took a spoonful of bisque before she said, "I've been wondering why your mother would write Peter's name on the back of a photo that obviously wasn't him."

I shook my head. "It makes no sense to me."

"But it does. There's no doubt she knew you would find that photo someday when she was gone. She left you a clue—a clue to pursue if you wanted to."

I immediately thought of Emmalyn and my last dream. She had told me to pay attention and look for the clues.

"So you're saying she wanted me to look for him and find him? If that's the case, then why didn't she tell me about him years ago? When there was still time. When he was still alive." I felt a surge of anger go through me.

Elaine nodded. "Yes. I certainly wish that she had. But she had reasons, I'm sure. Let me start at the beginning and maybe it will make more sense to you."

I sat and listened as she told me how my mother had been the waitress for their table in the dining room of Broadglen's every weekend.

"To be honest," she said, "I knew the first night we met her that Peter had fallen for her. And fallen hard."

She went on to tell me that she knew Peter was dating my mother over those months of spring.

"I liked her. A lot. I could see how happy Peter was, and we were very close."

"So what happened?" I asked.

"My father. I have no way of knowing for sure and Peter didn't either. But my father was an elitist snob. We came from money, Petra. Generations of it."

I felt another surge of anger but this time it was directed toward a grandfather I had never known. "So you're saying my mother wasn't good enough for Peter?"

She reached over to pat my hand. "Please understand . . . Peter certainly did *not* feel that way. I know that for certain. But my father? I won't lie. Had they continued their relationship, yes, my father would have made it extremely difficult."

"So Peter . . . my father . . . caved to family pressure?"

Elaine shook her head emphatically. "No. Don't ever think that. Because it's not true. Peter wanted to marry your mother. He loved her deeply."

"But she got pregnant and it was too much of an embarrassment?"

"Petra, my brother never knew about you."

"What? She didn't tell him she was pregnant? Why would she keep that from him?"

Elaine sighed and then took a sip of wine before saying, "I'm only now coming to understand why. It was because of the deep love she had for him."

Thoughts were swirling in my head. "Did he ever find out?" I whispered.

I saw an expression of sadness cross her face. "No. I'm afraid not. Peter died never knowing that he had a daughter."

I let out a sarcastic chuckle. "What a waste of two lives. What a waste of possible happiness. All because my mother fell in love with somebody . . . out of her league. And she wasn't willing to take a chance and risk it."

Elaine nodded. "I'm afraid so."

"What happened to my father? Did he marry somebody else? Have children?"

She paused a moment before saying, "He did marry. But not for many years. Peter was close to forty when he married Marion. They had no children. She passed away about fifteen years ago."

Fifteen years ago. My mother would have been only fifty-two—certainly still young enough to reignite that love and be with Peter. But with all the secrets and lies in her life, she probably didn't want to risk being rejected. Which was exactly what she did to him.

"So how did he come to acquire the paintings? Is that why you acted like you had seen me before when I came here last week? You knew I was his daughter?"

"I didn't know. Not for sure. But as soon as I opened the door and saw you . . . I saw a very strong resemblance to my brother. And your name. It's the female version of Peter. I was pretty sure you had been named for him. When I began to question you, the pieces began to fall in place. The location and the time frame fit the period when Rhonda was in his life. I couldn't prove it then, but yes, the paintings provided the final answer." She took a sip of wine before continuing. "Peter had shared his love for Rhonda with me from the beginning. He was absolutely devastated when she simply left Amelia Island with no word of where she was going. He tried inquiring at the hotel but got nowhere. We owned a manufacturing company in Jacksonville and Peter was there tending to business. There was an art gallery showing about ten years ago and he attended. He walked in and saw the painting of your mother on the beach. He recognized Rhonda immediately and sought out the artist. That was when he met Sebine LeBlanc. It was obvious that she was protecting Rhonda and gave him very little information. But she did tell him that in 1969 Rhonda had to come to stay with her to work and attend secretarial school. She never mentioned you and she wouldn't say where Rhonda was then living. Only that she had left Jacksonville many years before."

I shook my head. "So he wasn't able to find her." I felt an ache in my heart. "That's so very sad."

"Indeed it is," Elaine said, standing up and reaching for my hand. "Come with me."

She led me back down the hallway to a room filled with bookshelves from ceiling to floor. Walking to a wall covered with photographs, she removed two of them and passed them to me.

"Petra," she said, "Meet your father. Peter Maxwell."

I glanced down at an extremely handsome young man who appeared to be in his mid-twenties, standing at the helm of a boat, a huge smile on his face. His eyes jumped out at me. Dark brown eyes that were identical to mine. The shape of his face and his smile were also very similar. Tears blurred my vision as I looked at the second photograph. He was dressed in a suit, probably in his early sixties, very distinguished and handsome with salt-and-pepper hair.

I shook my head. "All my life . . . all my life I wondered about my father. A man I thought to be named Jim Garfield. And my mother's story was nothing close to what she told me. I'm very happy to now know the truth . . ." I began to say when something occurred to me. "So if Peter was your brother, that would make you . . ."

"Your aunt," she said, and pulled me into an embrace.

I felt the tears sliding down my face as I hugged her back. I had longed for family ever since I was a child, and now I had found a family member.

I pulled away and wiped my eyes to see that Elaine had also been crying. We walked back to the living room with our arms around each other.

She passed me a box of tissues and I blew my nose.

"I'm very grateful to finally have the truth," I told her. "But now I can't help wondering what happened when my mother went to live with Sebine. And who Jim Garfield is. There's probably no way of ever finding that out."

I saw a smile cover Elaine's face. "Oh, but there is. I think your aunt just might be able to help you with the final pieces."

She walked to the rolltop desk, opened a drawer, and removed a business card, which she passed me.

"Sebine LeBlanc is now ninety years old, but alive and well. She still lives in Jacksonville and she still paints. Not as much, from what I gathered from her website, but she keeps active. I have no doubt she would love to see you again."

I glanced down at her phone number and knew I'd be returning to Jacksonville again very soon.

# Chapter 19

I had a lot to process over the following week, and I found myself wanting to be alone. I had briefly stopped into the yarn shop the next day and was grateful only Chloe had been there. I explained to her about my lunch with Elaine Talbot, that she was my aunt, and that I still had more information to uncover, but I needed time to be alone. She understood.

Ben called and also understood my need to be alone right now. He told me whenever I was ready to talk to give him a call.

I had spent the past three days in T-shirt and yoga pants. Although I showered in the morning, I saw no reason for makeup or fooling with my hair. Lotte seemed to love the extra attention and having me constantly around. I could have done some work for my clients but since nothing was pressing, I chose instead to curl up on the sofa watching reruns of *Gilmore Girls*, knitting and snacking. And the entire time I was thinking about what I had learned from Elaine Talbot.

When I left her condo, she had asked if she could call me just to talk and I said of course. My newly found aunt was my last remaining family member, and I wanted a chance to build a relationship with her. She had called each day since Wednesday, and I had to admit I loved learning more about my father. I had found out that he had known Marion since they were children and their families had been friends. Elaine said she had no doubt it was a marriage of convenience. I found out that my father loved to read, was excellent at chess, enjoyed sailing on his boat, and could keep a crowd of people laughing. Although I had never met him, I knew that I loved him. So I came to realize over the past few days that I was grieving. Grieving for what could have been. For what I had never known but had lost.

The doorbell interrupted my thoughts. I jumped up to find Maddie standing there holding a huge arrangement of flowers from her florist shop.

She balanced the vase in one hand and reached out to squeeze my hand with the other.

"How're you doing, honey? Chloe told us about your meeting with Elaine Talbot."

I gave her a smile and nodded. "I'm doing okay. Really. Just trying to sort everything out in my head."

"Of course you are. Well, we're all thinking of you, and if there's anything you need, you let one of us know, okay? Oh, these are for you."

"Thank you so much. I'll see you soon at the yarn shop. I promise."

I carried the vase into the living room and removed the envelope. Thinking they were from the yarn shop group, I was quite surprised to see they were from Ben. Not Ben and Jonah. *Just Ben.*

*Thinking of you during a difficult time and missing you,* the card read. He had signed it, *With affection, Ben.*

I felt the smile that crossed my face. He was a very special man. I recalled how he had kissed me six days before, when we returned from Jacksonville. I had invited him in the house for coffee and when he was leaving, we automatically hugged each other but instead of pulling away, he bent his head and kissed me. I didn't find it odd in the least. Probably because throughout the day, at my house in Jacksonville and then later at his brother's home, there had been an element of sexual tension between us. So the kiss felt natural. And right.

I bent to inhale the wonderful fragrance of the flowers when the phone rang. I saw it was Elaine.

"I hope you don't think me a pest," she said when I answered.

I laughed. "Not at all." Actually, I found it endearing that I suddenly had an aunt who seemed genuinely concerned about me.

"I was just wondering if you had contacted Sebine yet."

"No. Not yet. I'm going to, but I just don't feel ready."

"That's understandable. How are you doing?"

I paused a second before saying, "I feel like I've had a death in the family."

"That's also understandable. You had a lot of information thrown at you in a short time. And you *have* had a loss, Petra. Don't diminish that fact. Allow yourself the time to grieve."

"That's what it feels like I'm doing. I only wish I'd had the chance to meet him."

"So do I," she said. "So do I. As I said, he would have adored you. Isn't it sad the choices people make in life? They make them for all the right reasons, but sometimes it's to the detriment of others. But of course, when one makes a choice there's no way of knowing if, years later, a different choice might have been the better one."

"I guess this just proves to me that life truly is a risk. Who knows, maybe I'll end up learning from my mother's missed chance."

"And that would make everything come full circle, Petra. I've always believed things happen in life as they're supposed to. Even though it might not seem it at the time. Well, if you don't think me a nuisance, then I'll talk to you tomorrow."

I smiled and said, "I look forward to it."

By the middle of the following week, I was ready to emerge from my cocoon back into the world of the living. The day before, another flower arrangement had arrived from Ben, but I still hadn't called him. Today was the day to do that. I didn't want to interrupt him during office hours, so I planned to call him that evening.

It was time to shower, put makeup on, fix my hair, and pay a visit to the yarn shop.

I walked in to find Mavis Anne, Chloe, Iris, and Louise sitting at the table knitting. All four jumped up to give me hugs.

"How are you doing?" Mavis Anne asked, touching my face.

I smiled and nodded. "Good. I'm doing okay now. I just needed some time to be alone."

"Well, that was quite the surprise, wasn't it?" Iris said.

"Come and join us." Chloe returned to the table.

"Imagine," Louise said. "You're Elaine Talbot's niece. She's such a nice person. I'm not surprised you two are related."

I laughed as I sat down. "Yeah, it's been quite an interesting week."

I proceeded to give them details about what Elaine had told me.

When I finished, Mavis Anne put a hand to her heart and shook her head. "Love isn't always easy. It's really a shame it couldn't have worked out differently for your mother and Peter Maxwell."

I let out a sigh. "Yeah, it's pretty sad. When I think of the lengths my mother went to in order to protect this secret all of her life, it makes the situation even sadder."

"And do you think it was all because they came from different backgrounds?" Chloe asked.

"According to Elaine, my father told her that when my mother broke up with him before she left for Jacksonville, that was what she indicated. He tried to convince her otherwise. That they could make it work, they could move away, but none of it was enough to convince my mother to stay."

"And of course her being pregnant must have compounded the situation," Iris said. "Did you learn anything about what she did when she lived in Jacksonville? How she met the fellow in the photo on the beach?"

"No, but I was very happy to learn that Sebine LeBlanc, the artist of the paintings and the woman my mother lived with, is still alive and living there."

"Oh, my goodness! Really?" Louise said. "Are you going to meet her?"

"I have her phone number. That was how my father acquired the paintings. He attended one of her gallery shows about ten years ago and bought them. He also got her business card. She was very careful to protect my mother, though, and refused to admit any more than the fact that my mother had lived with her for a few years. She never told him about me."

"What a shame," Mavis Anne said. "All of this might have been cleared up before they both passed away."

I nodded. "That's true. But I can't fault Sebine. It sounds like she was extremely loyal to my mother and was simply honoring her wishes."

"So when are you calling her?" Louise asked.

"Soon," I said. "I just need a little more time."

"I don't know Elaine well," Mavis Anne said. "But she's lived in this area for many years and I've met her at various fund-raisers. I actually remember when Peter passed away. Because he was a prominent businessman in the area, there was quite a write-up in the newspaper. Wasn't there another sister?"

I nodded. "Elaine told me about her the other day on the phone. Her name was Sheila and she was the youngest. It seems she was only twenty when she died. It was tragic. She ran away from home at age seventeen and got caught up in the drug culture of the day. She was found dead in Chicago from a drug overdose."

Louise's hand flew to her mouth. "Oh, my goodness. That *is* tragic. What a shame. So Elaine is the only one left in the family."

"Right. Elaine Maxwell Talbot . . . and me."

Everyone nodded and remained silent.

"Okay," Chloe said, jumping up. "I have a surprise for you." She ran to remove something from the armoire and held up the finished shrug. "I finished it. This is for you. Try it on."

I took the soft knitted piece and slipped my arms into the sleeves. "Oh, Chloe, this is gorgeous. You did a beautiful job."

"Thank you. I was hoping you would like it."

I spun around in a circle so everyone could see it. "I love it, but don't you want to keep it here in the shop?"

"No. This one is yours. I'm already making another one for the shop sample."

"And the yarn for the knit-along has arrived," Mavis Anne said. "We were just waiting for Chloe to show you the shrug. You can now sign up for the knit-along and purchase your yarn."

"It's about time," Louise said, and we all laughed.

"I think everyone will enjoy working on Petra's Past."

When I heard the name of the shrug again, I smiled. My past was turning out to validate my present.

I called Ben later that evening. I could hear the happiness in his voice.

"Oh, Petra. I've been worried about you, but I understood your need to have some time to yourself. How are you doing now?"

"Actually, very well. I think I'm in a good place. I feel bad that my mother had to resort to the decisions she did, but I also understand that she did it out of love. For me and for Peter."

"I think you're right," he said. "I've been thinking about your story all week. What she did was pretty brave. It had to be scary being alone, knowing she was pregnant and going to live with strangers. You can be very proud of her."

I felt tears stinging my eyes. "Yes, I feel the same way. Growing up, I never gave much thought to my mother having courage. But she did. I'm sure it wasn't always easy being a single parent."

"So where do you go from here?"

"Well, Elaine and I are looking forward to building a relationship and getting to know each other better. I still have a million questions about my father's side of the family."

I went on to tell him about Sebine LeBlanc.

"Oh, wow," Ben said when I finished. "This is really great news. She could be the one to finish unraveling the pieces for you."

"That's what I'm hoping. I plan to call her in the next few days. And if it goes well, I'm thinking of driving up to Jacksonville to meet her. Is there any chance . . . you might like to go with me?"

"Absolutely," he said immediately. "I'm glad you'd like me to go. You just let me know when. And by the way, Jonah misses you."

This really touched me. I had never been part of a child's life before, and to know that he thought of me meant a lot. "Aww, I miss him too. You tell him I hope to see him soon."

"Well, actually, we were wondering if you could come to dinner on Saturday. We'd *both* like to see you."

"That sounds great. Yes, I'll be there."

"Good. We'll see you around six."

I hung up the phone and smiled. I had been in Ormond Beach for two months and so much had happened. My entire life was turning around. It was going both backward and forward. And that was a very good thing.

# Chapter 20

On Saturday morning I decided the time had come to call Sebine LeBlanc. I got out the business card and dialed the number. An elderly woman answered.

"Yes. Is this Sebine LeBlanc?" I asked.

"It is. How can I help you?"

"Well . . . my name is Petra and I was wondering—"

"Petra *Garfield*?" I heard across the line. "Rhonda's daughter?"

There was no doubt that I had the right person. "Yes. I'm Rhonda's daughter. I'm sorry to bother you, but—"

"It's no bother at all," she said, interrupting me again. "Oh, my God! I always wondered if I'd ever hear from you. How did you find me? Your father?"

"Well, yes. Indirectly. I recently met his sister, Elaine, here in Daytona Beach. Actually, it was her paintings that brought all of this together. I was at her home and saw that she had one very similar to one that my mother had."

"Ah, yes. Probably the one of the back of my house and the patio. Peter purchased that one and a portrait of Rhonda on the beach when he was here about ten years ago. How is he?"

"I'm afraid he passed away three years ago."

There was a brief pause before she said, "I'm so terribly sorry. So very sorry. Did you have the chance to meet him?"

"No. I'm afraid not. I only found his sister last week."

Another pause. "I never should have listened to your mother ten years ago when I told her he had been here and purchased the paintings."

"You were still in touch with my mother?"

"Oh, yes. We stayed in touch right up until a few months before she died."

And yet I'd had no idea. "I never knew."

"No. Unfortunately, she never wanted you to know anything about her life here in Florida. Petra, I'm now ninety years old and though I'm in very good health, I would love to meet you or, I should say, see you again, before I die. Did you say you're in Daytona Beach?"

"I'm in Ormond Beach, and I would love to see you, Sebine. Would it be possible for you to fill in all the missing pieces of my puzzle?"

"Honey, that information has been hidden for way too long. I will tell you anything you need to know. Is there any chance you could visit me here in Jacksonville?"

"Yes. That wouldn't be a problem at all. When would be convenient for you?"

"Let me just check my calendar here," she said, and there was a slight pause. "I still give some painting lessons and I have a few other commitments coming up next week. Would next Saturday work for you? A week from today?"

"That would be fine. Yes. I just need directions."

I jotted down what she told me. "Thank you so much, Sebine. I really appreciate your meeting with me."

I heard a dry chuckle come across the line. "Oh, Petra. It's my pleasure. I always hoped that we would meet again. I'll see you next Saturday about noon. I want you to come for lunch. Are you married now? Because I want you to bring your husband too."

"No. Never married. Still single, but I do have a good friend, Ben. Would it be okay if he comes with me?"

"Of course it is. I look forward to seeing both of you. And Petra . . . thank you for getting in touch."

I hung up the phone with a smile on my face. Although I didn't really remember Sebine, I knew that I had been named for one very special woman.

I pulled up in Ben's driveway just before six. I looked in the rearview mirror to make sure I looked okay. I was wearing my new shrug, a pale yellow blouse, and tan capris. I had taken extra time with my hair and makeup, making me realize that Ben Wellington and his son were coming to mean a lot to me.

I rang the bell, and the door was pulled open by Jonah, who surprised me with a tight hug.

"Petra," he said, clearly excited. "I've missed you."

"I've missed you too," I said and laughed as Lucy and Ethel came sliding across the tile floor to greet me.

Ben walked toward me laughing, and he also surprised me by leaning forward and placing a kiss on my cheek, allowing Jonah to see the affection between us. "You look great," he said. "It's so nice to see you."

Jonah grabbed my hand and pulled me forward, his excitement notching up another level. "Come on. Come on," he said. "Come out to the lanai and see our surprise."

I walked out to the screened area and gasped as my hand flew to my face. Banners saying "Happy Birthday" were strung across the top of the screen. Brightly colored helium balloons floated over the pool. I saw gaily wrapped gifts on the end table, and the patio table had been beautifully set with white tablecloth, china, crystal, and a huge vase of red roses in the center.

My birthday. Today *was* January thirtieth. With everything that had transpired over the past week, I had lost track of time. But Ben had not.

I felt my eyes blurring with moisture as I said, "I can't believe you remembered my birthday. Because I forgot it was today. Thank you so much."

Jonah came to hug me again. "Did you really forget your birthday? Wow! I never forget my birthday."

I laughed and nodded as Ben gave me a hug. "Happy Birthday, Petra."

"How on earth did you know it was today?"

"Oh, I pay attention. When we were at Zak's house, we were talking about age and birthdays and you said yours was coming up on January thirtieth."

This man *did* pay attention. Another wonderful trait.

"Well, you guys have certainly surprised me."

Ben laughed. "Good. That's what we hoped. How about a glass of champagne?"

"Sounds wonderful," I said, sitting on the patio sofa, where Jonah promptly sat down beside me.

"Dad said I could have *one* sip, because it's your birthday," he proudly informed me.

"Really? Then this *must* be a very special day," I kidded him.

I realized that I had no clue when Jonah's birthday was. Or Ben's.

"When is your birthday?" I asked him.

"Mine is May ninth. I turn eleven. And Dad's birthday is October twenty-fourth. He says he'll be turning the big five oh."

I laughed and filed away that information.

"Here we go," Ben said, passing me a champagne flute and a small juice glass to Jonah.

The three of us lifted our glasses as Ben said, "Happy birthday, Petra. May this be your best year ever."

I certainly was beginning to think it might be.

I took a sip and heard Jonah say, "Yuk. I don't like this. Can I have a soda instead?"

Ben and I both laughed. "Absolutely," he said, sending me a wink. "Go get one from the fridge."

"It's really delicious," I whispered as Ben sat down next to me. "But I'm glad he didn't like it."

"Me too. He's growing up too fast as it is."

Jonah returned with a can of soda. "When can Petra open her gifts, Dad?"

"After we've had dinner."

"Okay. Can I go play with the dogs in the yard?"

"Yup, that's fine. We'll be eating in about a half hour."

When Jonah walked outside with the dogs, Ben reached for my hand and gave it a squeeze.

"I really *have* missed you. A lot."

"I've missed you too," I said, feeling a warm glow forming around my heart.

"I think I have to thank Jonah for going over to the dogs at Petco."

I laughed. "Well, we didn't have the best beginning, but yes, Jonah is the one who made the effort. I still can't believe that he took it upon himself to bring me those flowers and say they were from you."

A grin covered Ben's face. "Yeah, I never knew my son was such a matchmaker." He took a sip of champagne. "I think he's been lonely without a woman in his life."

"Well, having grown up with a single parent, I can say it's difficult for both the child and the parent. Many people do it and do it well. My mother did and you are too. But that doesn't diminish the fact that it's a little harder."

Ben nodded, and I wondered what he was thinking about.

"Oh," I said. "I called Sebine this morning."

Ben shifted to face me. I saw the expectant look on his face. "Really? How did it go?"

"Very well. She sounds so nice, and she was thrilled to hear from me. She's more than willing to talk to me and tell me whatever I want to know."

"Oh, Petra. I'm so happy for you. That's great."

"It is. And she invited me to lunch a week from today. Next Saturday at noon. I told her I'd be bringing you, and she's looking forward to seeing both of us. You can go, can't you?"

Ben pulled me into an embrace and kissed the side of my neck. "Absolutely. Thank you for including me."

We finished our glasses of champagne before sitting down to a dinner of roast pork, cheese potatoes, and squash.

"That was just delicious," I said, wiping my lips with the linen napkin.

"I helped Miss Betsy with the potatoes," Jonah said.

I gave him a smile. "And you did a super job."

"Can we have the cake and gifts now, Dad? I'll help you clear the table."

I started to get up, but Ben held up a hand. "Nope. You're the birthday girl, so no helping. Jonah and I have this covered, don't we?"

Jonah nodded his head emphatically. "Yup. We do."

I sat there feeling pretty special. I wasn't used to having two guys fawning over me. And I rather liked it.

They returned a few minutes later with Ben carrying a beautiful cake, birthday candles glowing, and both of them singing "Happy Birthday."

"Oh, what a gorgeous cake," I said.

"Miss Betsy made it for you," Jonah told me.

"I'll be sure to thank her."

Jonah came to stand beside me. "Blow out the candles. You have to make a wish."

I laughed as I followed his instructions.

"What did you wish for?" he asked.

"She can't tell you or it won't come true," Ben said and sent me a wink.

At that moment I couldn't think of a thing to wish for except to be able to stay in Ben's and Jonah's lives.

Jonah ran to get the presents and placed them in front of me. "You can open them now."

He stood next to me again, and this time I felt his body leaning into me. I was beginning to understand the magic of children. They just naturally made everything more fun. The expression "seeing things through a child's eyes" was taking on new meaning.

I began to unwrap the first gift, and Jonah said, "Those are from Dad."

Removing the last of the paper, I saw two novels. Both had been recently released and the stories centered on dogs.

"Oh, thank you so much. I had seen these on Amazon and have wanted to read them."

"Good," Ben said. "I hope you'll enjoy them."

"Now mine. Now mine," Jonah said with excitement as he passed me a box.

I removed the paper and opened the box to see L'Occitane bath products in the verbena scent I loved. Bubble bath, shower gel, and body lotion.

"Oh, I love these. Thank you so much, Jonah." I pulled him to me for a squeeze and he didn't resist, which meant more to me than the gift.

"Betsy helped me choose them."

I smiled. "Well, she has very good taste. Thank you again. I'll really enjoy these."

The three of us had cake and ice cream, and then we shared a small scoop of the ice cream with Lucy and Ethel.

By the time I walked in my front door just before ten, I knew this truly had been the best birthday I could remember. And the main reason for that was one particular man and his son.

# Chapter 21

The following morning I was sitting at the kitchen counter, sipping coffee and reading the Sunday paper, when the doorbell rang. I glanced at the clock and saw it was just before nine. Who would be visiting so early on a Sunday morning? I hoped it wasn't Ben because I was still in my jammies, no makeup, and my hair was a mess.

Lotte ran to the door, and I opened it to find Isabelle standing there loaded down with a pastry box, gift bag, and birthday balloons.

"Hey," I said, moving aside so she could come in. "What are you doing here so early?"

"Apologizing for missing your birthday yesterday," she said, walking to the kitchen and placing the items on the counter.

She turned around to pull me into an embrace. "Happy birthday, Petra. Can you forgive me for being a day late?"

I laughed. "Hey, I even forgot it was my birthday. So you're forgiven. Are those pastries from the French bakery?"

"They are."

"Then you're definitely forgiven. I just brewed the coffee."

I poured her a mug and got plates for the pastry.

"Now I feel really bad," she said. "So you spent your birthday alone?"

I reached for the *pain au chocolat*, took a bite and groaned. "Oh. My. God. This is so good. Thanks, Isabelle. I haven't had one of these since I visited here last year."

She laughed before taking a bite of a raspberry tart. "I know. La Gourmandise is the best French bakery around. We're lucky to have them right here in Ormond Beach."

I nodded. "And no, I didn't spend my birthday alone."

"Oh?" she said, and I saw her arched eyebrows. "Well? Give me the details."

"I was invited to dinner at Ben's home."

"Ben? Like in Dr. Ben Wellington?"

"Yup."

"Well, you're looking mighty smug. I guess this is my own fault for not staying in touch better. But I have all day. So start talking."

"Ben and I are friends. We had a bit of a rocky start but things have changed. Jonah has had a lot to do with—"

"Jonah? His son, right?"

"Right. He's a very special little boy."

"Hmm. Go on."

"Well, before I tell you about Ben, you need to know about my father."

"Oh, God! That's why my mother kept telling me to call you. She said you had a lot going on and I needed to get in touch with you. And of course she refused to tell me a thing."

I laughed. "Leave it to Iris. Well, I'd have to say this really all came about because of the animal shelter where I volunteer."

I saw the confusion on her face and started at the beginning on the day I went to pick up donations from Elaine Talbot.

When I finished, Isabelle was sitting with chin on her hand, totally engrossed in my story. I realized she must have been captivated, because she hadn't interrupted me once.

She blew out a breath and shook her head. "Wow. Wow, what a story. Who would have thought your mother found the love of her life only to walk away. That's so sad."

I nodded. "Yeah, it is. But I think she truly thought she was doing the best thing for both of them."

Isabelle took a sip of coffee, and I could tell she was trying to process all that I had told her. "I'm so sorry that you lost your father, Petra. Before you even had a chance to meet him. So how do you feel about this? Are you okay?" She reached across the counter and squeezed my hand.

"Yeah, I am. Of course I wish I had found out about all of this sooner, while he was still alive. But I'm grateful that I finally know the story. And the best part . . . I have an aunt."

She nodded. "That's really great. Are you staying in touch?"

I laughed. "Oh, yeah. Elaine calls me every day and we chat. I like her a lot, and I'm learning more about my father's side of the family."

"So how does Ben factor into all of this?"

"He's been there for me right from the beginning when I visited Elaine. I've shared all of it with him, and he's been a good friend. Ben came with me to Jacksonville to get the paintings at my house."

"I've been a shitty friend, haven't I? I should have been there for you."

I shrugged and rolled my eyes.

"I know. I have. And I'm sorry for that, Petra. I really am."

"Well, on the bright side . . . maybe Ben is the one who was *supposed* to help me through this."

"It sounds like it's serious."

"I'm not sure. I love being with him. And with Jonah. He's going with me on Saturday to meet Sebine."

Isabelle nodded. "I'm happy for you. I really am. And you seem different."

"What do you mean?"

"I've been with you through many boyfriends and relationships. I can't explain it, but this time . . . you seem involved. As if it really matters whether it works out or not. I always felt when you met a new guy, if it didn't work out, you were fine with that. But with Ben, I get the feeling you're investing in a possible relationship."

"You could be right, and I have to be honest. I'm surprised at the way I feel. Especially about Jonah. I never thought I could become attached to a child." I paused a second before saying, "But I think I'm attached to Jonah."

Isabelle got up to get the coffeepot and she refilled our cups. "I think that's a good thing. I always thought you'd make somebody a good mother. Somebody besides a dog."

I laughed and held up a hand. "Oh, I don't know about the mother thing. Jonah had a mother and she'll *always* be his mother."

"Of course, but having another woman in his life who is connected to his dad could have a very positive impact on him."

"Hmm. You could be right."

"Okay. So have you slept with him yet? How is he in that department?"

"Geez, Isabelle. We're not back in high school exchanging boyfriend gossip."

She let out a chuckle and nodded. "Right. So. How is he?"

"I don't know. We haven't gotten to that yet."

"Yeah, having a child in the mix can make that a bit more difficult."

"I think it's more the fact that we've been taking it slow. Getting to know each other. And hey, I remember when you were with Chadwick. You were stalling there too. It took some Victoria's Secret shopping to stir your sexiness."

She laughed and held up her palm. "Touché. Okay, I'll back off. But if you want to go shopping, I'd be happy to go with you."

I smiled. "I'm just fine, thank you. I have two bureau drawers full of those items."

"So you and Ben are going to Jacksonville on Saturday to meet Sebine? You don't remember her at all, do you?"

I shook my head. "No, I was just turning three when my mother and I moved to Pennsylvania. But when I saw the dogs in the painting, it did create a sense of déjà vu. A black lab and a golden retriever. I felt like I knew them."

"Apparently you did. At one time. Gosh, no wonder you've always had such a strong love for dogs. Possibly it has to do with these two dogs that you knew from the time you were born."

"Could be."

"Will you show me the paintings before I leave?"

"Of course. How're Chadwick and Haley?" I realized that our entire conversation had centered on me, something that hadn't happened in quite a while.

She went on to bring me up to date, and by the time Isabelle left, I felt like we had regained our footing as best friends.

I spent the rest of Sunday lazing around. So when I woke on Monday morning I decided I'd be spending most of the day working on my clients' accounts.

I had put in a good five hours when I decided to quit and have lunch. The phone rang as I headed to the kitchen, and I was pleased to hear Elaine's voice.

"Petra, how are you?"

"I'm good. And you?"

"Very well. I hope you won't think I'm a nuisance, but I was wondering if you could come by later this afternoon. I have something that I think you might be interested in."

She had jolted my curiosity. I said, "Sure. A couple of hours?"

"That would be fine. I'll see you then."

I hung up the phone, wondering what she could have.

I arrived at Elaine's condo just before three. She welcomed me with a warm hug as the dogs scampered around our feet.

"It's so nice to see you again," she said, leading the way to the living room. "Cordelia has prepared coffee and cookies for us."

I had only nibbled on a couple slices of turkey breast for lunch so the cookies enticed me.

"Thanks," I said, sitting down as she poured coffee into a china cup and passed it to me. "Help yourself to cookies."

I leaned over to place two on a small plate.

"First of all," she said, passing me a small square box, "happy birthday, Petra. I hope you had a good day on Saturday. I wanted to give you this."

I was touched by her thoughtfulness. "Oh, you didn't have to give me a gift."

She smiled. "You're not going to deprive an aunt of giving her niece a birthday present for the first time, are you?"

I also smiled, and she said, "Go ahead. Open it."

I removed the silver paper and opened the box. Lying inside against black velvet was an unusual bracelet. It had small gold links and interspersed between every few was a charm. One was a boat, one I recognized as the logo of Harvard University—a shield with the word VERITAS embedded in it. *Veritas* meaning truth. Two others were circular birthstones—one of which I knew was mine. A garnet for January. And the other was an aquamarine for March.

"It's just beautiful," I said.

"I had it designed. I hoped you would like it. The boat was taken from a pin your father had when he won a boating race. The one from Harvard is your father's class pin. And I've put a birthstone for both you and your father."

"His birthday was in March?"

She nodded. "March eighteenth. I wanted you to always have a remembrance of him. I wanted to be sure that you know he will always be with you."

I clutched the bracelet in my hand as I got up to hug my aunt. I blinked as tears blurred my vision. "Thank you. I hope you know how much this means to me. I will always treasure it."

She returned my hug and kissed my cheek. "I'm glad you like it. And I have a little surprise for you," she said, getting up. She walked to the dining room table and came back with a flat package wrapped in white paper.

"After you came here a couple of weeks ago, I began going through Peter's things. I still have some boxes of items that belonged to him, and when you're ready I'd like you to go through them and take what you'd like. But I found something that I thought you might want to have now."

I pulled away the paper to reveal an eight-by-ten black-and-white photograph of a couple standing on a boat, arms wrapped around each other, smiling at the photographer as if they didn't have a care in the world because love consumed them. And even staring at the first photo I'd ever seen of my parents, I saw and felt that love. My mother was so young, wearing white shorts with a pullover top. Her long brunette hair hung to her shoulders, and it was easy to understand why Peter Maxwell must have thought her so beautiful. He stood beside her, about six inches taller, and was very handsome with dark hair and smiling dark eyes.

I shook my head. "They made quite a striking couple, didn't they? Their love almost comes through the photograph."

Elaine nodded. "I thought the same thing. I found the snapshot tucked away in Peter's things. So I took it to be restored and enlarged. I think they'd both be very happy that their daughter now has this photograph."

And I knew she was right.

# Chapter 22

When Saturday morning arrived and Ben picked me up at ten, I found I was both excited and nervous to be meeting Sebine LeBlanc. I was wearing the beautiful bracelet that Elaine had given me and I had brought the framed photograph with me to show Sebine, along with the snapshot of the mysterious fellow on the beach.

I saw the sign for Palm Coast on I-95 and let out a sigh.

Ben reached over to hold my hand. "Nervous?"

I nodded. "Yeah. I have no reason to be, but I'm beginning to feel like Alice going through the looking glass."

He laughed and squeezed my hand. "You've certainly been hit with a lot of information over the past few weeks."

"I know, but it's all been good. It's just beginning to feel surreal. Going back to where my mother ran when she was pregnant with me. She must have been scared, uncertain what her future held, and the thing is . . . she had at least one other choice."

"What do you mean?"

"Adoption. Abortion wasn't legal, but she could have put me up for adoption. And yet, despite all the difficulties, she didn't."

"Which proves how much she loved you."

I nodded. "I never doubted that. Ever. But I don't think I knew just how much. It's a shame we find out things in life after the people involved are gone."

"Yeah, but I guess that's what makes life so interesting."

We pulled off of I-95 and followed the directions to Sebine's house. A short time later, we turned into the driveway and I stared at the gray brick two-story home with black shutters and a detached art studio.

"It's very pretty," I said, trying to imagine what my mother thought the first time she saw this house, which would become her home for three years.

I reached into the backseat for the bouquet of flowers that I'd asked Maddie to arrange and walked to the front door with Ben beside me. As soon as I rang the bell, the door was opened by an elderly woman. For a split second she looked vaguely familiar to me. This woman was of medium height, with wrinkles that gave her face character, and she wore her chin-length hair in a fashionable style. She struck me as a trendy woman, wearing black silk slacks, a white silk blouse, and black ballet slippers. Had I not known her age, I never would have taken her for ninety years old.

"Petra," she said softly, and immediately pulled me into a tight embrace. "I wasn't sure I'd ever see you again. Come in. You've grown into a beautiful woman."

I returned her hug and said, "This is Ben. My friend. And these are for you."

I looked behind her to see a beautiful labradoodle with a curly coat the color of cinnamon. "Oh, what a pretty dog."

Sebine laughed. "Ah, yes. This is Hannah. She's my constant companion. Come on in to the living room. Thank you so much for the beautiful flowers. Have a seat while I put these into a vase."

I sat on the sofa and Ben sat beside me as I looked around. The room had a cozy quality with an entire wall of books, comfortable furniture; I heard a Mozart symphony playing softly from speakers in the wall.

Hannah walked to me and I smiled as I patted her. "You're a very pretty girl," I said.

A few minutes later Sebine returned to the room and placed the vase on a side table before sitting down across from us.

She shook her head. "I almost wondered if I'd dreamed this. Finally hearing from you and getting to see you again." A smile crossed her face. "Your mother used to sit in that very spot knitting. You remind me a lot of her."

"How did she end up coming here? You didn't know each other before she came to stay?"

"No. It was a leap of faith on her part, coming to live with two strangers."

"Oh, you had a husband? You were married?"

A sad expression crossed her face. "No. Never married. But I had a partner. Back then she was referred to as my *friend*. But Lillian was my life partner. Our relationship would be much more accepted today. Lillian was the family doctor here in town. She had taken over her grandfather's practice and for the most part, people accepted us."

My mother had come to live with two lesbians? She had always been liberal and open-minded but she had never told me this. It made me love her courage a little more.

"Is Lillian still here?" I asked.

"No. I'm afraid not. She passed away five years ago. But we had a long and happy life together. I still miss her every day, though."

"I'm sorry for your loss."

"Thank you. My sister was in charge of the girls who came to work at Broadglen's. You knew Rhonda left Pennsylvania to work there, right?"

I nodded and she continued.

"When your mother found herself pregnant, she didn't know what to do. She *did* know she wanted the baby but for various reasons, she felt telling your father would be a mistake. So my sister contacted me, and Lillian and I discussed the situation. We wanted to help her. We wanted to allow her to live here where she'd have no pressure and would be able to make intelligent decisions for herself and her baby."

"That was extremely kind of you," I said. "It was a leap of faith on your part as well. And I'm sure my mother thanked you many times, but I also want to thank you for giving her that chance."

Sebine smiled. "I had the utmost faith in Rhonda the moment I met her. I knew she would do just fine. And she did. She was an excellent mother. She worked in Lillian's office until she returned to Pennsylvania. And she fulfilled the major request we made of her— got an education. Lillian and I both strongly felt that education is what opens a multitude of doors for women."

"You were feminists," I said.

She laughed. "Yes, we were, and I think by the time your mother left us, she was too."

Now I laughed. "Oh, trust me. She was. She worked at the university as a secretary for years, and she was always getting involved in issues. I was proud of her. She taught me to be my own person and to be strong."

"I'm not surprised," Sebine said.

"Right. But I'm beginning to see now that her beliefs—she developed them right here with you and Lillian."

Her smile widened. "I'd like to think that's true. We adored Rhonda. And you? We understood when she felt she had to return to Pennsylvania because her mother was ill, but oh, how we missed both of you. You were truly the apple of our eyes."

"Do you think if my grandmother hadn't gotten sick, she would have stayed here?"

Sebine nodded. "I do. She was happy here. She loved her job. She said many times that the four of us had formed our own family. And we had."

"Did she ever tell you why she didn't want to tell my father that she was pregnant?"

"Unfortunately, it all had to do with money and class. She felt Peter's world was so different from hers that any relationship between them could never work."

"What did you think?"

She let out a sigh. "I thought perhaps she was right. She never told Peter, but right before she made the decision to leave, she had been approached by Peter's father. He didn't even know she was pregnant but . . . he offered her money to leave the area and get out of Peter's life."

I gasped. "Oh, my God. What a terrible thing to do."

Sebine nodded. "It was, but I think it convinced your mother that there was no hope of a relationship with Peter. They could have left the area, of course, but that would have brought even more difficulties. I think for a young girl of nineteen, she made a very mature choice."

I always knew my mother was strong, but I was coming to see she had more strength than I'd been aware of.

"Your mother told me she had been invited to dinner once at Peter's home. His father was very condescending. She said she didn't want to come between Peter and his father, but she also knew she couldn't tolerate Mr. Maxwell's behavior. What ever became of the Maxwell home in Amelia Island? You said your father passed away. Does his sister still own it?"

I shook my head. "No. Elaine told me that my father sold it about ten years ago, after his wife passed away. The new owners have turned the property into an inn."

"Oh, he did marry?"

"Yes. But not till he was almost forty, and it was to somebody named Marion. He had known her since childhood."

"I remember that name. Your mother told me she met her once at the hotel dining room when Peter's father had her join them for dinner. Did they have children?"

"No. So I was his only child."

She nodded sadly. "I'm so sorry you didn't have the chance to meet him."

"But you did," I said. "Could you tell me about him?"

"Of course I will. But let's have lunch first. I have many questions for you as well, and then we'll continue with the past."

# Chapter 23

Following lunch, Ben and I joined Sebine on the patio for coffee. The moment I walked out there, I had another sense of déjà vu. It looked identical to the painting, except the Adirondack chairs were now painted red rather than blue.

The three of us sat down, and Hannah curled up at Sebine's feet.

"This is a lovely spot," I said. "And that's your art studio?" I pointed to the wooden structure next door.

"Yes, it is. We had many nice times out here when you were a baby. Your mother had you in a playpen and the three of us would sit here knitting or reading."

"Wasn't it an intrusion having a woman and her baby staying with you?"

"Oh, goodness. Not at all. Both of you brought happiness and love into our home. No, Lillian and I never once thought it was an intrusion. Quite the opposite."

I reached into the tote bag I'd brought with me and removed the framed photo of my parents. I got up and passed it to Sebine. "Elaine found this snapshot in my father's belongings and had it enlarged to give to me."

Sebine adjusted her wire-rimmed glasses and nodded. "So Peter did have one photo of the two of them together. I remember your mother *did* feel bad about that. That she didn't even have a photo to keep. She had told me about this day when they went out on the boat. Peter had a camera with him and asked a man on the dock to snap the picture." She became quiet as she stared at the photo and then said, "They certainly did love each other. By the time Rhonda moved back to Pennsylvania, she had become accepting of the situation and the way things turned out. And I have no doubt she was grateful for having Peter in her life—even for such a short time."

I reached back into the tote and passed her the black-and-white snapshot. "This is my mother on the beach with me. Is this Jim Garfield? The man she married?"

"Oh, my goodness," she said, looking down at the photo in her hand. She then shook her head. "No. It isn't. Petra . . . there was no Jim Garfield."

"She made him up? She was never married?"

Sebine nodded. "Yes, she did. She felt she had to. Society has changed tremendously since 1970. Being an unwed mother happened back then. Of course it did. But there was a huge stigma attached to that label. Even if a woman did marry, she often changed the marriage date so the child would never know the woman was pregnant when the marriage took place. It was a very judgmental time. So yes, Jim Garfield was fiction, and so was the story she told you about him."

"Then who is this?" I asked, pointing to the fellow in the photo.

A smile crossed Sebine's face. "Ah, that was Cal. Cal Hampton. His father owned the pharmacy in town. He was a very good friend to your mother. It didn't matter to him that she was single and pregnant when he first met her at the drug store. He genuinely liked her. But I also think he had a crush on her."

"And my mother wasn't interested?"

Sebine laughed. "Not in the least. But I know she felt grateful to have Cal as a friend. She never made any female friendships while she was here, so I know she appreciated his companionship. He took her to the movies, out to eat, and to the beach. But it was strictly platonic."

"Does he still live in the area?"

"No. Cal enlisted in the army and was killed in Vietnam, I'm afraid. He was only twenty-two when he died. His family and the community took it very badly. Especially your mother."

"What a shame," I said, as I realized that Cal's death was the inspiration for Jim Garfield's.

Sebine flipped the photo over and saw *Peter Maxwell* written there.

Confusion covered her face. "Your mother wrote Peter's name on the photo?"

"Yes, and when I found the photo after she died, I naturally assumed this photo was of him. And since he was pictured here with her when I was a baby, I began to think that he was really my father and not the man she married, Jim Garfield. It wasn't until I met Elaine that the pieces began to fall in place. But I still have no idea why she put my father's real name on the back of this photo."

"Oh, I think I do," Sebine said and took a sip of her coffee as I sat down across from her. "Your mother loved puzzles and mysteries. She was always reading mystery novels and doing various word puzzles. This was a clue for you."

"I don't understand."

"I have no doubt that she thought if you did find this photo some day after she was gone, you would see his name. The name of your biological father. And this would lead you to discover the truth and reveal all the secrets."

"So you think she actually wanted me to find out everything?"

Sebine nodded. "I do. As I said, I stayed in touch with your mother over the years after she left here. A number of times I had asked her if I could contact you. I knew when you had moved to Jacksonville. You were now living in the same city that I was. But your mother requested that I not get in touch. She was afraid something would slip. In all honesty, I don't think she ever wanted to have to be the one to explain everything to you. If you found out on your own after she was gone, she could accept that. So I think putting his name on this photo allowed her to think that might happen."

I let out a sigh and nodded. "Yeah, I think you're right. She was such a private person, and yet, she was quite liberal in her way of thinking. I'm not surprised that she would do this. She was still embarrassed, but she knew I would be much more willing to accept what society had once frowned upon."

"Exactly," Sebine said.

"And when you met my father ten years ago? My mother was still alive. Did you tell her you met him? Did he make the connection that you knew her because of the painting?"

Sebine nodded. "I had a gallery showing downtown and he was there. I had a painting of this patio and one of your mother on the beach. This stranger walked toward me, and I saw the look on his face as he stood in front of the portrait of your mother. He was truly mesmerized, and I knew it had nothing to do with the talent of the artist—it was the subject. And I also immediately knew he *had* to be Peter Maxwell. He confirmed this when he asked me if the girl in the painting was Rhonda Bradley."

"Wow," I said. "What was he like?"

She paused a moment before saying, "A man with a broken heart. The love he still carried for Rhonda was written on his face. He had a million questions, but I didn't mention you, and all I told him was that yes, she had come to stay with me during that time, that she'd attended secretarial school in the area and then returned to Pennsylvania. Of course he asked if we were still in touch and . . . I told him no. Maybe I shouldn't have, but I didn't feel it was my place to expose your mother's secret."

"And you told my mother about this meeting?"

"I did. Actually, he had given me his business card and said if I ever heard from her to please let her know how to reach him. I told her. But she was adamant in her refusal. She said it was too late. She felt the past should remain in the past."

I nodded. "Those were the words I heard all during my childhood whenever I asked her questions about my father or his family."

"We may not agree with her, Petra. But we do have to respect her choices and the decisions she made. It was her life, after all, and she lived it the way she thought best. Another thing I want you to know . . . I think she also made many of her decisions to protect you."

"Protect me? Why?"

"She knew the complications that could develop if she chose to tell Peter about her pregnancy. His father would have been heavily involved, despite Peter's efforts. Franklin Maxwell was well known in the area because of his business. And he had money. Lots of it. I don't think she wanted to risk possibly losing you."

Things were beginning to make more and more sense. I nodded. "I see what you're saying. The rich have their own moral code. Who's to say my grandfather wouldn't judge her to be an unfit mother. It wouldn't be the first time that money trumped what was right."

"Exactly. Do you have any other questions?"

I shook my head. "No. I don't think so. I feel you have provided the final missing pieces, and I can't thank you enough for helping me to unravel the entire story."

Sebine smiled. "It was my pleasure. Now you can tell me about your life and bring me up to date. This handsome man you brought with you . . . it must be serious?"

She took me off guard; I could feel a blush creeping up my neck. "Oh . . . well . . . I'm not . . ."

Ben reached for my hand and smiled. "We're working on it," he said. "We're working on it."

# Chapter 24

Ben and I left Sebine's house around four. Just like when I had met Elaine, I was left with a lot of new information to process, but I felt good. Part of me felt sad for my mother and what she had lost, but I also realized it had been her life and her choices. What made me feel good was that I now knew about the love my parents had shared for each other. I was the product of that love.

"Doing okay?" Ben asked, reaching for my hand as we headed back to Ormond Beach.

I shot him a smile and nodded. "Yes. I am. I really am."

"Good. I'm sure having the final pieces provides some closure for you."

I nodded. "It does. It really didn't seem to bother me that much growing up. A kid just learns to accept what the parent tells them and if it's pretty much nothing, you get involved in your own life and move on. But recently, over the past year, it's been nagging at me to know more. Finding that photo was the first step, and according to Sebine, my search has probably ended the way my mother hoped it would."

"I'm glad you're in a good place. And I'm glad you let me be a part of your discovery."

I smiled, and we became silent, each lost in our own thoughts.

I noticed that Ben took the exit off I-95 to Flagler Beach and A1A.

"It's close to dinner time," he said. "I thought we'd stop at Betty's for some great seafood."

"Wonderful idea."

We both enjoyed a delicious fried clam dinner. The clams at Betty's were flown in fresh from Ipswich, Massachusetts, and never failed to be exceptional.

I took the last sip of my wine. "That was excellent," I said. "I'm glad you wanted to come here."

When we got to Koi House, I said, "I'm not sure if you have to get home to Jonah, but would you like to come in for coffee?"

"Jonah is at a sleepover tonight at a friend's house. So, yes. Sounds good."

We walked in to find Lotte dancing in circles, delighted I was home.

"Come on, sweetie," I said and saw the note on the kitchen counter from David. He had come over twice to let Lotte out in the garden. "It's been a few hours since you went out."

I had asked David to look in on Lotte while I was gone, so I thought it was only courteous to give him a quick call and let him know I was back.

"It was my pleasure," he said, after I thanked him. "I hope your journey proved worthwhile."

"It was," I told him. "I'll give you and Mavis Anne all the details tomorrow. Ben is here and we're going to have coffee."

"How nice. Enjoy the rest of your evening."

After the coffee was brewed and I got Lotte back inside, I filled two mugs and passed one to Ben. "Let's take this into the family room," I said.

He followed me to the sofa and sat beside me.

I let out a sigh.

"Are you okay?" he asked, and not for the first time I noticed his genuine concern.

"Yes. I'm fine. It's been a draining few weeks, but in a good way. The best part of all of this is that I now have an aunt I never knew I had. And I'm very pleased that Sebine wants me to stay in touch. I hope you'll go back to visit her with me in a few months."

"I'd love to. I very much enjoyed meeting her. She's an interesting woman."

"She is. I'm looking forward to getting to know her better. She certainly is a strong woman. It couldn't have been easy having a lesbian relationship in the fifties and sixties in this country. Yet she and Lillian were together for a lifetime. And my mother . . . I think both Lillian and Sebine were a positive influence on her and passed on their strength and confidence."

"And there's no doubt that your mother passed that on to you."

I nodded.

Ben placed his mug on the table and edged closer to me, pulling me into an embrace.

"I'm very glad I met you. You've also been a positive influence on me."

I looked up at him and felt my eyebrows arching. "Really? In what way?"

"Well, after Emily's death I had to go through a period of grief, but I think her betrayal left me feeling somewhat bitter—maybe angry is a better word. I was angry that she lied to me about our agreement not to have another child at that time."

"And how do you feel about that now?"

"I'm beginning to see that, like your mother, she did what she felt was right. I can't fault her for that. I think I was stuck in a sort of limbo when I met you. Just going along day to day, working, caring for Jonah . . . but without much emotion."

"And you think that's changed?"

I felt him pull me tighter and nod his head.

"Yes. I do. I feel *you* changed that. You brought brightness to my life. And a refreshing pleasure. Not to mention you've made my son very happy, and he adores you."

I sat up straighter and faced him. "Really?"

He laughed and nodded. "Yes. Really. You must know how much Jonah thinks of you. He's been playing matchmaker from the beginning."

"And his father?" I asked. "Is that why he wants to be with me? Because his son likes me?"

"While it's very nice that he *does* like you . . . no, that isn't close to the reason. I like you for the person you are, Petra. But even more important . . . I like who *I* am when I'm with you. You make me see things differently. You help me to truly enjoy each moment."

Before I could reply, his lips brushed mine and we kissed. The kiss deepened into passion, and by the time we broke apart, we were both breathing heavily.

"I like you too," I whispered. "I'm glad you came into my life."

We continued kissing as Ben slid me down on the sofa. Desire shot through me: I knew I wanted him. After a few minutes, I pulled away to stare into Ben's eyes.

"Would you think me a seductress if I invited you upstairs to my bedroom?"

Ben stood up and reached for my hand. "I would think we're both on the same page," he said in a husky voice.

Sunlight was streaming through my bedroom windows when I woke. I moved slightly to see Ben sleeping, one arm flung across my body, and I smiled. It had been a beautiful and passionate night. Making love with Ben made me feel complete. I had been with other men over the years, but I had never experienced the same sense of satisfaction and emotion. He was a proficient lover, taking his time to pleasure me before we came together in a joint climax. There was no doubt in my mind—not only was Ben Wellington a good man, he was a good lover.

It was then that I recalled my dream after we had finally fallen asleep. Again, Emmalyn had come to me. This time she was out by the fishpond in the garden. Still wearing the formal red evening gown, she appeared to float along the side of the pond. I stood there watching her, and when she turned, I saw the dazzling smile on her face.

"You found the clues," she said. "You found them and unraveled your pieces."

She held up a mesh fabric of brightly colored ribbons. "They all fit together now. Every piece has been put together, and you are left with the completed work. Life is good. Enjoy it."

And that was the end of the dream. I felt a twinge of sorrow because I knew I would not dream of Emmalyn Overby again. But I also felt a sense of renewal—a fresh energy for what lay ahead.

I felt Ben stir and looked at his handsome face. "Good morning," I said. "Sleep well?"

"Good morning, beautiful. And yes. The best sleep in ages."

He turned to pull me into his arms and kissed the top of my head. "That was quite an intense night, wasn't it?"

"It was the best."

"I'm glad we're still on the same page," he said, and I laughed.

"And now, the least I can do is feed you breakfast. What time is Jonah due home?"

"Not till noon. What time is it?"

"Eight."

"Can I use your shower?"

"Of course. But you'll have to share it with me."

He laughed again. "Twist my arm."

Before we actually made it downstairs for breakfast, we made love again.

I had prepared cheese omelets, home fries, and bacon. Ben was tending to the English muffins on the grill.

"Are we eating inside or out?" he asked.

"I'm sure Mavis Anne has seen your car in the driveway, so no sense pretending you didn't stay the night. On the patio."

I got the table outside set with placemats and napkins and then went in to fill two crystal glasses with fresh orange juice.

By the time we sat down to eat, I found that I was hungry.

"This is delicious," Ben said, taking a bite of omelet.

"Thanks. Love makes . . ." I started to say and then stopped. I didn't want to sound presumptuous.

But Ben reached for my hand and said, "You're right. Love does make everything better. And I *have* fallen in love with you, Petra. Looking back, I think I loved you even as I was telling you off at Petco."

I laughed. "Well, I have to be honest and say I did not love you at that moment."

"And now?" he questioned.

"And now . . ." I let out a sigh and nodded. "Yes. I have no doubts. I do love you, Ben."

He gave my hand a squeeze. "I was hoping you'd say that."

# Chapter 25

By the time June arrived, I had known Ben for six months. And I could honestly say they were the best six months of my life. I had brought him with me a number of times to visit my aunt, Elaine. We had returned to Jacksonville twice to visit Sebine. And we had spent quality time with Jonah, who seemed delighted to have me in his life. We attended sports events, spent time on the beach, took him to current movies, and sometimes we just hung out and played old fashioned-board games together, like Monopoly or Clue.

And during this time I had fallen more in love with Ben and become more attached to Jonah. I wasn't sure where, exactly, we were headed, but I did know that I would be very empty without both of them in my life.

Ben had informed me a few days before that he had a surprise for me. He wanted to take me away for a few days. But despite my repeated attempts to get more information, all he would tell me was we were driving there and I needed to pack a bag for two nights.

I had made arrangements with Mavis Anne to have Lotte stay with her, and I was putting together a tote bag for Lotte with her food and toys. I then got her bed, clipped on her leash, and said, "Okay, girl, let's take you over to Mavis Anne for your getaway."

David opened the door with a huge smile on his face as he bent down to scoop Lotte into his arms. "Here's our little sweetheart," he said and leaned over to place a kiss on my cheek. "Come on in, Petra."

I followed him to the sitting room where Mavis Anne sat knitting a gorgeous Irish knit sweater.

"Oh, Petra. And Lotte." She put her knitting aside as Lotte jumped up in her lap. "We're going to have such a nice time together," she said, ruffling the top of Lotte's head. "All set for your surprise trip?"

I nodded and smiled. Mavis Anne loved a good romance, and she was like an involved grandmother when it came to Ben and me. All the women at the yarn shop waited for my updates on what we were doing or where we were going.

I recalled Louise saying, "Honey, we're living vicariously through you. So don't leave out any details."

"Yup, I'm ready. I can't imagine what Ben has planned."

"Well, whatever it is," David said, "I have no doubt it will be a wonderful weekend."

"I agree," Mavis Anne said. "My Jackson used to like to spring little surprises on me."

Once again I marveled how her love had endured over the years even though he had passed away at such a young age.

I went over to pat Lotte. "Now you be a good girl while you're staying here and I'll see you on Sunday."

"Have a great time," they both said as I left.

Within the hour Ben pulled up in the driveway and used the key I had given him to come inside.

"I'm here," he called. "Is my beautiful date ready?"

I came from the back of the house and smiled. "She is. My piece of luggage is by the front door."

Ben pulled me into an embrace and kissed me. I could tell he was excited about his surprise.

"Then let's go," he said, picking up the leather bag.

He drove west on Granada and when he turned onto I-95 we were heading north.

"Hmm, north," I said.

He laughed. "Yup. North." And he refused to say any more.

We talked during the drive and I was surprised when he turned on the indicator light to exit I-95.

"Amelia Island?" I said.

"Yes."

I wasn't sure why he would choose this area for my surprise.

"First, we'll go to lunch down near the water, and then there's someplace I want to show you."

We had a great lunch of shrimp and grits at Marina Seafood Restaurant, the oldest restaurant on the island. Just steps from the harbor, we enjoyed a view of the water and boats from our table.

I took a sip of my Bloody Mary. "Great lunch and a very pretty view. Now will you tell me where we're going?"

"Soon," Ben said, a grin covering his face. "I never knew how impatient you could be."

I laughed. "See, we're still getting to know each other. Maybe by Sunday you won't care for me at all," I kidded him.

"Highly unlikely," was his reply.

When we left the restaurant Ben drove toward another part of the island, and a few minutes later, he pulled up in front of a sprawling structure. The sign attached to the post told me it was a DoubleTree hotel.

"Is this where we're staying?" I asked.

"No. This is the former Broadglen's. Where your mother came to work in 1969. I thought you might like to see it."

I looked at the huge oaks that towered above the property as Ben drove up the long drive. He pulled into a parking spot and we got out.

"Want to walk around a little bit?" he asked, and I nodded.

*So this was where it all began,* I thought.

Ben took my hand and we followed the walkway to the side of the building and then to the back. The Atlantic Ocean was in front of me, and surrounding the property were upscale cottages, which I assumed were for tourists to rent. But I knew they had to have been the cabins that back in 1969 housed the Broadglen's staff.

"So this is where my mother lived and worked," I said. "I imagine she was quite happy to escape the Pennsylvania winter to come here."

Ben nodded. "Yes. I'm sure. It was a good opportunity for a young woman in the late sixties."

"I wonder what ever happened to her good friend, Cynthia."

"That was the girl she came here with?"

"Yes. My mother told me a little about her, but she said that by the time she returned to Pennsylvania, she never heard from Cynthia again. I guess their lives took different paths. Cynthia left that summer of sixty-nine to go to Woodstock."

"No kidding? I bet that was quite an experience."

I laughed. "Yeah, I'm sure. And then she left with her boyfriend for San Francisco. He was a musician and looking for a break out there, but I don't think it ever happened. My mother said the last time she heard from Cynthia was when she got a Christmas card postmarked Birmingham, Alabama. I guess her boyfriend was originally from there."

"Maybe they married and settled there. It's too bad they lost touch, though."

"Yeah, but I always got the feeling my mother was okay with that."

We walked to the other side of the property as I watched the boats on the Atlantic.

"Thank you for bringing me here," I said. "I've often wondered what this place was like, but never took the time to come here."

"Maybe that's because you were supposed to come with me."

# Chapter 26

We got back in the car and Ben drove about ten minutes before pulling up across the street from a large two-story brick structure surrounded by a black wrought-iron fence.

I looked at him with confusion.

"*This* is where we're staying," he said. "It's the old Maxwell home, your ancestral property, and now it's the Sail Away Inn."

I leaned over him to get a better look. This was where my father had grown up. I felt tears stinging my eyes. What a thoughtful gesture on Ben's part. I had mentioned to him that eventually I would like to come and see the property but had made no plans to do so.

I kissed his cheek. "Thank you. Thanks for making this happen and bringing me here."

"I was hoping you'd feel that way," he said before turning the car to enter the long driveway leading to the parking area.

We got out, removed our bags from the car, and walked up the steps to enter the reception area. I looked around and felt a shiver. This room was filled with antique furniture and had an Old World feel. I assumed this had probably been the living room and my father had spent many hours here.

"Hello," the woman behind the polished wood counter said. "Welcome to the Sail Away. I'm Sarah and this is my husband, Nigel." She pointed to the tall man standing beside her. I detected a British accent right away. They appeared to be in their early forties.

"Ben Wellington. We have a reservation."

I saw the beautiful staircase leading up to where I thought our room was.

She flipped through some cards and said, "Ah, yes. Mr. Wellington. You'll be with us for two nights." She reached for a key and passed it to Ben.

"You have a beautiful place here," I said.

"Thank you. We purchased it about ten years ago from the original owner, Peter Maxwell. It was his family home. We had to do some remodeling and updating, but we didn't want to change the beauty of the house. Much of the furniture and paintings that you see belonged to his family. They were included in the sale."

"So you met Mr. Maxwell?" I asked.

Sarah nodded. "Yes. He was such a nice man and very helpful in answering our questions about the history of the house. We were very sorry to hear he passed away a few years ago."

I nodded but said nothing.

"You're booked to stay in the Boat House," she said and pointed to her right. "It was a small cottage at one time, but we have expanded the structure to include a bedroom, sitting area, and a large bathroom. Just walk through that side door, follow the walkway, and you'll come out to a clearing overlooking the beach. You'll see the Boat House in front of you. There's a dock there and the boat moored is for your use during your stay."

"Thank you very much," Ben said, reaching down for his bag.

"If you need anything at all, just give us a call. There's a phone in the room."

Ben nodded, and I followed him out the door to a beautiful garden area with umbrella tables and chairs arranged with a view of the ocean.

We walked along the walkway. I wondered if Peter had taken my mother out here. I would never know for certain, but I had a strong feeling that he had.

I looked up and saw the white clapboard building. French doors covered the entire front and looked out to the beach and ocean beyond. I saw the dock a short distance away and a boat bobbing in the water.

Ben slipped the key in the lock and we walked into a cozy sitting area. The décor was nautical with white, yellow, and pale blue colors adding softness.

I set my piece of luggage down. "This is just beautiful," I said.

"I'm glad you like it."

Ben pulled me into his arms for a kiss, and then we stood for a minute gazing out at the picturesque view.

"Let's look around," he said, reaching for my hand.

At the back of the sitting room was a small galley kitchen. To the left of the sitting area was a large bedroom with king-size bed, bureaus, and night tables. Off the bedroom was a good size bathroom complete with Jacuzzi tub.

"Did you bring bubble bath?" Ben asked, and I laughed.

"No. But we can certainly buy some."

We walked back to the kitchen area and found a bottle of champagne cooling in an ice bucket on the counter. I picked up the note beside it and read a welcome from Sarah and Nigel.

"This was so nice of them," I said.

"It was," he agreed. "Shall we try some?"

"Absolutely." I walked to the French doors as he uncorked the bottle and I heard a pop.

I looked out to the sky and the ocean and felt a sense of peace come over me. In that moment I felt the spirit of both my parents. I felt their love and I whispered, "Thank you."

I was grateful to now have the entire story of how I came to be. I also thought of my mother in a different way. I may not have agreed with her choices, but I admired the strength and resilience she showed throughout her life. I only wished that both of them could have remained on this earth much longer.

"Here you go," I heard Ben say as he stood beside me.

I reached for the champagne flute.

He touched the rim of mine and said, "Here's to us. Here's to whatever our future will bring."

I nodded. "I love you, Ben."

"And I love *you*."

We took a sip of champagne, and then sat on the sofa to enjoy the view in front of us.

By Saturday evening we were sunburned, full of delicious seafood, and completely satiated from making love.

After sleeping late, we went downtown and found a great place for brunch. We walked around Centre Street, holding hands, browsing in shops and enjoying these moments of being together. We spent time in the bookshop and I found some books that I thought Mavis Anne, David, and Clive might enjoy as a thank you for caring for Lotte.

When we returned to the Boat House, we took the boat out on the water. It was a gorgeous day with a wonderful breeze off the Atlantic. We had been out about an hour when Ben dropped the anchor. We had taken wine and cheese with us, and I curled up beside him on the bench seat as we enjoyed it.

"Have I thanked you for this wonderful weekend?" I asked.

"Oh, I think you have. I think you've shown me in many wonderful ways."

I smiled and let out a sigh. "This has been so special. Being with you has been special in itself . . . but being here, in this place, has been so meaningful for me."

"I was hoping you'd feel that way."

I thought of something my mother used to say to me. "You know, my mother always said the past should remain in the past. But I think she got that wrong." I took a sip of wine as I formed my thoughts. "I think sometimes we have to dig into the past in order to go forward into the future. I grew up thinking somebody named Jim Garfield was my father. And I accepted that. I don't think that old saying, you don't miss what you don't have, is true."

"What do you mean?" Ben asked as he slowly made circles with his fingers on my forearm.

"I think somewhere, deep inside me, I just knew there was more to me. More to my story. I can't explain it, but I think . . . I think the soul knows. Many times people ignore this, but when you decide to look for answers, it's a good thing. In addition to closure, I think it allows us to truly understand why we had many of the feelings that we did."

"And is this a good thing?" Ben questioned.

I gazed out at the water and the horizon in the distance and nodded. "Yes. I think it is. Who knows why I could never connect with anybody until I met you. But I couldn't. My relationships were always superficial. Until you. Love has everything to do with it, of course. But sometimes I think love isn't necessarily enough. If both people aren't in a good place . . . there's no connection, or the connection eventually ends."

"So you're saying that putting all the pieces together has helped you in this way?"

I nodded. "I believe it has. I think it has enabled me to take a step back and view things in a different way. Everyone has a story. We might not always be happy with the final results of the story, but it's their story to tell. Knowing my mother's story made me realize that she wasn't willing to take the risk of telling my father she was pregnant. And this has made me understand that life itself is a risk. If we hold back, if we don't embrace the love or emotions we feel, we will definitely protect ourselves. But . . . we could also be missing great happiness and fulfillment."

Ben leaned down to brush his lips across mine.

"Did I tell you that you're a very wise woman?"

I smiled as a cool breeze came off the ocean.

"It's getting chilly," he said. "Let's head back. It's starting to get dark."

We sat on the cushioned glider on the dock, holding hands and sipping wine.

"This has been a wonderful weekend, Petra. Thank you for making it so special."

"I think we did that together."

He gave my hand a squeeze. "I'm just wondering . . . where do we go from here?"

I had given that some thought as well.

"I'm not sure."

"Two things I know for sure. I don't want to pressure you. Wherever we do end up, I want you to want it as much as I do. And secondly, I want to spend the moments with you. You've become a very important part of my life."

I nodded. "Well, I've made a decision over the past month. I've decided that no matter what, I want to remain in Ormond Beach. So I've contacted a real estate agent and I'm putting my house in Jacksonville up for sale."

I saw the smile that covered Ben's face. "That's an excellent start."

"I thought so too. And I've been giving it some thought . . . I want a permanent relationship with you. I can't picture my life without you and Jonah as part of it."

He pulled me closer. "I'm glad you shared that with me. So does this mean that eventually you just might consider marriage?"

I let out a contented sigh. "Ben Wellington," I said, "that is precisely what I mean."

I leaned my head back and looked up at the black sky dotted with silver stars and I smiled. I knew for certain that my mother had been content with the choices she had made in her life. But I also had no doubt that Rhonda Garfield would be very happy and proud of the choices that her daughter was now making.

## Author's Note

The lovely shrug, Petra's Past, mentioned in this novel was designed by Maria Villegas. Maria is the owner of Yarn and Arts in Fort Lauderdale, Florida.

Thank you so much for designing this piece! And also a huge thank you for your support with my books and hosting such fun book signings at your shop.

If you're in the Fort Lauderdale area, be sure to stop by this very nice shop and tell them Terri sent you.

And if you have a question on the pattern, email Maria at: mvillegas@yarnandarts.com. Or give her a call at 954-990-5772.

# Petra's Shrug

## Designed by Maria Villegas

**Materials:**
Malabrigo Arroyo superwash 335 yards per skein = 4 (1340 total
  yards)
32-inch circular needle size U.S. 6 (4.0 mm)
Stitch markers

**Gauge:**
5.5 sts and 24 rows = 4 inches (10 cm) in stockinette stitch on U.S. 6
  (4.0 mm) knitting needle, or size needed to obtain gauge

**Abbreviations:**
K = Knit
K2tog = Knit 2 stitches together
KFB = Knit into front and back of stitch (1 stitch increase)
M1 = Make 1 stitch by picking up bar between stitch on needle and
  next stitch, putting it on the left needle, and knitting into the back
  of the stitch (1 stitch increase)
P = Purl
pm = Place marker
P2tog = Purl 2 stitches together
Rem = Remaining
RS = Right side of knitting
rm = Remove marker
Sl1 pw wyif = Slip 1 stitch purlwise with yarn in front
St(s) = Stitch(es)
St st = Stockinette stitch (K on RS, P on WS)
D & U = Drop stitch from needle and unravel it down to KFB rows
  below
WS = Wrong side

*Note: Sleeves and body are knitted sideways in one piece starting
with ribbed sleeve pattern. Scarf is knitted separately and sewn to
body at neck edge.*

**Instructions:**
Cast on 62 sts. Continue in rib pattern as follows:

**Rib Pattern**
RS: K1 P1, repeat to end of row.
WS: Knit to end of row.
Repeat these 2 rows until work measures 7 inches, ending with a
   RS row.
Continue body pattern as follows:

**Body Pattern**
Row 1: K4, purl to last 4 sts, K4.
Row 2: K to last 4 sts, M1, K4 (63 sts).
Row 3: K4, purl to last 4 sts, K4.
Row 4: K.
Row 5: K4, purl to last 4 sts, K4.
Row 6: K to last 4 sts, M1, K4 (64 sts).
Row 7: K4, purl to last 4 sts, K4.
Row 8: K.
Row 9: K4, purl to last 4 sts, K4.
Row 10: K to last 4 sts, M1, K4 (65 sts).
Row 11: K4, purl to last 4 sts, K4.
Row 12: K.
Row 13: K4, purl to last 4 sts, K4.
Row 14: K to last 4 sts, M1, K4 (66 sts).
Row 15: K4, purl to last 4 sts, K4.
Row 16: K.
Row 17: K4, purl to last 4 sts, K4.
Row 18: K to last 4 sts, M1, K4 (67 sts).
Row 19: K4, purl to last 4 sts, K4.
Row 20: K.
Row 21: K4, purl to last 4 sts, K4.
Row 22: K to last 4 sts, M1, K4 (68 sts).
Row 23: K4, purl to last 4 sts, K4.
Row 24: K16, pm, KFB, K to end (69 sts).

Repeat Rows 19 thru 24 nine times more (9x), each time knitting an
   additional 5 stitches before marker, and increasing by 2 stitches
   every 6 rows as shown, until you have 87 sts on the needle.

Work even in st st (K on RS row, P on WS row) for 7 inches, ending with RS row. Now get ready to unravel stitches (D&U) as follows:

Row 1 and all WS rows: K4, purl to last 4 sts, K4.
Row 2: K to last 6 sts, K2tog, K4.
Row 4: K.
Row 6: Same as Row 2.
Row 8: K.
Row 10: Same as Row 2.
Row 12: K to first marker, rm, K1, D&U, K to end.
Repeat rows 1 thru 12 until you have dropped all stitches after each marker.

Work even in st st, decreasing (K2tog) 1 stitch on the right side ONLY four more times, maintaining K4 borders, and ending with a WS row.

Work in Rib Pattern for 7 inches, ending with RS row. Bind off second sleeve.

**Scarf (60 inches long):**
Cast on 25 sts and proceed as follows:
Row 1: KFB, knit to last 2 sts, K2tog.
Row 2: Sl1 pw wyif, purl to last stitch, then sl1 pw wyif.
Repeat these two rows until scarf is 60 inches long. Bind off loosely to match cast-on.

On each side sew sleeve ribbing plus approximately 7 inches to armhole. Mark center of back neck and center of scarf. Attach scarf to neck side of shrug.

Read on for a taste of Terri DuLong's first Ormond Beach novel, available now!

# PATTERNS OF CHANGE

## An Ormond Beach Novel

"DuLong reminds me of a Southern Debbie Macomber but with a flair all her own."
—Karin Gillespie

\*\*\*\*\*\*\*\*\*\*\*\*\*\*\*\*\*\*\*\*\*\*\*\*\*\*\*\*\*\*\*\*\*\*\*\*\*\*\*\*\*\*\*\*\*\*\*\*\*\*\*\*\*\*\*\*\*\*

*New York Times bestselling author Terri DuLong turns a new page in breezy Ormond Beach, Florida, where a woman looking for a fresh start discovers her dreams coming true in ways she never imagined . . .*

Chloe Radcliffe was ready to shake the dust of Cedar Key off her feet and sink her toes into the warm sands of Ormond Beach with her soon-to-be husband. But when tragedy struck, she found herself alone, unraveled—and unsure where she belonged . . .

A series of vivid dreams of a Victorian house with a beautiful fishpond convince Chloe to take a leap of faith and rent a condo in Ormond Beach. There, she makes fast friends with a group of knitters and the owner of a tea shop, who also happens to have a house nearly identical to the one in Chloe's dreams—and she's willing to rent her the property. Just as Chloe begins casting on her grand plans for the home, her tangled past comes back to haunt her—but her dreams and newfound friends just might point her toward the love she's been missing all along . . .

**INCLUDES AN ORIGINAL KNITTING PATTERN!**

# Chapter 1

Sitting on Aunt Maude's porch watching the April sun brighten the sky wasn't where I thought I'd be ten months ago. Having experienced two major losses, I found myself still in the small fishing village of Cedar Key... and like the boats in the gulf, I was drifting with no sense of purpose or direction.

Life had proved to me once again that it can change in the blink of an eye. I certainly found that out four years ago when my husband, Parker, left me for a trophy wife. But eventually I pulled myself together and made my way from Savannah to this small town on the west coast of Florida. Straight to the shelter and love of my aunt. At the time, I'd been estranged from my sister, Grace, for many years, but eventually Grace and I renewed our bond and now we were closer than we'd ever been.

The ring tone on my cell phone began playing and I knew without looking at the caller ID that it was Gabe's daughter, Isabelle—she was the only person who called me before eight in the morning.

"Hey," I said. "How're you doing?"

A deep sigh came across the line. "Okay. I just had another battle with Haley about going to school, but I managed to get her out the door. How about you?"

"Yeah, okay here too. Just finishing up my coffee and then I'll be heading to the yarn shop to help out."

I wasn't even gainfully employed anymore because I'd given up my partnership with Dora in the local yarn shop when I thought I was relocating to the east coast of Florida... with Gabe. And now Gabe was gone.

Another sigh came across the line. "It's funny. I didn't see Dad all that much, but I knew he was *there*. Do you know what I mean?"

"I do. Sometimes I think we just take it for granted that those we love will always be with us."

Losing Gabe in the blink of an eye was a heartbreaking reminder of the fact that life was indeed fragile. We had made great plans for a bright new future together. When he arrived in Cedar Key to spend the winter months, he had signed up to take some men's knitting classes at the yarn shop. I knew immediately that I liked him, and the feeling was mutual. Eight months later we'd made a commitment to relocate together to Ormond Beach on the east coast. Gabe was also an expert knitter and we had put a deposit on a lovely home just outside the city limits, where he would tend to the alpacas we'd raise and we'd both run a yarn shop downtown. But that wasn't to be.

"Exactly," Isabelle said. "And poor Dad didn't even make it to Philly to sell his condo. This might sound selfish, but if I had to lose him, I'm glad it happened right here at my house." I heard a sniffle across the phone line. "At least I was with him at the end."

We both were. Gabe had wanted to make a stop outside Atlanta on our way to Philly to visit his daughter and granddaughter. But on the third day of our stay, sitting on Isabelle's patio after dinner, a grimace covered Gabe's face, he clutched his chest and he was gone. I jumped up to perform CPR while Isabelle called 911 but by the time the paramedics arrived, it was too late. A massive coronary had claimed his life. Just like that.

"No, it's not selfish at all," I said. "I'm glad I was with him too."

"We've both had a time of it, haven't we? I lose Dad and then two months later, Roger decides he doesn't love me anymore."

It was actually the breakup of Isabelle's marriage that had brought the two of us closer. While she had been civil to me when we'd first met the previous June, she had been a bit cool. I remembered how she had emphatically informed me that she wasn't called Izzy or Belle. "It's *Isabelle*," she'd said.

I chalked it up to father-daughter jealousy on her part. Although she wasn't at all close to her mother, who had taken off to Oregon years ago after her divorce from Gabe, I had a feeling that Isabelle didn't want another woman in her father's life. But when her husband up and left her, I was the first person she called. Sobbing on the phone, she related that she was experiencing the same thing that had happened to me—her husband had fallen out of love with her. Common troubles have a way of uniting women.

"Any further word on the divorce settlement?" I asked.

"Yes, that's why I'm calling. It's been decided that I will get the house. At least until Haley is eighteen, so that gives me five years to figure out what I'm doing. And when we sell it, we each get half."

"That sounds fair enough."

"Yeah, except that Haley is so unhappy here. Between the loss of her grandfather and her father leaving, it's been a difficult time for her. And to make matters worse, things at school aren't going well either."

I knew Haley was a bright girl and a good student, so I was surprised to hear this. "What's going on?"

"Well," she said, and I heard hesitation in her tone. "In the ten months since you've seen her, Haley has really packed on some pounds. Unfortunately, I think she's taking comfort in food. And you know how cruel kids can be. Especially thirteen-year-old girls."

"Oh, no." I didn't know Haley well, but when I met her for the first time we immediately clicked. Unlike her mother, she didn't display any frostiness toward me. Quite the opposite. She seemed to genuinely like me and I liked her. "What a shame. Gosh, I know kids have always been mean but today, from what I hear, they seem to have taken it to a new level."

"You have no idea. Hey, how's Basil doing?"

I smiled and glanced down at the twenty-pound dog sleeping inches from my foot. I guess you could say that Basil was my legacy from Gabe. I had gotten to know the dog well during the months that Gabe was on the island, and we had taken an instant liking to each other. When Gabe passed away, there was the question of what to do with Basil. Although I know that Haley would have loved to keep him, Isabelle had insisted that wasn't possible and even hinted that perhaps he should go to the pound. That was when I stepped in and offered to give Basil a home. I think gratefulness has a lot to do with loyalty, because Basil hasn't left my side since we flew back to Florida from Atlanta. Basil in his carrier, in the cabin with me, of course.

"Oh, he's great. I'm so glad I took him. He's a great little dog and sure keeps me company."

"That's good. Well, give him a pat from Haley and me. Any decision yet on what you're doing? Do you think you'll stay in Cedar Key?"

"I honestly don't know, Isabelle. I'm no closer to a decision now than I was after Aunt Maude died two months ago. And Grace has been hinting that she and Lucas might want to move to Paris permanently."

My sister had married a wonderful fellow four years before. Lucas owned the book café in town, but he was originally from Paris, and it was beginning to sound like he wanted to bring his family back to his roots in France. Which included my sister and three-year-old niece, Solange.

"Oh, gee, and where would that leave you? Would you put your aunt's house up for sale?"

"I just don't know. I think Grace is trying to go easy with me right now. She doesn't want to add any more pressure, but it's not fair of me to hold them back if that's what they want. Besides, in this economy, property just isn't selling on the island. My building downtown has been on the market for ten months."

"Yeah, true. Well, listen, Chloe, I need to get going here. You take care and keep in touch."

"Will do, and give Haley a hug from me."

I disconnected and looked down at Basil, who had his head on his paws but was looking up at me with his sweet brown eyes.

"Well, fellow, time for us to get moving too."

He jumped up, tail wagging, ready for whatever I suggested.

I headed into the house for a shower and breakfast before we opened the yarn shop at ten.

Dora and I took turns opening the shop, and today she wouldn't be in till noon.

"Come on, Basil. Time for coffee first," I said, unclipping his leash and heading to the coffeemaker.

Dora had her own dog, Oliver, who was now elderly and didn't come to the shop with her anymore, so she was more than happy to have Basil with us during work hours. He was a good boy and enjoyed greeting customers, and I think he was a hit with them as well.

Very well mannered, he had just turned two years old. Gabe had gotten him as a puppy from a rescue group. His ancestry was of unknown origin, but he strongly resembled a cross between a Scottish terrier and a poodle. When designer dogs became popular and Gabe was questioned on Basil's breed, he'd jokingly refer to him as a Scottiepoo.

I had just poured the water into the coffeemaker when the door chimes tinkled and I turned around to see Shelby Sullivan enter the shop.

"Hey, Shelby. Just in time for coffee. It'll be ready shortly."

"Great. I found a nice pattern to make Orli a sweater, so I need to get some yarn."

Shelby Sullivan was a best-selling romance author, born and raised on Cedar Key, and an addicted knitter, especially when she was between novels.

"How're Josie and Orli doing? I imagine they appreciate the sweaters to keep them warm in the Boston area."

Shelby laughed as she fingered some yummy lavender alpaca yarn. "They're doing great and they seem to have survived their first winter up there and all the snow. Although I'm told it's not unusual to get some even in April."

Shelby's daughter, Josie Sullivan Cooper, had married the love of her life and the father of her daughter, Orli, the previous October. The wedding had been the event of the year on the island and thanks to Shelby's expert guidance, it had been on par with many celebrity weddings. Josie's husband, Grant, was an attorney in Boston and the three of them resided on the North Shore of the city.

"I saw on the national weather that the temps are still pretty chilly up there," I said, handing her a mug of coffee. "I'm sure it's quite a change from the tropical climate they're used to."

Shelby nodded. "Thanks. Yeah, but they both seem to love being in Boston and that's what matters."

I smiled as I recalled the control freak that Shelby used to be. But a scare with uterine cancer the year before had put life in perspective for her. She truly did seem to be less stressed and more understanding of Josie, allowing their mother-daughter relationship to strengthen.

"How about you?" she asked. "How are *you* doing?"

I let out a sigh. "I'm doing okay. As well as can be expected, I guess, but I'm beginning to feel like my life is on hold. In limbo."

"Two major losses in your life within eight months will certainly do that. When the time is right, you'll know which direction to take."

"I hope so," I said and took a sip of coffee. "I feel fortunate that we had Aunt Maude these extra years. We knew her heart was bad. The house is just so empty without her around."

Shelby placed eight skeins of alpaca on the counter and patted my arm. "I'm sure it is. Maybe you should still consider going over to

Ormond Beach. You know . . . something different. New beginnings and all that."

"It just wouldn't be the same without Gabe. All of our plans are gone."

"Yes, they are, but that's part of life. It constantly changes whether we want it to or not. Believe me, I found that out last year. But, Chloe, that doesn't have to be a bad thing. Life is always full of surprises, and some of them can be quite wonderful. If we pay attention. Maybe you should go over there for a visit. Allow yourself to chill out and renew your energy."

"Alone? You mean go to Ormond Beach alone?"

Shelby laughed. "First of all, you wouldn't be alone. You'd have Basil with you. But yeah, find a nice place to stay for a while. No pressure. No commitments. I don't think women do this nearly enough. It's good to be alone sometimes. It allows us to reconnect with ourselves. Especially during times of change or confusion."

"Hmm," I said, slowly beginning to warm to the idea. "Maybe you're right. Maybe a change is what I need for a while."

"Give it some thought, Chloe. We just never know what's around that next corner," she said, passing me her credit card to pay for her purchase.

# TERRI DuLong

# PATTERNS OF CHANGE

## An Ormond Beach Novel

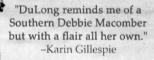

"DuLong reminds me of a
Southern Debbie Macomber
but with a flair all her own."
–Karin Gillespie

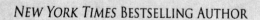

NEW YORK TIMES BESTSELLING AUTHOR

# TERRI DULONG

# STITCHES IN TIME

*An Ormond Beach*
*Novel*

Born and raised north of Boston, **Terri DuLong** was previously a resident of Cedar Key, Florida. She now resides on the east coast of the state in Ormond Beach with her husband, three dogs, and two cats. A retired registered nurse, she began her writing career as a contributing writer for *Bonjour Paris*, where she shared her travel experiences to France in more than forty articles with a fictional canine narrator. Terri's love of knitting provides quiet time to develop her characters and plots as she works on her new Ormond Beach novels.

You can visit her website at www.terridulong.com or her Facebook fan page, www.facebook.com/TerriDuLongAuthor